Acting on Impulse

By Mia Sosa

Love on Cue
Acting on Impulse

The Suits Undone
Getting Dirty with the CEO
One Night with the CEO
Unbuttoning the CEO

Acting on Impulse

LOVE ON CUE

MIA SOSA

AVONIMPULSE
An Imprint of HarperCollinsPublishers

This is a work of fiction. Names, characters, places, and incidents are products of the author's imagination or are used fictitiously and are not to be construed as real. Any resemblance to actual events, locales, organizations, or persons, living or dead, is entirely coincidental.

Excerpt from *Pretending He's Mine* © 2018 by Mia Sosa.

Digital Edition SEPTEMBER 2017 ISBN: 978-0-06-269033-3
Print Edition ISBN: 978-0-06-269034-0

Cover design by Nadine Badalaty
Cover photographs: © Peopleimages / Getty Images (couple); © Shutterstock (details)

FIRST EDITION

17 18 19 20 21 HDC 10 9 8 7 6 5 4 3 2 1

*This book is dedicated to my
favorite spot in Romancelandia,
where happily-ever-afters are guaranteed,
love is love, and only cakes are moist.
It's a special place, and we need it now more than ever.*

Hollywood Observer

9:00 a.m. PDT 5/1/2017 by Observer Staff
Los Angeles, California

Fans hoping to see more of Carter Stone will soon have their wishes granted. The popular television actor, best known for his roles as Nina Blake's love interest in *My Life in Shambles* and as the adorably awkward but gorgeous neighbor Clinton in the second season of *Man on Third*, recently completed work on a super secret project in Philadelphia that will feature Stone on the big screen. According to a set insider, most of the principal photography was completed several months ago, but Stone's part required a delay in the production schedule. Color us intrigued. Our sources couldn't tell us whether Carter will be in the buff for this role, but we've got our fingers crossed.

Chapter One

Carter

I'M STANDING IN the middle of an airplane aisle, inching my way to row 12, when I spot her. I don't know her name, nationality, age, or occupation, but I know this: Someday I'm going to marry the woman sitting in 12D.

Okay, maybe that's an exaggeration—for all I know she could be someone else's wife, or a serial killer—but hey, I'm an optimistic guy. Plus, she's in my row, so I know fate is in play.

Don't roll your eyes. It's not polite.

I lift the baseball cap from my head and whip my hands through my hair, trying to bury the cowlick that's been the bane of my existence ever since *Seventeen Magazine* dubbed it my "adorable nod to imperfection." That was eight years ago, and among my friends and family, the embarrassing mention might as well have happened yesterday. Knowing from experience the errant lock of hair won't budge, I concentrate on her instead.

She's gorgeous. What I can see of her, at least.

It begins with her bottomless dark eyes, which are set in an intense gaze as she watches the parade of travelers making their way through the cabin. Although she's probably just anxious to know who her seatmates will be, I can't help wondering what it would be like to have all that attention focused on me. Her hair is a riot of dark brown curls that I could easily wrap around my fingers. From this vantage point, I can't see her lips, but that might be a good thing, since what I *can* see is enough to fry my brain.

Look, before you decide I'm a shallow jerk for choosing my life partner based on appearance alone, consider this: Sexual compatibility is a strong indicator of long-term wedded bliss. I'm not saying that I'd marry this woman if she were as engaging as my dad's proctologist—yes, I've heard stories—and I'd never be able to marry someone who didn't at least *feel* comfortable around children or puppies—but this instant lust is promising. The truth is, I'm excited, and I haven't been eager about anything other than acting in years.

An older couple two rows ahead of me parks their luggage in the center aisle, and my future wife pulls her headphones out of her ears and jumps up to assist them. She edges out of our row with a warm smile. I peek around the jerk in front of me, the guy who buried his face in his phone when the couple asked for help, and that's when I see it: the finest ass I've ever seen. For a few seconds,

I don't know what to focus on: face, ass, face, ass. *Who am I kidding?* My gaze falls to her backside. Yes, Mom, you've taught me better, but you are not standing where I'm standing as I look at the bounty that's before me.

She's dressed in expensive-looking casual wear, and the pants covering said backside leave little to the imagination. Granted, her oversized off-the-shoulder top probably was meant to cover all that finery, but she's stretching to place the couple's carry-on bag in the overhead compartment, and I'm the shameless beneficiary of her Samaritan act.

After a few more seconds of unabashed ogling, I return my gaze to her face. Her brown sun-kissed skin is smooth and seemingly unadorned. I imagine she's got some kind of makeup on, though, because I've watched my younger sister, Ashley, spend an hour plastering her face for what she calls a "barely there" look. Whatever this woman is or isn't wearing, it works.

The elderly woman squeezes my future wife's hands, thanking her with a bright smile, and the bronzed goddess reciprocates. Her lips are shiny—with gloss perhaps—and made for wickedness. My heart does this weird thing: a thump and a catch, then a thump-thump and a catch, almost like the beats are off track and are working to right themselves. *Fuck me, this is weird. And yet right—in a weird kind of way.*

I make my living convincing audiences that love at first sight exists. Turns out I'm a shitty actor because there's not much pretending involved. It happens. Because I'm pretty sure I'm experiencing it right now.

Hoping this muddled feeling will level out, I stretch my neck and shake out my hands. I can't demonstrate my game if I'm sidelined by queasiness. Now that the elderly couple is tucked away in their row, I click the latch to open our overhead compartment. Wanting to make my best first impression on my seatmate, I puff out my chest and stand tall, eager for our eyes to meet. We're seconds away from the moment to end all moments, the one I'll tell our kids about a decade from now.

And then my dream lady ruins it.

She again jumps up. "Oh, hey." Pointing to my bag, she says, "Looks like you're going to need a little help there."

Confused by her assumption that a strapping man like me can't handle my own luggage, I tug on my overgrown beard—and wince. That's when I remember my appearance is not my own. Instead, I'm embodying my latest character, an emaciated twenty-seven-year-old man suffering from drug addiction and possessing a troubling aversion to grooming. I'd like to think that she'd be able to see beyond my skinny frame and unkempt hair and recognize her soul mate, but folks, it ain't happening.

I quickly recover from this twist in our love story and stop her with a wave. "It's okay. I've got it. I'm stronger than my body suggests."

A faint blush appears on her cheeks.

And there goes the thump and a catch again. Fuck. Do I have a heart defect I don't know about?

She takes great interest in her footwear. "Of course. It's the helper in me. I didn't mean to—"

"No need to apologize," I say as I hoist my travel bag above my shoulders and slide it into the compartment. With my arms pressed against the overhead bin, I wait until she's looking at me again and give her a wink. "We're fine."

I typically don't cut off people when they're talking to me, but I'm worried that my future wife's embarrassment might lead her to ignore me during the flight. That's definitely not how I've scripted this in my head, so if she thinks it's a little rude, she'll have to forgive me. It's for the greater good.

I smooth my jeans and confirm that I've got the middle seat, conveniently close to her but away from curious onlookers who might recognize me. Given that I look like the fourth and forgotten member of ZZ Top, that's unlikely to happen anyway. Pointing to my boarding pass, I tell her, "Mind if I slip in here?"

"Sure," she says with an easy smile.

She's still standing, so she steps into the aisle, giving me a glimpse of her ass as she moves one row back to let me in.

As I crawl into the tiny space—it's been a while since I've traveled coach class—I catch a whiff of her scent and close my eyes. Not sure if it's perfume, body wash, or what, but it smells like vanilla and reminds me of the candles my mother used to buy at the local craft store. That right there is a sign. My mother would most heartily approve of this woman.

Now to find out her name.

I turn in my seat, prepping myself for a short conversation—too much too soon isn't part of the playbook—but then I realize she's not next to me. I raise myself off the cushion and pretend to stretch as I turn my head to scan the back of the plane. She's a few rows back, standing and chatting with a guy who doesn't appear to have anyone sitting next to him.

Oh, hell no.

Do I have to go to the restroom? You bet.

Before I stand, a bell rings and a flight attendant announces that there will be a short delay while the ground crew clears debris from the runway. Perfect.

I rise and make my way through the aisle, pushing down the bill of my baseball cap so no one notices me. But, of course, someone does. For all the wrong reasons.

A little girl with huge brown eyes and a mop of bright red hair tugs on her mother's shirt and says, "Mommy, that man looks like a bear."

The cutie's pronouncement is loud enough that several nearby passengers chuckle. Even the object of my fascination turns and laughs. I grin at the kid, and she growls in her best imitation of a bear. So freaking adorable, that girl. Enjoying her fascination with my beard, I channel my inner Leonardo DiCaprio and growl right back.

Now I've done it.

The little girl's eyes go round, and her eyes water. Then she lets out a shriek like the hounds of hell are chasing her. Unfortunately, I'm the hounds, and everyone on the plane, including my future wife, knows it.

The girl's mother tries to quiet her, rocking her and telling her everything will be okay. Their seatmate, meanwhile, throws daggers at me with his eyes.

"He's so scary looking," the little girl chants over and over into her mother's chest.

"Sir," the flight attendant says behind me, "we're getting ready to take off soon. Could you please return to your seat?"

Bewildered by the past ten minutes of my life, I nod and amble back to my row. How the hell did things go south that quickly? Fantasy woman returns, and my stomach drops when I catch the look of sympathy on her face. I slide down into my seat, give her a pathetic smile, and cover my face with my baseball cap as though I'm settling in for a nap. I need to regroup before I can speak to her. And I refuse to listen to the preflight safety demonstration unless the attendant can teach me how to save me from myself.

So now I know another thing: Whatever I tell my kids about how I met their mother, it's going to be a lie. A big, fat fucking lie.

Philly Water Cooler

5/5/2017
Heard Around Town
By Lisa Blane | <u>Leave a comment</u>

One year ago, Philly residents swooned over the story of how two-time Olympian and current Philadelphia councilman Mason King met Tori Alvarez, a personal trainer, at a community service event hosted by Get Fit America. Alvarez challenged King to a push-up competition, and King accepted, but only if the prize was a date with Ms. Alvarez. The badass trainer won and sparks flew. It appears those sparks have fizzled, however, as sources tell us King and Alvarez are no longer an item. We at *Philly Water Cooler* aren't surprised, but the couple's meet-cute would have been the perfect story to share with their grandkids.

Chapter Two

Tori

POBRECITO.

I think the poor guy's embarrassed that he made the little girl cry. I watched the whole exchange, though, and it was kind of cute. Normally, I'd try to coax him out of his shell, but I know what it's like to be the subject of unwanted attention, and I understand the need to block out the rest of the world.

This trip to Aruba, for instance, is my way of hiding from the aspects of my life that I don't want to deal with.

Well, one thing specifically: my boyfriend.

Scratch that.

My *ex-boyfriend*.

The one who announced in a radio interview that he was taking a "breather" from the dating scene—in direct response to a question about whether there was anyone *special* in his life. Guess who thought she was special? Go ahead. I'll wait.

I've heard about men breaking up with their girlfriends via text messaging, and I'm sure it's a wretched experience. But trust me, listening to your breakup on a local radio show sucks big balls. Like *huevos* the size of a tuberous bush cricket—relatively speaking, that is. Stay with me here. You see, while some men walk around like their balls make up 14 percent of their body, this insect's balls actually do. Nothing like a spirited game of Trivial Pursuit to round out your cultural literacy. And yes, I was tipsy, *pero* that morsel of uselessness made an impression on me, penetrating my apple martini haze and settling in my brain for eternity.

The *pendejo*—that's *dumb ass* for you non-Spanish speakers—didn't even have the decency to warn me about his little publicity stunt. And yes, I'm sure that's what this is. Somehow it benefits Mason, but he'll try to explain it away. Escaping Philly for a short but much-needed trip ensures that I won't suffer through Mason's pitiful attempts to justify his asinine behavior—at least during that critical period when my anger might lead me to inflict bodily harm on him.

No. Take a deep breath, Tori, and focus on the many positives. I won't have to worry about a local news crew taking pictures of us during the seventh-inning stretch of a Phillies game. And no reporter's going to corner me at a political fundraising event in a harebrained effort to get me to spill secrets about Councilman Mason King. This is my chance to relax without worrying about whether to filter my language, hide my cleavage, or smile for the occasional camera. I made a vow to enjoy this attachment-free vacation, and I intend to keep it.

As the plane taxis down the runway, I close my eyes, enjoying the rumble of the engine and the vibrations under my feet. Minutes later, the pilot switches off the seat belt sign and gives us the local forecast: no threat of rain for several days—which is perfect since that's how long I'll be staying on the island.

The man next to me shifts, but his hat is still sitting atop his face. My gaze falls to the armrest between us. He's thin, but he's also tall, and his wrist size suggests that he should be larger than he is. Given the sunken cheeks and wan complexion that accompany his lean frame, I'm guessing he's sick. I'm hesitant to disrupt his nap, but there's no one sitting in the window seat, and I could use the extra elbow room.

I tap his hand. "Excuse me, sir."

He removes the cap and sits up, his movements quicker than I'd expected them to be. "Yeah?"

The man stares at me, his eyes alert, a small smile lifting his lips at the corners. The mouth catches my attention, but the eyes seize it. I don't think I've ever seen a pair like his. Ice blue and rimmed in black, they sit in stark contrast to his other features: the raven hair on his head, the dark brows, and the full beard that covers the lower half of his face like a shaggy carpet. If a blond man had eyes like his, I'd probably think nothing of them, but on this guy, the effect is startling.

He doesn't otherwise look well, though, and I give him a sheepish grin because I feel a hairbreadth's shy of shitty for disturbing him. "Sorry. I didn't mean to wake you."

"Are you sure about that?"

I drop my head a fraction, acknowledging the insipidness of my own words. "Well, you're right, I did mean to wake you. Looks like no one's sitting with us, so I figured we could spread out a bit."

He spins his head and torso toward the window seat as though he needs to see for himself that, indeed, no one is there. "Yeah, yeah, sure. I'll move. Not a problem."

His languid movements make me regret the interruption.

I'm not a nosy soul, but I venture into personal territory anyway. I don't know why, but I just want to be certain. "Are you feeling okay?"

His eyes widen as he refastens his seat belt. "Yeah, I'm fine. Just exhausted. I mean dead-on-my-feet tired."

I give him a nod in understanding. I've definitely been there. "I won't bother you anymore, then. Sorry I woke you."

If he'd waved off my interruption with a friendly salute or smile, I'd have thrown on my earbuds, closed my eyes, and settled in for a short rest. But that's not what he does. Instead, he turns on his side and stares at me with those piercing eyes, and I swear that we're not on a plane, but in a bedroom, and he's staring at me as we lie on a bed facing each other. The vision causes me to shrink back and gasp, and I can tell that he has no idea what's going on in my head because his thick eyebrows shoot up as though he's not certain I'm mentally stable.

ACTING ON IMPULSE 17

Unfortunately, at the moment, I can't assure him that I am. Because...*what the hell was that*?

This time he's the one who's concerned. "You okay?"

My words trip over themselves. "Yeah, yeah. I'm fine. I'm exhausted, too. Just feeling a little loopy." I point at the air around me. "Flying, probably."

He nods and holds out his hand. "I'm Carter, by the way."

Our hands meet in an awkward handshake, his confident grip clashing with my delicate finger dance. "Tori."

"Short for Victoria?"

I get that question often. "No. Just Tori."

"I have a feeling there's nothing *just* about you."

Oh no. That was awful. But the guy's had a bad day, and he's exhausted, so I don't give him my infamous side-eye. "So what's taking you to Aruba?"

He nibbles on his bottom lip as he ponders my question. If it's a calculated move, boo. But if it's an unstudied mannerism, I dig it. I dig it a lot. I'm watching. He's nibbling. What am I even doing?

The pause approaches an uncomfortable territory seconds before he answers. "I've been banished. I got into it with someone, work-related crap, and I've been told to take some time off. So here I am. You?"

"I haven't taken a vacation in two years. And a situation in my personal life's gone wonky all of a sudden, so I thought this would be the perfect time for some relaxation and reinvention."

"Nice," he says. A sliver of his hair falls forward, the tip of it landing just above his eyebrow. He swats at it with the enthusiasm of someone trying to avoid a mosquito bite.

"So what did the someone do?" I ask.

He frowns. "What?"

"The person you got into it with. The one who caused your banishment. What happened?"

His face relaxes in understanding. "Ah." But he doesn't answer my question.

"Sorry, if that's too personal…"

He shakes his head. "No, no. It's just…the person…he took advantage of me, and I didn't expect it."

"I'm sorry. I've been blindsided recently, too. But here's how I see it. Now that whatever happened is out in the open, you can learn from it and move on, right?"

He draws back and squints at me. "Right. It's as simple as that."

I know that tone well. It rings with male condescension and ends with a "well, actually." "Am I detecting a sheen of sarcasm on your skin?"

"Christ," he says. Then he bursts out laughing. "You're not defensive *at all*." With his head cocked to the side, he holds out his hands. "See there? *That's* sarcasm."

My cheeks blaze under his inspection. And although I don't want to give him the satisfaction, I laugh anyway. Because he's not wrong. The debacle with Mason has left me raw. "Did you know the phrase 'The quick brown fox jumps over the lazy dog' uses every letter in the English language?"

He narrows his eyes. "What are you doing?"

Without an ounce of embarrassment, I say, "Changing the subject."

"In that case, did you know only female mosquitoes sting humans?"

A man who's willing to engage my love for trivia? Oh my. If I were on the market, I'd be sold. Instead, I mentally swat at the butterfly zipping around in my stomach. We'll have none of that, thank you. "Well played, Carter. There's hope for you yet."

"I was thinking the exact same thing about you," he says with a grin. "First time in Aruba?"

"Yes. You?"

"Same. Where are you staying?"

Okay. Does he think I'm stupid? I'm a single woman traveling alone. My intended whereabouts shall be guarded like state secrets. Well, given how often government employees divulge confidential info, maybe that's a bad analogy. But you know what I mean. So what do I do? I fib. "Oh, I'm not even sure yet. A friend is meeting me at the airport. He's taken care of the arrangements." I lift my brows and rub my hands together. "A surprise."

The brightness in his eyes dulls, like a headlight dimming in the black of night. He stares at me, eyes unblinking, for several seconds. "Hope you have a great time," he finally says. Then he loosens his grip on the armrest. "I'm going to catch some much-needed z's, so…"

Damn, that was abrupt. "Sure, sure. You won't hear a peep out of me."

He reclines his seat and places the cap back on his face. "Peep all you want. I'll be out in a minute."

My body is still angled in his direction, poised for more conversation. And now I feel kind of silly because he's tuned me out in less than ten seconds. I gather the existence of my fake boyfriend has relegated me to the unbangable-and-therefore-uninteresting zone. Well, *screw* him. But then my conscience batters me with guilt, because maybe he *is* sick and maybe he's been screwed already.

Well, no matter. His dismissive attitude lights a fire under my freshly ditched ass, bringing the last few days of my life into focus. After one last glance at his sleeping form, I put on my earbuds and close my eyes. I'm going to have fun on this vacation, sure. Dance on a few tables, in fact. But men? They're off-limits to me. No rebound hookups. No one-night stands. Not even a kiss on the cheek.

I decree it.

Chapter Three

Carter

My wife is dead to me.

Okay, before you accuse me of being dramatic, bear in mind that I'm an actor. This is minor drama compared with the stuff I've experienced in my real and fictional lives. Still, her defection hurts. I'm not experiencing gut-wrenching pain, of course. No, it's more like a pang that settles just below my heart, in that fucking annoying space my younger sister always tickles when she's trying to get a rise out of me.

I'll live. If Tori's with someone, she plainly wasn't fated to be with me. But damn. Just damn. I'd enjoyed talking to her. Lyrical and comforting, her voice reminds me of the wind chimes that hung over our front porch and lulled me to sleep when I was young. And her smile has the power to distract me from completing my sentences.

She's entertaining, too. The kind of person who requires your undivided attention in a conversation.

The thing is, I'd already imagined her meeting my parents, but now I know that'll never happen. And nothing's worse than experiencing a sliver of magic and learning later that there's no more magic to be had. She probably thinks I'm a jerk who just blew her off, but in reality, I couldn't think quickly enough to hide my disappointment.

I shift my hat and look at her with one eye. There's no point in disturbing her, and pondering what might have been won't be useful, so I settle into my seat and prepare to sleep the remaining duration of the flight. With luck, I won't dream about the woman one seat away from me.

A TAP ON my shoulder wakes me.

"Hey, sleepyhead. We're here."

Tori shoots up from her seat as I get my bearings.

I stretch my arms wide. "Haven't slept that hard in a long time. Thanks for waking me."

"No problem," she says as she gathers her stuff. "Didn't want you to get trampled by the folks behind us. Getting into the aisle after you've missed your turn is about as hard as merging into traffic on the 405 in LA."

I'm still disoriented from my four-hour nap, but that gets my attention. "You know that area?"

She nods as she speaks, and a few of her curls bounce around her shoulders. "Very, very well. I have a cousin who lives in Costa Mesa. Are you from LA?"

I shouldn't say too much here, right? No, that wouldn't be wise. "It's where I live now. Transplant."

If she thinks it's odd that I haven't volunteered the location of my hometown, or that my flight originated at Philadelphia International, she doesn't show it. Instead she nods and turns away. She then bends to peek out the window of the row across from ours, and I'm proud of myself for resisting the urge to gawk at her ass.

We slip into the aisle, and I grab my bag from the overhead bin.

She shifts from side to side as she waits for the people ahead of us to make their way off the plane. Leaning backward, she looks at me over her shoulder. "This is the worst. The waiting. I'm the most impatient person on the planet, so this is high-level torture."

I lean against the top of the aisle seat. "A small price to pay for the rest and relaxation that awaits you."

I glimpse part of her smile.

"Yeah, you're right," she says. "Thanks for the perspective."

"My pleasure."

We say nothing else to each other as we shuffle off the plane. Once we're through the jet bridge, she waves at me. "Have a great time."

"You do the same."

She hoists her bag on her shoulder and strides away.

I watch her veer in the direction of the women's restroom, and my steps slow as I catch a last look at her curls bouncing through the entrance. That's it. She's gone. And it's tragic, but I'll survive.

I follow the signs to ground transportation on the airport's lower level. When I get there, a blast of warm air hits me full on. The airport isn't packed, and everyone proceeds through the building like they're being captured on slow-motion video.

A driver who looks like he was plucked right out of a casting call for a Tommy Bahama ad holds a cardboard sign with my name neatly written on it in big block letters. He shakes out his shoulder-length blond hair and flashes a megawatt smile, complete with the kind of gap that would make the latest "quirky" model super famous. "Mr. Williamson?"

It takes me a few seconds to answer to my given name. "Yes, that's me."

"Good to meet you, sir," he says as he grabs my bag from me. "I'm Derek. I'll be driving you to the Caribé Resort. Shouldn't take us more than ten minutes."

"Great. Lead the way."

As we walk out to the bay for short-term parking, I power on my cell phone and check my messages. Three missed calls from Julian, my best friend and agent. I hit the call button as I climb into the car.

Julian addresses me without preamble. "Did you get into any fights on the way there?"

"Nice to hear from you, too. And no, I didn't get into any fights. What's the latest?"

"Okay, so here's what Legal has been able to learn. The doctor claims he had nothing to do with selling the photos. Says his medical assistant was the one who snapped them for her own stash and then got the stupid idea to sell them to the magazine."

That's not what the jackass said when I confronted him in his office and took a swing at his jaw. Now he's throwing his assistant under the bus to save his license? What a prick. "You don't believe that, do you?"

"No, I don't believe it. But the question is, what do you want to do about it? The studio's not pressed. To the execs, this only adds to the mystery surrounding the movie, but they assure me that if you want to pursue an invasion of privacy action, they'll support it."

"You mean they'll stand behind me, but they won't bankroll it, right?"

"You catch on fast, my friend."

"What about a complaint with the licensing board?"

"That's easy, but we'll have to drag in his medical assistant. Legal says she's a forty-two-year-old single mother of three."

Shit. My older sister, Kimberly, is a single mother of two. I picture what losing her job would do to her and my niece and nephew. More than anything, the hit to her pride would devastate her. Not worth it. Particularly since I know the doc's assistant wasn't the one who sold those photos to the tabloids. Plus, when I decided to become an actor, I signed up for the inevitable intrusion into my personal life. It's not right, but it happens. And since I was under the doctor's care specifically for a movie role, I'm not too sure it's entirely personal anyway.

Still, I'm not thrilled about having my physical meta-morphosis plastered on the inside of a rag mag. And the doctor's face knows it. I'm not proud of myself for hitting the guy, but I'd be lying if I said the blow wasn't satisfying. "I'll let it go as long as he doesn't try to pursue charges. Let's keep the complaint in our back pockets just in case. But for now, I just want to spend a few uncomplicated days in the sun."

Julian clears his throat. "Speaking of which, you know to keep a low profile, right?"

I chew on my bottom lip to stem whatever smartass remark is bound to fly out of my mouth otherwise. I've never gotten used to the idea that my best friend has a right to tell me how to behave.

"Carter?" Julian's voice is impatient. As usual.

"Yeah, yeah. Low profile. Got it."

"You don't have to take any extraordinary measures. Just don't go looking for publicity, okay? The studio thinks it'll spark interest in the film. Mystery begets curiosity. And curiosity begets ticket sales."

"Right."

"Okay. We'll talk when you get back."

"Fine." A quick glance out the window confirms we're still on airport grounds. Which reminds me of Ashley, who's working as a flight attendant this month. Next month, it'll be something else. "Wait. Ashley's flying into LA tomorrow. Can you check in with her?"

The pause on the other end of the line isn't a surprise. Julian hates when our conversations switch from professional to personal during a single call. But after several more seconds of silence, I realize the length of this delay is atypical. "Julian?"

"Yeah. I'll give her a call."

"And see her, too, Julian? Because I'd like to be sure she's okay."

His voice is gruff when he asks, "Why wouldn't she be?"

"She broke up with the douchebag."

His name is Johnny Doche, and there was no way he wasn't getting that nickname, whether or not it fit. Unfortunately for Ashley, it does.

"Good riddance," Julian says.

"Agreed. So you'll see her?"

"If she's willing to see me, then yes, I'll see her. Anything else?"

"Nope. That's all. Love you lots. Smooches."

"Damn, man. If you weren't my best friend, I'd drop you as a client."

I chuckle at the thought. "If you weren't my agent, I'd drop you as my best friend."

A car at the intersection honks at my driver for jumping out in front of him before the light changes. "Gotta go, Julian. See you on the other side of sanity."

"Later. And don't forget: Keep a low profile."

"Right."

The livid driver and mine gesture at each other like they're dabbing at the Super Bowl. Now that I'm off the phone, Derek turns his head and gives me a what-are-you-going-to-do shrug. "Sorry about that," he says. "Every once in a while, someone on the island forgets the rule."

I lean forward as I peer out the windshield. "What's the rule?"

"No stress. Just rest. There's no such thing as 'having to be somewhere' in Aruba." Derek glances at me through the rearview mirror and gives me a toothy smile. "If you're here for fun, you picked the right time."

"Why's that?"

"The Caribé's hosting the Miss Aruba Pageant this weekend. Wall-to-wall women at the resort."

Christ. *Not* what I need right now. Particularly since I've been asked to keep a low profile. I'm on the phone with my assistant within seconds. "Jewel, it's Carter—"

"I see your international cell service is working. I wonder who arranged that—"

"Thanks, Jewel—"

"Was your driver at the airport at the appointed time?"

"Yes, thanks—"

"And are you on your way to the five-star resort where I booked a last-minute reservation in an opulent suite?"

My groan fills the taxi's interior. "I am. From the bottom of my heart, Jewel, thank you. For everything you do. For brightening my day with your sunny disposition. For just being. For all of it, you have my unending gratitude, okay?"

"Which you'll demonstrate by giving me two days off next week, right?"

Holy shit, she's something. "Right."

"Well done, Carter. By the way, sarcasm does not look good on you."

"So noted."

"Now what *else* can I do for you?"

The clickity-clack of her long fingernails tells me I don't have her full attention. Nothing new. "I need to book another hotel room."

"Why? Is the one I arranged for you too small for your ego?"

"You're about to lose the two days off."

She laughs. "Okay, okay. What's wrong?"

Mindful of my audience, I explain the situation without revealing too much. "The Caribé's hosting the Miss Aruba Pageant this weekend. Not a good idea."

"You're still in character, though, right?"

"Yes, but this beard's itchier than a crotch full of crabs. I—"

"Crotch full of crabs, huh? You'd know that why?"

I'd never replace her. She seriously brightens my day. But damn she controls every one of our conversations. Every. Single. One. "Not all metaphors are based on personal experience. Anyway, I need to get rid of the carpet on my face, and when I do…"

"Fine, fine. I'll see what I can do. I'll text you the new info when everything's set."

"Great. But don't try to be cute about my accommodations. Simple is fine."

"You doubt my abilities? I'm hurt."

She's not. This is merely future ammunition for her. "I don't doubt your abilities. I think you're fully capable of pranking me one hundred percent of the time. The coach-class ticket was a nice touch, by the way."

She snorts. "Glad you think so. Just making sure you stay grounded, Carter. Wouldn't want you to lose touch with the masses."

"And your days off are disappearing in five, four, three—"

"No, don't. I'm on it. Simple accommodations forthcoming. No pranks included, I promise."

"You're a goddess, Jewel."

"Who will not be in the office Monday or Tuesday of next week. Bye."

She hangs up on me. Again, nothing new. Jewel calls herself my phenomenal personal assistant, or PPA. The acronym is perfect because she's also my personal pain in the ass.

Derek looks at me through the rearview. "Change in plans?"

"Yep. Sit tight." Which he'll have no problem doing since we appear to be stuck in traffic anyway. "We should have a new location soon."

I return to my emails, and sure enough, Jewel's text comes through ten minutes later.

> **Tried to book a secluded villa but no availability on short notice. New hotel is Eagle Bay Beach Club. Mix of families, newlyweds, and singles. Low-key according to travel agent. Have fun. And watch out for crabs!**

I gift her with a thumbs-up emoji and share the new location with Derek.

"You got it," he says as he maneuvers an illegal U-turn. "So the idea of wall-to-wall women doesn't appeal to you?"

Why is everyone in my personal business this week? I shake my head as I continue to read my emails. "Usually, yes. This week, no."

Derek nods at my succinct response and returns his attention to the road.

There's nothing of importance in my inbox, so I search Google and find the Eagle Bay Beach Club's website. The image gallery displays a sprawling ten-acre property on the northernmost point of Aruba's hotel row. A typical beachfront resort with all the amenities a single guy could need or want. Well done, Jewel.

A minute of whistling-while-he-drives later, Derek again tries to engage me in conversation. "So what do you do?"

The response falls from my lips without much thought. "I'm in between jobs right now. Taking a vacation while I figure out my next steps."

"Not a bad place to figure out next steps. You look familiar to me. Are you famous or something?"

His narrowed-eyed gaze suggests that he's ready to pounce and say *I knew it*. But retreating into my shell will only make Derek more curious, so I snort and give him an open smile. "If I were famous you wouldn't be asking me that question."

Derek purses his lips and nods his head slowly. "Right. Of course."

I glance in the rearview.

Derek's squinting as he looks back at me, one question away from asking too much. *Fuck*. I should probably keep the beard while I'm here.

Minutes pass. I drum my hands on my lap as I pretend to enjoy the scenery outside my car window. "It's gorgeous in Aruba. Wish I had enough money to live here year-round."

I scan Derek's face for any signs that he knows who I am. As his face relaxes into a plane of serenity, the tension in my own muscles dissipates.

"You don't have to be rich to live on the island, trust me," he says. "That's the real draw of the place, in fact." He maneuvers the car around a taxi unloading its passengers and parks in the circular driveway. His long whistle is meant for my ears. When he knows he has my attention, he juts out his chin in the direction of the cab at the curb. "Actually, that's the real draw of the island."

I follow the trajectory of his gaze with my own. Good gravy, I'd know those curls and that ass anywhere. They belong to the woman who will never be my wife. Well, well, it's good to see you again Tori-not-short-for-Victoria.

What are the odds?

I whip out the billfold in my back jeans pocket and watch her like an assassin keeping an eye on his target in a crowded square. She strides down the walkway leading to the resort's lobby and glides inside, an eager bellhop walking by her side and chatting her up. Reenergized, I spring out of the car and chuckle to myself. If it weren't for the beauty pageant, I'd be at another hotel. Now Tori and I will be spending some time together after all. Not exactly how I thought this day would play out, but Fate, you're a cunning mistress, and it's my duty to follow your lead.

Chapter Four

Tori

THE BAR ADJACENT to the pool area boasts a lovely view of the sun setting over the ocean. A few feet away, three men tend to an open-fire barbecue pit, filling my nostrils with the smell of smoked meats and taunting my empty stomach. The sticky air coats my skin like a layer of scented lotion. Makes me feel like I bathed in coconut oil and reminds me of my grandmother's best dessert, *tembleque*, a creamy coconut pudding that literally jiggles on the plate. When I was young, I'd scramble underneath her arm as she kneaded dough for her *empanadillas* and tap the *tembleque* to watch it shake. Abuela Clara would promptly swat my hand away and shoo me from the kitchen, and I'd smile on my way out of the room, listening for her ever-present throaty laugh.

Abuela's long gone, but her wisdom is with me today: "*You'll always know when you matter to someone. Sometimes it's something said. Other times it's something done. But it's always in their eyes. Even when the person's angry, the eyes will show they care.*" She said all of this in Spanish, with her head cocked to the side and a weathered hand on her hip. I'd nod, pretending to understand, but her sage advice didn't sink in until now.

Mason never looked at me as though I mattered. Abuela would have said that was the only sign I needed. I'm not bitter. Not exactly. Mostly, I'm pissed at myself for remaining in a relationship that gave me so little and exposed me to so much. The manipulative little shit didn't deserve me.

A breeze washes over me as though it's signaling the time to forget the past and live in the present. With so much natural beauty around me, doing so is easy. The sunset casts a majestic glow over the pool area. I snap a picture of it and post it on Twitter: "Sometimes the best thing you can do for your mind and body is relax and enjoy your surroundings. #Aruba #vacation #longoverdue." Other times, the best thing to do is tip your head back and guzzle a cocktail. I draw in a deep breath and lift my finger to get the attention of the nearest of the two male bartenders.

He reaches me in seconds, thanks to a dramatic shuffle across the length of the bar, and leans across the counter. "Just you, pretty lady?"

I sigh. "Yup. I'm alone in paradise. All the good ones are taken."

He casts a sideways glance at his coworker and grins. "Well, let's make you feel better. What can I get you?"

"A pineapple upside-down cake, please."

The bartender bites his bottom lip and furrows his thick brows. "Not familiar. But I'm sure I can make it. Tell me what you need."

I use my fingers to tick off the ingredients. "Vodka, bourbon, pineapple juice, Peach Schnapps, and a maraschino cherry to top it off."

He winks at me and leans his elbow on the counter. "Know your drinks, eh?"

"I was a bartender in college," I explain.

He extends his hand for a fist bump, and I oblige him. "What's your name, handsome man?"

"Damon."

"Nice to meet you, Damon. I'm Tori."

"A pleasure, Tori," he says with a sweet smile before he turns away.

I watch him work, admiring how he imbues every movement with energy, his hands sweeping everywhere as he gathers the liquor for my cocktail. A sheen of sweat kisses his impossibly smooth skin. It's the perfect canvas for just about anything, and my tongue is all too willing to serve as a paintbrush. He and the other bartender step around each other, a clumsy dance that makes them laugh, and then I catch the way they almost lean into each other at one point, a look of longing passing between them. The moment's so thick with tension I catch my own breath.

Ah, okay, no licking the bartender, then.

His apparent unavailability is a good thing. It reminds me that I'm not here for a fling anyway. I'm here to unwind and let loose. Also on the to-do list: forgetting that I dated Mason King for over a year. Thankfully, my pineapple upside-down cake will help me achieve both.

Except the drink that's placed before me is in a martini glass, its sexy maker apparently under the misimpression that I intend to sip it daintily. "Damon?"

"Yes, ma'am?"

"I'm going to need another one of these in a few minutes," I say, pointing to the cocktail.

"You got it, Tori."

He drops a napkin next to my drink and heads off to the other side of the bar. I cup the glass with both hands and take a long gulp. The liquor slides down my throat in a satisfying rush. The resulting burn intensifies and then abates, a warm sensation flowing like lava from my chest to my stomach. I'm hopeful this is the first step toward oblivion. Pineapple upside-down cake, don't fail me now.

"Is this seat taken?" a man's voice to my right asks.

Shit. I'm not in the mood to fend off someone this early in my vacation. My mistake, though. I should have ordered room service and thrown a pity party in my pj's.

I peer into my martini glass. "That seat's not taken. Nor is the one next to it. Or the one next to that one."

My voice is low and husky, irritation laced with a layer of "Get lost, dude."

"Don't misunderstand me. I don't want to sit next to you," he says. "I was just hoping to snag the stool."

Good cover, I suppose. Without raising my head, I give him a dismissive wave. "It's all yours then."

"Boyfriend not showing up anytime soon?"

Ha. Hardly. "Definitely not." And this is beginning to sound like the worst pickup attempt in the history of pickup attempts. With the cocktail still in hand and poised to connect with my lips, I turn to give my would-be harasser the "say anything else and you die" stare. My eyes cross instead. *Him.* Momentarily confused, I drop my head and bump my mouth against the rim of the glass. Damn. That's going to leave a mark. My gaze whips up to his face. "You."

"Yes, it's me," my skinny, icy-eyed seatmate says.

"Okay, this is super creepy. You know that, right? I mean, I meet you on a plane and now you're asking if it's okay to take the chair next to mine? What gives?"

He tilts his head and considers me. His cool gaze doesn't stray from my eyes, and I really want to squirm. My muscles go rigid as I wait for him to say something. Finally, he quirks his lips as if he knows something I don't. Then he lifts the stool. As he walks away, he says, "I didn't follow you here, if that's what you're thinking."

That's *exactly* what I was thinking. "You're telling me this is nothing more than a coincidence, then?"

"Exactly," he says over his shoulder.

I roll my eyes. "Right."

"Sorry to bother you. Have a nice evening."

Out of the corner of my eye, I observe him plant the stool behind me, next to a table—*with no chairs.*

I guess if he wanted to sit at the table he *would* need the stool. But my suspicious nature nevertheless refuses to believe his presence here is pure happenstance.

His cell phone rings, and the background noises fade as I try to listen in on his end of the conversation. *Who's the stalker now, Tori?*

"Yes, Jewel," he says with an exasperated sigh. "It's perfect. You're perfect. I never should have doubted you."

A bit of silence as he listens to the person. Then, "No, hell, no. I'm not saying that."

He inhales deeply and lets out a long, slow breath. "Fine. You are a phenomenal personal assistant," he says, and then he mumbles, "my PPA for sure. Are we done here?"

The person on the other end of the line cackles—so loudly I hear it despite the hum of the island music and bar chatter around me.

My seatmate—his name escapes me—then says, "Enough with the crabs already. And yes, you've more than earned your two days off by scoring me reservations at the perfect resort. Good-bye."

He ends the call and slides the phone across the table as though he's willing himself not to pick it up.

If someone made these reservations for him, I suppose it's unlikely he stalked me from the plane. Dammit. Looks like an apology is in order. And what's a fate worse than standing idle on a plane as I wait to disembark?

Yep, you guessed it: admitting I made a mistake.

I trudge to his table, where he sits with his back to me. He straightens his shoulders when my shadow appears, and of course I should say something, but I'm transfixed by the soft waves of his inky-black hair. I'm not inclined to reach out and touch the strands. I'm not. But I press my hands together anyway, just in case my brain engages in mutiny.

My throat doesn't cooperate when I open my mouth to speak.

He turns his head in my direction. "To quote someone I *don't* know, 'This is super creepy. You know that, right?'"

His humor and the shaky smile he gives me break the logjam of awkwardness.

I sidle up to his bar table and rest my hands on it. "Look, I shouldn't have assumed you were a stalker. I'm sorry about that."

He points his thumb behind his shoulder in the bar's direction. "That just then, or the lie you told me on the plane?"

"What?"

"On the plane, you claimed to be meeting someone at an undisclosed-to-you location. That wasn't true, right?"

"Not that you're entitled to that info, but yes, you're right. I'm not apologizing for that, though. You don't ask a woman traveling alone where she's staying."

He pretends to scribble something on a nonexistent sheet of paper. "I've made a note of that in my book of small-talk etiquette. Thanks for the tip."

I bite the inside of my cheek and debate what to say while he pretends not to care whether I disappear altogether. I mean, yes, he's picked up his phone and appears to be unable to draw his eyes away from it, but his shoulders are almost touching his ears, suggesting he's tense and waiting for my next move. Typically, I'd say something snide or sarcastic and ensure that my seatmate never speaks to me again. But he's done nothing to suggest that he's a bad guy, and for a moment on the plane, he'd almost charmed the panties off me. Plus, I've discovered that drinking alone is a drag. I could use his company. If nothing else, having him around will ward off any weirdos. "Come join me at the bar. I'll buy you a drink."

My voice is frustratingly tentative when I hold out the olive branch. This guy unbalances me, and worse, I don't understand why.

"Do you even remember my name, Tori-not-short-for-Victoria?"

"I don't. Sorry."

He squeezes his eyes shut and purses his lips. "I'm hurt. The name's Carter. Carter Williamson." His eyes remain shut as though the revelation that I don't remember his name truly offends him.

Right. It comes back to me then. "Hey, Carter-I-won't-forget-your-name-again-Williamson."

My pronouncement earns me a smile and a quick once-over. "That's great to hear," he says. "But I think I'll pass on the drink."

It takes me more than a few seconds to register that he's turned me down. Huh. I gather he's still pissed that I lied to him about my companion, but I don't care. *Move on, Tori. You're not meant to be friends with him.*

I stride back to the bar and plop down on the stool. "Damon, let's cancel the fancy cocktail order. A row of vodka shots instead, please. Preferably the good stuff."

Damon stops wiping the bar counter and drapes the towel over his shoulder. "You sure about that?"

"Very."

Damon makes a show of preparing the shots, his broad chest and arms flexing as he reaches for the glasses and a slim bottle of vodka. He draws an audience, the people standing near the bar gathering around for the entertainment.

After a spiral toss in the air, he spins and catches the bottle behind his back. The crowd cheers. Never breaking eye contact with me, he unscrews the cap, pours the vodka, and places the shot near my clasped hands. "As you wish."

With deft hands, I slide the rim of the glass across my lips. I take a deep breath before I down the entire shot, and then I breathe out, slamming the glass on the counter. The small group of revelers roars with approval. One down, six more to go.

Damon shakes his head, his eyes lighting up with humor. "Not a novice, I see."

"Certainly not."

I demolish the second shot in a similar fashion, and the warmth that's spreading in my belly makes me sway to the beat of the band's steel drums.

Carter drags his stool to the counter, the scraping sound interrupting my hard-earned buzz. His face—a challenging jigsaw puzzle of sharp edges, hollow cheeks, and intense eyes—compresses into a look of concern. "Tori, you might want to—"

"Oh no!" I say as I shrink away from him.

He flinches. "What?"

"You have the telltale posture of a mansplainer. Body leaning forward. An elbow on the bar. The pointed finger. You were going to say something about my alcohol tolerance, weren't you?"

A flush works its way across his cheeks as he drops his jaw. Then he snaps his mouth shut and grins.

Pointing an accusing finger, I smirk at him. "I *knew* it. Don't worry, Carter. I can handle it." I look him up and down, and he straightens under my assessing gaze. "In fact, I bet I could outdrink you any day."

With my challenge issued, his composure returns. Shifting in his seat to face me, he places the balls of his feet on the bottom rung of my stool. "You really think you can outdrink me?"

I paste on a bright, fuck-yeah smile. "Yup."

"How would we determine that?"

"The first person to beg for mercy, or fall flat on *his* face, loses."

"And what would I get if I took you up on that bet and won?"

I size him up: the scruffy beard, the adorable cowlick, the shy smile. "I'll help you catch the attention of someone…man, woman, or both."

"A woman," he offers.

I shrug as I caress my empty glass. "Whatever works for you."

His mouth drops open as he watches me. Finally, he draws back and shakes his head. "So you think I need help picking up a woman?"

"Let's just say my help couldn't hurt."

"You're cute."

He says that as though he knows it will annoy me. And it does. He vacillates between being tentative and bold, and I can't shake the feeling that he doesn't know which version of himself he wants to be. This is more than I want to think about during my vacation, though. "Okay, John Grizzly Adams. Never mind."

His hand drops over mine in a flash. "No, no. I'm intrigued. What do you want in the unlikely event that I lose?"

It takes more time than it should to answer his question. I'm focused on the tingle that spread over my fingers when he touched me. Not a welcome development. Now, what was the question? Ah, right. What happens if he loses? I shake my head to clear it before I respond. "Your company when I jog on the beach in the morning. I'd love to keep to my regular exercise routine and take advantage of the beautiful scenery, but I'm not enthused about running alone in an unfamiliar place. I'm not asking you to be my protector, mind you. Just company. I run with a partner at home, for pacing. Think you could handle it?"

"Sure, no problem. I'll be your running mate."

Interesting that he didn't ask any questions about the extent of my run. Maybe he's a serious runner, too. Then again, he's a guy. He probably thinks he's got this bet on lock. Either fact could explain his lack of due diligence.

I rub my hands together. "Excellent. One condition, though."

"What's that?"

"We have to start with a level playing field. I've already had two shots."

I've also drained a cocktail, but I have an advantage anyway. My tolerance for alcohol is as high as my intolerance for mansplaining.

He considers me for a few seconds and ends his survey by drumming a staccato beat on the bar counter. "Deal."

Damon sets four more shots of vodka in front of me. I grab two and hand them to Carter. "Then drink up, buttercup. We don't have a lot of time. You'll need a good night's rest 'cause we'll be running at six in the morning."

Chapter Five

Carter

THIS APPEARS TO be the best kind of situation: a win-win.

Whatever the outcome, I get to spend time with Tori. What she doesn't realize, however, is that she made a bet with a man whose iron stomach and indestructible kidneys are legendary among his friends. The outcome of this competition is all on me.

As I study her eyes over the rim of the shot glass, I'm faced with an interesting quandary. If I win the bet, I'll have to pretend that I need her help gaining the attention of a woman at the resort. If I *let* her win the bet—c'mon, that's the only way it could happen—I'll have to run with her each morning at the ungodly hour of six o'clock. The former involves acting, an activity that for obvious reasons comes naturally to me, while the latter involves opening my eyes before the butt crack of dawn, a time of day when I'm not at my best. Ultimately, it's an easy choice.

I raise the glass to my lips and knock back the liquor in one gulp. The second shot goes down just as easily. "Now we're even."

Tori rolls her shoulders forward and back, drawing my eyes to that irresistible expanse of skin on a woman's body: the area between her collarbones. It's a magical place. The center of a compass rose. Whether you head east, west, north, or south, you simply cannot go wrong. Tori's not wearing a necklace to mar the view, and she has fantastic collarbones. Some might even call them delectable. Yes, "some" is the royal "me."

Tori waves her hands in front of my face. "Hey, Carter. Shots already affecting you? You look a little dazed."

I draw back and shake my head. "What? No. Just a little tired, remember?" Jesus, Carter, how fucking lame can you be? Very, apparently.

She pretends to hold her laugh, but we both know she thinks I'm a joke, which she confirms when she says, "Okay, let's get on with this, so I can tuck you in for a nap."

All right, now she's spouting fighting words. Game on. I pick up one of the shots and gesture for her to do the same. She does so with a lick of her lips. I'd trade shots with her for days if it meant I got to watch that again and again.

"The trick to this," she says, "is to draw in a deep breath before you take the shot and exhale slowly afterward."

I lean into her, drawn to the idea of her taking deep breaths in my presence. "Is that so?"

She scrunches her brows like a caterpillar inching its away across the ground. Okay, she probably wouldn't appreciate my thoughts right now.

"Yes, that's so," she says, her voice haughty and tight.

Giving her my best I've-got-your-number smile, I toss my head back and gulp the vodka. "I think I'll do this my way."

"Suit yourself, John Grizzly."

She applies her technique admirably, and I'm impressed by her stamina. By my count, this is her third shot, and she doesn't seem fazed at all. The bartender walks over and sets several more shots in front of us. Tori places her hands on the counter and raises her body to lean into him. A smile plays across his face when she whispers something in his ear. Even though I have no right to *anything* about this woman, let alone the right to be jealous that she's talking to another guy, I clench my jaw as I watch them interact. *Get a grip, Carter.*

Before we can trade more shots, she presses me for information about myself.

"Where are you from?" she asks.

My answer comes without hesitation. "A small town in Connecticut. Harmon."

"Is there such a thing as a big town in Connecticut?"

"Spoken like a native New Yorker." I shudder. "Or a Californian."

Tori blushes. "Wrong on both counts, although I should note the latter would be a travesty. Philly, born and raised. When did you move to California?"

"When I was nineteen, and you're stalling." I slide another shot glass her way. "Ready?"

"Always," she says with a dimpled grin.

We each take our respective shots, both grimacing as we slam the glasses down.

Despite my efforts to redirect the conversation, she doesn't miss a beat. "What do you do in the Golden State?"

I knew we'd reach this point, but I wish it hadn't come so soon. Our rapport so far has been easy and light, unblemished by the collateral bullshit associated with my career. The assumptions. The ass-kissing. The *agendas*. I'm not looking forward to seeing the humor in Tori's eyes switch to something else when she learns who I am. It'll surely come. It always does. Shit. This week, a doctor sold photos of me to a gossip magazine, so I know this isn't paranoia.

Here's how this usually plays out: She learns I'm Carter Stone, and the feisty, wisecracking woman in front of me turns into someone else. Someone she thinks I want her to be. Someone befitting the arm of a rising *Hollywood heartthrob*. And if she's ambitious, she'll devise a way to make our connection beneficial to her. I'd rather not see that person tonight, though.

Besides, what are the odds I'll see Tori after this trip? It would be nice to spend time with a woman who isn't trying to get something out of me. I resolve to do nothing more than enjoy her company while we're on the island, in which case the details are unimportant. Broad brushstrokes will suffice.

"I'm a Hollywood insider, and I do a little bit of this and a little bit of that. I work on studio sets a lot."

All true.

Her eyes go wide—just as I'd feared. "Know any celebrities?" She leans in and gives me a conspiratorial wink. "Any gossip to share?"

"I know a few, but I don't gossip."

She pouts at me and scans my body.

The skin around my collar gets itchy under her prolonged observation. "What are you doing?"

She winks at me. "Someone must have misplaced the microchip that programs your ability to have fun when they manufactured you. I'm looking for the place to reinsert it."

My jaw drops. What? Me, boring? No fucking way. I'm the life of the party. Always.

Before I can make my case, Tori whips her head around and surveys the area beyond the bar. Not more than ten feet away, a lit path leads directly to the resort's pristine beach. Two men work in the sand, one balancing a thick pole in his hands and the other setting up a steel stand.

Tori grabs another drink and gestures excitedly with her other hand. "Limbo," she bellows for the benefit of everyone within a three-mile radius. Jesus, this woman's got pipes.

She jumps up from the stool and downs her shot. "Just what we need to get this party started." She lifts a brow and motions for me to take another shot. "Catch up, Carter. Don't think I'm not counting."

That makes me laugh—and for some reason I'm unable to stop.

Tori halts and turns back to me. "You okay?"

I snap my mouth shut, wave her off, and stand on wobbly legs. Whoa. The vodka's hitting my system sooner than usual. "Doing just great. Don't worry about me." I hold my arms out and stand as still as I can. "See? I'm fine."

She catalogs my demeanor as she rubs her bottom lip. "I've had five shots. You've had four. Ready to call it quits?"

I place my hands on my hips and roll my eyes. "Ugh. *As if.*"

Tori bursts out laughing as she walks in circles. It's…odd.

I straighten and regard her from head to toe, and because she won't stop moving, my head is spinning. "Now it's my turn to ask if you're okay."

She stops circling me and crosses her legs at the ankles, her face tight in concentration. "Um. I need to pee. Be right back."

She runs off in the direction of the public restroom. Several hotel guests hover near the dance floor waiting for the game to begin. I choose not to be one of them, so I plop back onto the stool.

The bartender sets an elbow on the counter, affecting a casual stance, but his laser-like gaze tells me he's on a mission. "Forgot to card you, my man. Hotel policy."

I pull my wallet from the side pocket of my cargo shorts and show him my Connecticut license. He gives it a once-over and nods.

"Let me guess, you're already feeling protective of Tori," I say as I tuck the license back into my wallet.

He smiles. "Well, yes. But Tori's also protective of herself. You may have an eye on her, but she wanted to be sure we had an eye on you, too. Nice to meet you, Carter Williamson of Harmon, Connecticut."

Grinning, I salute him—and mentally applaud Tori's efforts to ensure her own safety. I'm also gratified to know she was probably asking Damon to card me when she leaned into him before.

She returns minutes later and slaps her hands on the bar. "Time to take your fifth shot, John Grizzly Adams."

"The Grizzly thing's wearing a little thin, Tori. Time to expand…your…arsenal."

Jewel touted Aruba for being a tropical paradise with pleasant weather, so why the hell are my face and neck burning?

She lifts a brow. "I have a feeling you'll be providing me with more reasons to tease you very soon."

The shot glass appears at my fingertips. She and the bartender must have a secret code. I down it easily. "Now we're even."

She tugs on my hand. "Now, we limbo."

I tug her back. "No, thank you."

She laughs and crooks her finger at me as she walks backward. "C'mon, Carter. Have a little fun."

Fun? I'm usually all over it. But I'd prefer to tell a joke rather than be one. "Go ahead. I'll watch."

She pauses and crosses her arms in front of her. "What's the matter? You're worried you'll look silly?

You'll have so much more fun when you learn not to care about what others think of you."

She's probably right, but my *life* revolves around letting other people judge me. And I care what they think. Very much. If she wants to sue me about it, she can join the class-action lawsuit against me; my mother happens to be the lead plaintiff.

Tori shrugs her shoulders and spins around, sashaying her way down the lit path to the beach. I blow out a harsh breath when I finally focus on the back of her dress. From the front, it looks like nothing more than an oversize T-shirt with a modest V-neck. Now that she's standing, I can see the back is another story, however. The cotton is shredded just above her ass and at her shoulder blades. Have mercy. Backyard barbecue in the front, Lollapalooza in the back.

The tempo of the steel drums increases, mimicking what's happening to my already-taxed heart. For a minute, I lose Tori in the throng of people lining up for limbo. Then a toned limb shoots up in the air, and a set of bracelets jangle together as they slide down its owner's arm. She emerges from the crowd and skips under the stick. A lone male about my age follows her, his eyes trained on her back.

"Damon, a few more shots, please," I call back behind my shoulder.

He pushes four more shots my way. "The bar is now closed."

According to the clock behind him, it's only fifteen minutes past nine. "A little early for a resort to be closing its bar, don't you think?"

"Let me rephrase. The bar is closed to you." He juts his chin out in the direction of the limbo game. "And to her."

"Fair enough."

I return my gaze to Tori, who's acquired a friend in the short time it took me to get more alcohol. He's wearing an aloha shirt and a goofy grin. The next time Tori goes under the limbo stick, he places his hands on her shoulders and follows closely behind her.

I polish off shots six and seven as I watch them.

The bartender sidles over to me. "You might want to get over there. Looks like he's trying to replace you."

I shoot up from my stool, but the blood rushes to my head, forcing me to sit back down. I should step in. She doesn't know this guy from Adam. Never mind that she doesn't know me, either. At least she's taken steps to vet me.

This time I place my hands on the bar counter before I rise. That's not so bad. I slog through the sand as I balance Tori's remaining shot glasses in my hands, stumbling a few times because the sand is wet and tightly packed. Only a few limbo participants remain, including Tori and her new friend.

Tori's up next. Well, hell. Her turn under the stick, which is only two feet off the ground, is jaw-dropping. She digs her toes into the sand and bends like a contortionist. The move outlines her body in a way that's so indecent I almost look away. Almost.

For some reason, her friend catches her as she lunges forward to steady herself. He must have hit the stick when I wasn't paying attention, or maybe he abandoned the game because he simply wants to get his hands on Tori. Either way, the bartender's correct. It's time for me to reassert myself.

Tori's all laughter and smiles, and I'll admit to being just a little disappointed that she's having so much fun without me. Maybe I should just turn around and leave her alone. This guy might be goofy, but he'll probably tell her who he really is. I pivot in the bar's direction, but someone grabs my wrist and stops me.

"Carter-I-won't-forget-your-name-again-Williamson. I'm glad you decided to join us," Tori says. Each word is drawn out, and her eyes are glassy.

Victory is near, friends.

With a playful flourish, I present her with her shots. "Your drinks, my lady."

"How do I know you had your two?"

She slurs the word *two*. Uh-oh. Tori's approaching shit-faced territory.

"You can ask Damon." I turn and wriggle my fingers at the bartender, who wriggles his fingers in kind.

Tori communicates with Damon, pointing first at the shots and then at her chest and sticking her thumb up. He gives her a thumbs-up in return. Down the hatch the vodka shots go in quick succession, and Mr. Aloha arrives for no good reason whatsoever. The prick.

Tori places the empty shot glasses on a nearby table and jumps up. "Ready to limbo?"

I smirk at the guy beside her. "Yeah, I'm game."

The resort staffers lower the stick half an inch and egg me on. My back and stomach are strong. I've got this.

With my fingers laced behind me, I lean back and dig my feet in the sand to ground me. I'm almost there when I step on a sharp object. The pain causes me to jump, which catapults me forward. My neck collides with the stick, and I'm immediately dropped on my ass like I'm auditioning for the WWE. I roll onto my back and just lie there. From this vantage, I can see that the sky is clear and filled with stars. Really fucking pretty, actually.

Tori drops to the sand by my head. "Oh God. Carter, are you okay?"

I massage my neck and laugh. "Yeah, I'm fine."

Wide-eyed, she asks, "Are you *sure*?"

"Yeah, yeah."

Then she lowers her head, her shoulders shaking violently.

I sit up on my elbows and place my hand on her arm. "Hey, hey, I didn't mean to scare you. I'm fine."

When she lifts her head, she regards me with tear-stained cheeks and proceeds to roar with laughter. "I knew you'd give me another reason to tease you."

Fuck. She's laughing at me? This is what I get for going outside my lane.

She rises and helps me to my feet. "C'mon, I think it's time for you to call it a night."

I brush off her assistance at that point. "I said I was fine."

She backs off and holds her hands up. "Okay, okay. No need to get so testy. The bet was made in good fun, but I think liquor brings out the cranky pants in you. We can consider it withdrawn if you like."

Cranky pants? Christ. Once again, I need to regroup. "Fine."

She smirks at me. "Fine."

Then she walks away. Hmm, no. She's definitely stumbling in the sand.

I try to do the same, but I'm too dizzy to do anything but stare after her. I want to say I'm sorry for acting like a pissed-off child. Really, I do. But the numbness in my mouth is making it difficult to call out to her. After a few more wobbly steps, Tori spins around, her mouth open and poised to speak.

Without warning, my stomach roils. My vision blurs, too, although I can still see Tori ahead. And as gravity pulls me to the sand, her eyes go round.

Why the hell is she running toward me?

Chapter Six

Tori

FOR THE SECOND time in five minutes, I drop to the sand near Carter's head. He's not out cold, but he's not looking great, either. I place two fingers above his nose and mouth. He's still breathing, thank goodness, but he's on his back, which isn't safe. With as much strength as I can gather in my current state, I roll him to his side.

It tickles me that he's such a lightweight.

He winces when he sits up, his eyes glossy and droopy, and when he tries to stand, he lets out a deep, tortured groan. I scoot out of the way when he predictably crashes back down.

"You're trying to do too much," I tell him.

He pins me with an incredulous stare. "How is it that you're completely unaffected by the seven shots of vodka we drank? Are you a mutant?"

"It's a talent of mine. Always been this way, too. Comes in handy when making drinking bets with unsuspecting men who assume their gender guarantees them a win."

He falls back onto the sand. "I didn't assume anything because of my gender. I assumed I'd win because my stomach and kidneys have never failed me before."

"Don't take offense at my question—"

"Don't tell me how to feel about your question before you ask it."

That shuts me up, just as he likely intended. I *like* this guy—because I would have responded the same way. "Are you at your typical weight?"

He shakes his head, squeezing his eyes shut as he does so. "I've lost a few pounds recently. How'd you guess?"

"You don't look comfortable in your own skin. You move as though you're used to carrying more weight. And I'm a personal trainer, so I see this all the time. You have the look of someone who's operating at fifty percent."

He shrinks back and shields his face with his hands. "Stop, the flattery is too much to bear."

Goodness, he's such a drama king, and I refuse to feed into it. "My *point* is that your blood alcohol level depends on a bunch of factors. Gender. Personal tolerance. Weight, too. You want to drink like you just did? At least pack on some pounds first."

"Believe me, I'm working on it."

"Good. Do you need help getting up?"

He places his hands in the sand and twists himself into a standing position. "I'm good."

"Need me to ask Damon to get you to your room?"

"Are you *trying* to kick me when I'm down?"

"I'm *trying* to help you."

He raises his head to the sky. "I'm just going to stand here and stare at the stars."

I think he fully intends to do just that, but he's swaying like a palm tree; one strong gust of wind and he'll topple to the ground.

"I'll sit, actually," he says as he plops down and crosses his legs. "You're welcome to join me, though."

So I join him, because…why the hell not?

After a few seconds of silence, he points at the night sky. "See that constellation of stars over there?"

My brain is too fuzzy to focus on stars, but okay, I'll play along. "Yeah, sure."

"That's Indicitus Minor."

A spectrum of colors—black, navy, and indigo—blanket the moonlit sky, and I do see a bunch of stars, but nothing's readily recognizable. "Really? What's it supposed to look like?"

He laughs and scratches his beard. "I have no idea 'cause I just made that shit up."

I push on his shoulder and shove him away. "Charming."

"Sorry. I've just always wanted to say something like that. Sounds appropriate when you're looking at stars on the beach."

"Ha. Anyone ever tell you you're special?"

"All the time."

There's an edge to his voice that suggests he doesn't appreciate that fact. I tip my head to the side and consider him. Brooding male alert. He's a good-natured person, so his reaction to my question begs for further exploration. "You sound unconvinced. You don't think you're special?"

"Most people tell me what they think I want to hear."

"But if it's true why does it matter?"

"Because even if it's true, a person's motivation for saying so is just as important." He picks up a stick and drags it through the sand. "To me."

I get his point—most people would, I think—but I'm more interested in why he's so grumpy about it. "So—"

"Enough about me." He tosses the stick and dusts off his hands. "What's your story, Tori? Why are you here vacationing alone?"

"My boyfriend broke up with me, and I wanted to get away to clear my head."

"Sorry."

"Don't be. You didn't do anything wrong. I'm to blame."

Carter rears back. "Wait. He broke up with you, and you're to blame. How so?"

I didn't expect Mason to manipulate our relationship in public, but given the nature of his career and ambitions, I suppose it was inevitable. The odds were always against us. To Carter, I say, "I should have anticipated that we weren't a good match, that's all. The signs were as bright as a fireworks display. He's an attention seeker, and I'm the exact opposite. Our demise isn't all that surprising."

Carter, who's again sifting sand through his fingers, pauses and clears his throat. "Ah." Our gazes lock, and then he drops his chin, breaking the connection. "You seem to be taking it well."

He's right, of course. And that's telling in a way I hadn't focused on until this moment. "Now that I've had time to consider what he did, I can see that I was more upset about being duped than being dumped. But it's all good. *Siempre pa'lante, nunca pa'tras.*"

Carter's brows snap together. "What does that mean?"

"It means I've got to keep moving. Onward and upward. Never backward. My ex is in my past, and that's where he'll stay."

"Just like that?"

I nod. "Just like that. I suppose I shouldn't be upset with myself for being thrust in a bad situation, but if I let it continue, well, then the blame really is on me."

"How long did you date?"

"About a year."

Carter angles his head and stares at me, his eyes flickering with…interest, maybe? "He was a lucky man for about a year."

My breath quickens, and a tingle runs along my spine. His words are like a verbal caress that's too intimate to ignore. "That's sweet of you to say, but you don't know me well enough to come to that conclusion."

"Are you the kind of woman who changes completely when you're dating someone?"

"No," I say on a laugh.

"Then my gut tells me he was a lucky man for about a year."

I part my lips and take in a slow breath. "Thank you."

He breaks our eye contact, and I'm grateful someone's thinking clearly.

"So where do you train in Philly?" he asks.

"At a fitness club in Center City. I'm the manager."

He widens his eyes and leans back. "Now I see where you get your taskmaster tendencies."

This man gives me a permanent grin. If I'm not careful, I'll break my vow to avoid a vacation hookup. And that would be foolish. I mean, I haven't given Mason his official walking papers, so why is this even a consideration?

He drops onto his back, apparently not caring that the sand will infiltrate his hair. It's a luxury I'd never be able to afford; sand and curly hair simply don't mix well. "Congratulations, Tori-not-short-for-Victoria," he says as he yawns. "You've gotten me trashed."

I stand up and dust off the back of my dress. Now's as good a time as any to escape temptation. "Then my work here is done, Carter. I've got to get up bright and early for my run, so I'll bid you adieu." After tugging on the hem of my dress to make sure it's covering my backside, I salute him. "You're off the hook, but let the record reflect that I did in fact outdrink you."

I wait for a witty retort, but none is forthcoming, because Carter's eyes are closed and he's snoring. So much for his stamina.

When I reach the bar, I raise a finger to get Damon's attention.

"What can I do for you, princess?"

"Mr. Williamson's back there taking a nap. Can you make sure he doesn't stay there all night?"

Damon ducks and peers at the beach. "Found him. Yes, I'll take care of it."

He hands me the guest check, and I charge the drinks to my room.

"He seems like a good guy," Damon says.

"He does. Funny, too."

"Maybe you won't be alone on this vacation after all, huh?"

"Maybe," I say with a coy smile.

Although my decree still stands: No rebound hookups. No one-night stands. Not even a kiss on the cheek. *Nothing.*

THE NEXT MORNING, I rise at six and throw on my running gear. The view from my balcony convinces me to slow down, though. The sky is clear, not a skyscraper or puff of smog in sight, and dolphins are skimming the water's surface. I take in a deep breath of the salty air. Then my stomach growls, jockeying for my attention, as if to say, *Beyotch, forget the view and feed me.*

Breakfast is my favorite meal, but I can't whip up an omelet in my room. And I'd never order room service this early in the day because I'm convinced those calls annoy the staff and they put "special sauce" in your scrambled eggs to spite you. A granola bar it is, then.

I hold the bar in one hand as I check my phone. I'm not surprised to see several missed calls from Mason, which makes me chew harder. The Do Not Disturb feature on my phone is a lovely tool. It's the technological equivalent of my roommate and best girlfriend, Eva. If she were here, she'd send Mason straight to voice mail, too.

After a quick brush of my teeth, I leave the room and take the spiral stairs to the hotel courtyard, where I'm surprised to find Carter sitting on an iron bench surrounded by hibiscus plants. He and his workout clothes don't mesh with the stunning backdrop. It reminds me of the plywood scenes my sister and I used to stick our heads through at carnivals, the ones that made us look like farmers with ears of corn and radishes in our hands. Here, it's Carter's head sticking out of the hole cut into the majestic island backdrop.

I glance at his feet. "You're running with me?"

"Sure."

Hmm. How to put this? He's a man, so I'm guessing I'll have to be delicate here. Fragile egos, you know. "Carter, you got wasted last night. Running this morning might be more taxing than you realize."

He tries to wave my concern away. "I'll be okay. I might not be dripping with physicality, but I'm actually a pretty fit guy."

I stare at the physique of which he speaks. The personal trainer in me can't help it. He's underweight, perhaps due in part to a freakishly overactive metabolism, but he otherwise looks healthy. Yesterday's Caribbean sun has warmed his pale skin, giving him a not-quite-but-on-its-way-to-healthy glow. "Fine. Let's head out to the beach and stretch."

He points to my waist. "Wait. What's going on with that fanny pack?"

"It's *not* a fanny pack. It's called a waist pack, and it will hold my water during the run. Does it offend your fashion sensibilities?"

He wrinkles his nose. "It certainly does. I wouldn't have agreed to run with you had I known you'd be wearing *that*."

I stare at him for several seconds while I figure out if I'm hallucinating. "Are you serious?"

He stretches his neck, and then he shakes his head. "No."

I can't help snickering. Damn him. "You're stalling. Have you changed your mind about running?"

"I'll admit to being nervous. Your calves are intimidating as hell. I didn't see them well last night. Makes me think this is going to be painful."

Holding in my laughter, I turn away and wave goodbye. "Suit yourself," I say over my shoulder.

As expected, Carter catches up, and we walk in silence toward the beach.

We park ourselves under a divi-divi, its leaves creating an irregular swath of much-needed shade across what will soon become sun-drenched white sand. It's an iconic tree in Aruba, for sure. Kind of like a bonsai tree in reverse, its artistry emanating from the trunk that's seemingly carved into submission and forced to point in the direction of the winds. Every online travel guide included it on the must-see list, and now I understand why.

Carter traces the tree's tightly coiled branches. "This is incredible." Wearing an intense gaze, he circles the trunk, which splits into branches that jut out at an almost ninety-degree angle. "How do they get like this?" He resumes his exploration, his long fingers ghosting over the plant delicately. Would he worship a woman's body with the same reverence? Dammit. Why did that thought pop into my head? It's time to get Carter away from any island vegetation, obviously.

"A natural wonder," I say as I point and flex my calves before dropping into a walking lunge. "Hey, Carter, join me, huh?"

Carter turns away from the tree and rotates his hips in a circular motion. "You do this every day?"

I shake my head and move into a stork stretch. "I do some form of physical fitness daily, but running is usually reserved for the weekends."

Carter mirrors my stance. "You said you run with someone at home?"

The question reminds me that Eva envisioned this beach scenario differently. "Find yourself a local," she advised, "and have cake by the ocean." When I gave her a blank look, she smacked her forehead and said, "Sex, Tori. Have sex. The kind where you get nasty sand burns."

Until then, I'd had no idea what the lyrics to "Cake by the Ocean" were about. But I can always rely on Eva to educate me. After I met her during my first year at Temple, my pop culture literacy reached Mensa levels. "Yeah," I tell Carter. "My roommate usually runs with me."

"I'll try to do him justice, then," he says.

Fishing for information much, Carter? "Her."

He smiles brightly. "Ah."

"The concierge mapped out a four-mile route starting at Palm Beach, running along the main road that parallels the water, and ending at the California Lighthouse. If you're game, we can run there and back for an eight-mile workout."

His eyebrows shoot up, and then he coughs. "Yeah, that should be fine."

We start at a jogging pace. The road is clear and largely populated by early morning runners like us. I'm enjoying the rhythm of our footsteps and the crashing of the nearby waves.

Not even five minutes into it, Carter slows to a stroll and points ahead. "Look. It's a Dunkin' Donuts." There's wonder in his voice, like he's spotted a unicorn.

"There's a Starbucks at the hotel," I say, unimpressed.

"Not the same thing at all," he says as he veers toward the door.

Okay, I'll give him this one. Abuela's *café con leche* can't be replicated. Even my mother's version is only a close approximation, so if DD is his thing, who am I to judge? Nevertheless, I pull him back and point two fingers at my eyes. "Focus."

He tilts his head and drops his shoulders. "Right."

Five minutes later, he again slows down when he sees a row of street vendors. "Look, Tori. Bracelets. And charms. And stuff." Now he's waving his hands like Vanna White. And pretending to be excited.

"Carter, if you didn't want to run why'd you agree to join me?"

He stops and dons an innocent expression. "Me? Not want to run? What makes you say that?"

Now I employ the infamous side-eye. "The fact that we've only managed an eighth of a mile in ten minutes."

"Sorry, I'm easily distracted. But that's not fair to you. Let me buy a drink and then we can get going. Do you want something?"

I shake my head and point to the fanny pack he detests so much.

He motions to a vendor selling fresh coconut water. "One, please." He turns to me. "This is okay, right?"

"Actually, it is. Full of electrolytes and not a lot of sodium. Good choice, Carter."

He beams at me, and then he pays the vendor. As we walk, he sips the coconut water through a straw. "Oh, that's good. Nothing like the ready-made ones in the stores." He holds the coconut in front of me. "You sure you don't want any?"

I lean over and take a sip. It has the characteristic sweet and nutty flavor I adore. "That's how they tasted when my grandfather pulled them off the tree in his backyard."

Carter stares at my lips but quickly drops his gaze to the ground.

"What?" I say as I wipe my mouth.

He takes another sip of his drink. "Nothing. So...your grandfather had a coconut tree?"

"Yeah. In Puerto Rico. He'd twist one off the bunch and chop the tops off with a machete. My sister and I would wait for him to pour the water into our cups. We'd have the ice and straw ready."

"Do you still see him?"

"No. My grandparents passed away a long time ago. My grandfather first and then my grandmother about five years later. I have lots of great memories of them, though. Are your grandparents still alive?"

"On my mother's side, yes. And my grandfather still chases my grandmother like they're youngsters. Grandpa James is a player."

I chuckle, imagining Carter's grandfather literally chasing his grandmother around the house. "Good for them."

We walk in silence a bit, and there's this ease to us being together that makes me feel like I've walked along this road with Carter before. I decide just to enjoy it, taking in the scenery and enjoying the morning breeze. Somewhere along the way, though, we acquire a small following, in the form of two stray dogs.

My chest tightens. I've never encountered a wild dog, but I've seen enough stories in the news to know they're nothing to be cavalier about. "Carter, don't flick the juice off your hands and don't make any sudden movements. We have stray dogs behind us."

Ignoring my instructions, Carter whips around and jumps back. One of the dogs, a mangy mixed breed with short ears, bares its teeth, and the other dog, a black Lab mix with matted fur and saliva hanging from its mouth, begins to bark aggressively.

My heart races like a Thoroughbred—and I sure as hell hope I'll be able to move like one, too. "Drop the coconut and run," I yell.

This time Carter listens to me and chucks the coconut across the road, and then we run like we're being chased by wild dogs—*because we are.*

But within seconds, the gap between us and them widens, and it becomes clear that these dogs either can't or aren't interested in expending any energy to catch us. Still, Carter looks like he's competing in an Olympic track meet or reenacting Tom Hanks's infamous sprint in *Forrest Gump*, and I match him stride for stride, the dogs nowhere close to our heels. I'm so overwhelmed by the ridiculousness of the situation that I burst out laughing as tears stream down my face. "Run, Carter, run!"

Carter laughs, too. "I'm trying, Tori. I am. You think they're faking us out?"

"That would be diabolical."

Just in case, we run at full speed for another quarter mile, and after the dogs' barking fades, we slow to a trot, and then stop altogether. I drop my hands to my knees and suck in all the air I can get.

Carter pants by my side. "Never again. I'm *never* running with you again."

"Hey, at least I got you to run," I say with a smile.

He narrows his eyes. "I'm not amused."

I pat him on the shoulder. "Let's walk the rest of the way to the lighthouse. I think this run was doomed from the start."

"There *is* a God," Carter mutters.

I expected to run a minimum of four miles this morning and came nowhere close to that distance. Despite the change in plans, I'm glad Carter joined me. This was a much better way to spend the morning, and how many people can say they were chased by wild dogs in Aruba?

I loop my arm through Carter's and drag him along. "C'mon, Carter."

I don't think anything of the physical contact until he stiffens, and then I sever our connection. "Sorry."

Carter stops in the middle of the sidewalk. "No. It's fine." He tugs my arm from behind my back and loops it with his. "I like your hands on me, Tori. I just wasn't expecting it."

He turns his head and pins me with a heated stare.

Warmth pools in my belly. Whoa. Shying away from his gaze, I face the hill ahead of us and point. "Look. We're almost there."

Carter clears his throat. "Let's get going, then. It must be an amazing view."

We climb the hill, and as we approach the lighthouse, the terrain changes, the grass transitioning to stone-filled land. The rocks are jagged, and I slip a few times before we reach the top.

Carter reads the plaque at the entrance to the observation area. "Says it's named after a ship that was wrecked somewhere near here."

The lighthouse is impressive, but the view enthralls me. It's nothing but sky, waters in various shades of blue, and small patches of sea grass to remind us that perfection is impossible. Carter and I stand next to each other, taking it all in, remaining silent because nature is doing the talking now.

Finally, he speaks. "Wow. I know that's inadequate, but wow."

I'm gratified to hear he sees it like I do. "Exactly."

Beside me, Carter's stomach grumbles.

"Let's get you back to the hotel," I tell him. "You've taxed yourself enough for one day."

"The taskmaster has a heart."

I press my thumb and index finger together. "A small one."

He laughs and holds out his hand when we get to a patch of rough ground.

"So, will you be staying in Philly awhile?" I ask as we begin the hike back.

He gives me a sideways glance. "Not sure how long, but I'm not in a rush to get back to LA. Why?"

"I could train with you for a few days. Show you a few exercises. I'd even draw up a program for you if that's something you'd be interested in."

It takes me a minute to realize the import of my offer. Shit. He probably thinks I'm manufacturing reasons to see him again. But he obviously needs someone's help, so why not me?

"I'd love that," he says. "It would be nice to have a friend in Philly."

Right. *A friend.* Given my recent breakup with Mason, Carter's offering exactly what I need: friendship. So why am I disappointed to hear that he's placed me squarely in that zone? Argh.

Stop, stop, stop. Don't do this, Tori. Keep it simple. Keep it light. Keep it fun. "Hey, I'm planning to go paddleboarding tomorrow. One of those excursions booked through the resort. Interested in joining me?"

He slides two fingers above his upper lip as he ponders my question. I'm staring so intently that I notice the tiny dots of perspiration that have settled there. Suddenly I'm thirsty.

"I'd love to," he says, his eyes crinkling at the corners as he smiles down at me.

Because I'm more excited about spending time with him than I should be, I quickly add another task on my to-do list: help Carter find his own island fling at the first opportunity. Maybe seeing him flirt with someone else will rid me of my *unfriendly* thoughts. A woman can always hope, can't she?

Chapter Seven

Carter

YOU'RE THINKING I should have declined her invitation, right?

Here's why I didn't.

One, I *like* Tori. In the short time I've known her, she's bested me in a drinking challenge, convinced me to limbo, and saved me from certain death at the hands of stray dogs. The bothersome scenes in my life fade to black when I'm around her.

Two, I'm constitutionally predisposed to engage in activities that demonstrate my skills, and stand-up paddleboarding fits the bill. Whenever I visit home in the summer, my sisters and I head out to Stonington for a few hours of paddleboarding, so this is well within my wheelhouse.

Three, I'm 99 percent certain Tori will be wearing a bikini. That thought alone puts an extra bounce in my step and gets me from my room to the travel tour's meeting point in less than three minutes.

A small group of people stand in a loose circle in the resort's lobby. Tori's not among them, though. To their right, a stocky man with brown leathery skin speaks to the hotel concierge in the local language. I think it's called Papiamento.

When the man spots me, he calls me over. "Hey, my friend, are you joining us this morning?"

"Paddleboarding?"

"Yes, yes. I'm Howie, your guide." He points to a man tinkering under the hood of a van parked in the circular driveway. "That's Raul. He's my right-hand man and driver. We're just waiting for two more and then we'll head out."

While we wait for Tori and someone else, the members of our group make the customary introductions. There's a couple on their honeymoon and a mom vacationing with her teenaged daughter.

The group engages in a few more minutes of small talk, and then Tori strolls toward us, and dammit, the guy who was sniffing around our first night on the island is trailing behind her, his gaze trained on her ass. Tori's wearing a short-sleeved scuba shirt and swimming shorts. She looks as adorable as ever, and I don't even care that she's not showing more skin. I'm just happy to see her again.

Tori introduces me to Mr. Aloha Shirt, whose real name is Stevie. It doesn't suit him or his beady eyes, so let's just call him Skeevy for the moment.

We file into the third row of the passenger van, and Tori takes the seat between Skeevy and me. He's pointing out landmarks to Tori as we travel from the resort to the excursion site. From the front passenger seat, Howie shares facts about the island and asks whether anyone has paddleboarded before. The female honeymooner, Skeevy, and I raise our hands. Skeevy leans into Tori and whispers in her ear. She doubles over in laughter.

"Hey, Howie," I yell. "It's hard to hear you back here. Could you talk a little louder?"

"Sure, sure," he yells back.

Skeevy leans forward and smirks at me.

I solemnly swear to smack him with my paddle at least once today.

Howie tells us about the wildlife we're likely to see during the trip, and twenty minutes later, the van slows near a lagoon. We pile out of the van, and Howie and Raul distribute the boards.

The water's clear and calm. Perfect conditions for paddleboarding. The scenery's breathtaking, too. Mature red mangroves line one side of the lagoon, and nothing obstructs my view of the seascape. It's eerily quiet, adding to the island mystique, but then a flock of birds shake the trees' leaves when they escape the brush, reminding me that we're the trespassers here.

"Why don't you guys who've done this before go ahead," Howie says. "I'm going to help the others."

Tori's face is flushed, and she looks like she can hardly contain her excitement. I walk several feet before dropping the board into the water, making sure that my fin isn't stuck in the sand. Biggest mistake first-time paddle-boarders make? Trying to stand on the board as soon as they get on. I look over at the mother-daughter duo, who aren't waiting for Howie's instructions, and yep, they're struggling for that very reason.

"Get on your knees first," I tell them.

They take my advice, and the mother gives me a thumbs-up.

The water's cooperating today, so I mount the paddle-board with ease. I'm only seconds in when Skeevy's board skims mine, and the moment when I'll smack him with the board is upon us. "What's your problem, man?"

Skeevy gives me a shit-eating grin as he struggles to stay close. "No problem at all. Just doing a little reconnaissance."

"What does that mean?"

He jerks his chin toward the beach, where Howie is instructing Tori on how to stand on the board. "She's what I mean. You planning on hitting that?"

Jesus. I grit my teeth in lieu of knocking him into the water. I'm hardly averse to admiring a woman's body in my head, but talking with him about Tori like she's a piece of ass for the taking is a hard limit for me. He probably thinks he's earning points per the Bro Code, but I don't subscribe to such bullshit, especially not with two sisters of my own. This guy doesn't deserve to be anywhere near Tori. "No, I don't plan on hitting that, asshole, and I'll make it my life's work to make sure you don't hit that, either. You don't deserve her."

My hold on the grip is so firm my fingers are aching. But my anger subsides when I return my gaze to the object of our conversation. She peels off the scuba top to reveal a black triangle bikini top and the best motherfucking set of abs I've seen on a person in years. Her stomach is a fascinating study in hard and soft lines, captivating my attention because her skin is brown and smooth and utterly touchable. And she has powerhouse thighs. I bet she looks glorious on a leg press. Oh, fuck me. This is a disaster. She's stripping, and I'm wearing board shorts that cannot mask my um…interest. I'm just as bad as Skeevy, and I don't deserve her, either.

She unbuttons her shorts and they drop to the sand. I suspend the paddle in midair, unable to focus on my strokes. Behind me Skeevy whistles, which pulls me out of the spell Tori's cast on me.

Howie calls out to us. "You guys all right out there?"

"Yeah," I reply as I reposition the paddle to resume my strokes. But somehow I've gotten closer to the shore than I'd intended, and the paddle hits sand, causing the board—and me—to upend in an epic wipeout.

My gaffe probably would have gone unnoticed, but Skeevy draws attention to it with his exaggerated laughter and finger-pointing. Skeevy needs to be handled. This minute. I mount the board with revenge on the brain. But before I can maneuver the paddle to whack his board, water splashes behind me and Skeevy yelps.

"You all right back there, Skeevy?"

He's moaning, so I turn around to check on him.

Skeevy's in the water now, his hands wrapped around his foot and his face twisted in pain. "It's Stevie, you dick," he says through clenched teeth.

I look back at the shore and yell. "Howie, something's wrong with Stevie."

Howie shades his eyes and wades in. Tori and her amazing black bikini trudge through the water, too. Great. Now the guy's going to get sympathy points. He probably planned this.

Howie checks Stevie's foot. "Sea urchin. Rare for this area, but they do come in with the tides from time to time. I guess today's your lucky day."

And mine, Howie. And mine.

"Looks like you've got about eight stingers," Howie says. "Let's get you out of here. Carter, can you give me a hand?"

I take Stevie's arm and lace it over my shoulder. "Ready?"

"Yes," Howie says.

"Ow, ow, ow," Stevie says over and over.

I feel bad for the guy. What? I do.

When we reach the sand, we help Stevie sit, and the group circles him.

"Is there anything I can do to help?" Tori asks.

Miraculously, Stevie's able to push through the pain and make a request. "Yeah. Could you pour some water over my head?"

What the fuck is water going to do? *This dude.* He's back to Skeevy now.

Tori grabs a water bottle from Howie's cooler and pours the entire contents over Skeevy's head while Howie tries to remove the stingers from his foot.

"Tori," Skeevy says in a breathy voice. "Could I squeeze your hand while he pulls out the stingers?"

Tori's eyebrows snap together and then she rolls her eyes. "Sure."

The little shit looks up at me and smirks as he clasps Tori's hand in his.

Howie glances between us, and his eyes narrow as his gaze settles on Skeevy, finally hip to the fact that there's no bromance between us. "I don't have the right tools for this."

"Hey, Howie. You know what works for easing the pain?"

"Vinegar," Howie replies.

I clear my throat. "Or uric acid."

Howie laughs. "That's an old—"

I elbow Howie in the side. "You've seen it work before, right, Howie?"

Howie's eyes go wide. "Oh, yeah, yeah. Plenty of times. Just a little bit of piss—sorry, ladies—and the pain fades away."

"Seriously?" Skeevy asks in between hisses.

Howie and I nod enthusiastically.

"Yeah, then we'll get Raul to drive you back to the resort," Howie tells him. "The doctor should be able to pull the stingers out with tweezers. Unfortunately, my first-aid kit doesn't have any."

"What do you say?" I ask.

Tori, who's been biting the fingernails of her free hand, chimes in. "You should do it, Stevie. Think of the van ride. It'll be torture if you don't."

"Okay, okay."

Oh, damn. Skeevy's cool with this? What did I do to deserve this series of events?

Howie and I help Skeevy to an area past the jetty dividing the lagoon from the more turbulent waters on the north side of the beach.

I reach into my pants, preparing to do Skeevy a solid, but he stops me. "No, not you. And there's no need for you to hang around."

Howie shakes his head and mutters under his breath.

I back up with my hands in the air. "No problem. As long as you get the help you need." I spin around and walk back to the group, reveling in the knowledge that Skeevy will forever be known to Tori as the man who let someone piss on his foot to relieve a little pain.

Tori meets me halfway and hands me a water bottle from Howie's cooler. "Everything okay?"

"He didn't let me do it. Took one look at my junk and said it intimidated him."

Tori's eyes glisten with tears as she drapes a hand over my shoulder. "Oh, Carter, you're *too much*."

I take a swig of the water, hyperaware of her touch. Under different circumstances, I'd be stoked that she's feeling more comfortable around me. But I can't aim for anything more than friendship, so any physical contact between us tortures me instead.

Minutes later, Skeevy returns with Howie at his side. A thin sheen of sweat covers both his forehead and the area above his upper lip.

"Feel better?" I ask him.

"Not really. No. He couldn't…produce."

Howie gives me a pointed look. "It's probably for the best." Our tour guide is all business now. "Raul, let's get him back to Eagle Bay. And make sure the doc on staff sees him immediately. Be back to pick us up in an hour. If there's any problem, let me know."

"No problem, boss," Raul says.

The group watches Raul and Skeevy's departure. The latter hobbles to the van while everyone wishes him a speedy recovery.

When Raul drives away, Howie pins me with a bemused expression and shakes his head.

"What?" I ask him.

"Did you seriously think I'd piss on his foot?"

I shrug. "It was worth a shot."

"I'm amazed I took it that far," he says. "Let's finish this trip without any more shenanigans from you, okay?"

"Yeah, okay." As everyone grabs their boards and paddles, I pull Howie to the side. "I can help Tori."

Howie chuckles, and his gaze settles on the water. "I'm not so sure she's going to need your help."

I follow his gaze. Tori's already dropped the board, and she's kneeling on it like she's done this a million times. "Find your sweet spot," I call out to her.

She steps to the middle of the board and rises slowly, her hands perfectly positioned on the paddle.

"She's a natural," Howie observes. "Guess you'll have to find some other way to get close to her."

I draw back and give him a "what-who-me" expression. "It's nothing like that. I'm just enjoying her company."

"Well, you went to great lengths to *just* enjoy her company."

"C'mon, Howie. I didn't plant the sea urchin."

Howie nods. "True. But that piss business? You must want her badly." He claps and yells out to Tori. "Great job." Then he hands me my board. "Don't go too far out, Casanova."

I mount the board and catch up to Tori easily. "How's it going?"

"This is so much fun. I can tell I'm going to be sore tomorrow, though."

Her face is dotted with water droplets, and she has a streak of sunscreen down her nose. Her hair is pulled into a bun. And of course, Howie's right: I want her badly. But I'm not going there, because pursuing her as Carter Williamson would be wrong, and she doesn't deserve to be screwed—*figuratively*—by two guys in one week.

I focus on our counterparts to get my mind off Tori. The lagoon is wide enough that the group can spread out, but everyone's within my field of vision. The male honeymooner appears to be having the most trouble, so Howie's focused on that couple.

"Ready to do something more than paddle in circles?" I ask her.

She bites her bottom lip. "I'm not sure."

"Yes, you are," I assure her. "If you can swim, you'll be fine."

"Okay, I'll follow."

We paddle out toward one end of the widest section of the lagoon. Within seconds, a passing motorboat causes a few ripples.

"Eeep," Tori says behind me. *"Ay Dios, me voy a morir!"*

I turn my head and frown at her. "You're not going to die, Tori."

She bends her knees to regain her balance. "Wait. You understand Spanish?"

"Only what I can remember from high school. I had a Spanish tutor."

"Ooh. Tell me something else."

I lower the paddle into the water and use my elbow to wipe my brow. *"Estoy caliente."*

Tori barks out a laugh. "Ha-ha. *Despacito*, Justin Bieber. You're supposed to say *tengo calor*. *Estoy caliente* means you think you're hot, as in sexy. Common mistake."

I give her an overtly smoldering look. "Who says it was a mistake? Are you saying I'm not sexy?"

She stops paddling, and her cheeks flush. "No, I never said that. You're sexy. *Very* sexy." She dips her chin and blinks as though her brain has now caught up with her mouth. "I mean…you, ah, you've definitely got that…lumberjack swag. With the beard and all."

I smirk at her. "Uh-huh."

I'm not even a little annoyed that she struggles to give me a compliment. It feels *real. Right.*

Tori's choked voice crashes into my thoughts. "Carter, we're drifting apart." Her eyes are wide, and she's whipping her head back and forth as her board takes her farther away from me.

"Just keep paddling toward the beach. I'll catch up with you."

She maneuvers herself around and paddles in the shore's direction. The strain in her face disappears when she realizes she still has control of the board. Only when I know she's comfortable again do I paddle to meet her. Once I'm close, we move through the water side by side, and as we approach the sand, we race to the finish, Tori's laughter floating in the air like a cool breeze on an oppressively hot day. Just a day by the sea with a woman I like—a lot.

Still, I can't let a few days in the sun blind me to reality. Tori and I wouldn't have this easy connection if she knew the truth about my profession. So I'll enjoy our time together for what it is. And then we'll both return to Philadelphia the way we came.

Alone.

OUR GROUP, EXHAUSTED and disheveled, returns to the resort in the early afternoon. Tori and I make plans to have dinner together.

A couple of hours later, Tori meets me at the entrance to the open-air restaurant on the north side of the resort. She's wearing a one-piece tank-top-and-shorts combo that accentuates her long legs. Her hair is slicked into a side ponytail, a mass of curls draped over one shoulder, and her eyes are rimmed with black eyeliner.

"Your hair looks great," I tell her.

She flicks her ponytail. "Very necessary, too. My hair lost its battle with the humidity today. To the victor goes the frizz."

Paper lanterns dot the perimeter of the restaurant and bathe the space, giving it a warm glow. A band plays soft jazz on an elevated platform in a corner.

As we wait to be seated, I breathe in the salty sea air and listen to the waves crash against the shore.

The hostess arrives and tells us we're free to sit at the bar or choose a table wherever we'd like. The bar is populated by a rowdy bunch, half of them standing, while most of the people at the tables are twosomes who appear to be enjoying a night of romance under the stars.

Tori and I are silent as I weigh our options. The intimacy of sitting at a candlelit table might tempt my brain to go to places it shouldn't, but I'd prefer not to be jostled by the drunkards at the bar.

Tori lifts her brows. "Um. Table?"

"Yeah," I say.

I'll just keep it light. Easy and breezy always works.

After we order from the bar menu, I ask Tori about her plans for tomorrow.

She folds and unfolds her linen napkin. "I'm going to spend it on the beach. Nothing else. Just me, a book, and sunshine."

I gasp, pretending to be shocked. "You're going nude?"

She tosses the napkin at my face, and I catch it with one hand.

Tori doesn't know that a napkin can become art in my hands, but I'm planning to school her. I fold it in half diagonally.

She reaches over, her pretty mouth curved into a playful smile. "Hey, what are you doing with my napkin? It's rude to touch someone else's stuff."

"If that were true, no one would have sex," I say as I roll the napkin.

"Without asking for permission," she clarifies.

"Fair point. Tori, can I touch your stuff? You'll be glad I did."

She blushes. "Fine. But you better make it worth my while."

I throw innuendo at her, and she pitches back sass. I could do this with her all day. And if I'm not too careful, I'll miss her more than I should miss anyone after a jaunt in the Caribbean.

I fiddle with the napkin and present it to her. "Voila. Tori, will you accept this rose?" It's the same question countless bachelors and bachelorettes have posed to their dozens of "one true loves" on that train wreck of a show.

She gazes at me, smiles, and leans forward. "Absolutely not. You just had your tongue down the throats of four other women. You probably have mono."

I laugh until my sides hurt. Then I toss the napkin back at her.

"So you've worked in a restaurant, too?" she asks.

"Catering, mostly, which included all the setup. It's left me with an impressive skill set."

The candle in the center of the table highlights the twinkle in her eyes. "Any woman would be lucky to have you."

"Sarcasm notwithstanding, I agree with you."

She rolls her eyes.

The band takes a short break, and an up-tempo song plays through the speakers. The drums add a thumping beat that's hard to resist, and soon Tori and I are both swaying in our chairs.

"If you don't mind my asking, how old are you?" I ask.

She's snapping her fingers to the music as she answers. "Twenty-nine."

Shit. She *is* older than me. Not by much, but still…

"How old are you?" she asks.

"Twenty-seven. I've been told I act mature for my age, though."

She sits back, opens her eyes wide, and cackles. "Whoever told you that is a liar."

"And whoever taught you manners is a terrible teacher."

She tips a nonexistent hat and gives me a lopsided grin. "Touché."

"Let me put this age difference in perspective."

With her eyes squinting at me in amusement, she gestures for me to continue. "Please, Carter, break it down for me."

"When I was born, you were learning to pee in a potty. That's it. That sums up our age difference."

She shakes her head. "No, what sums up our age difference is the absolute certainty that I would never willingly mention *peeing in a potty* in casual conversation."

We stare at each other for several seconds, and then we both howl with laughter. While we're still doubled over, the server delivers our drinks: a beer for me and a glass of passion fruit juice for her. Minutes later, he brings an assortment of appetizers to our table, including grilled barbecue chicken so good Tori and I are both licking our fingers before we're done.

"You're right about what you said earlier, actually," she says, sucking barbecue sauce off her thumb. "I have the worst manners when I'm with you."

I study the way her lips close over the digit. Perfection. "I could say the same about myself," I say in a low voice.

She drops her hands to her lap like she's a Catholic schoolgirl who's been told to sit up straight by a nun. It's fascinating to watch her react to me. One minute, she's playful. The next minute, she's shy. Playful appears to be her comfort zone, and I wish she'd stay in it.

"It just means we're comfortable around each other," I say, hoping to send the message that there's no risk in flirting. "And I'm not complaining."

She nods and leans forward, her hands reappearing on the table to fiddle with her straw and glass. But she avoids my gaze. After a few seconds of worrying her bottom lip, she straightens, her jaw set in determination. "I've been thinking about our wager."

"What about it?"

"Well, I'm feeling generous, so even though *you* lost the bet, I'd like to help you anyway."

I'd forgotten about the bet, and since I'm spending tons of time with Tori already, I have no interest in her assistance. "It's okay. I'll manage on my own."

She clasps her hands in front of her and pleads. "Please, Carter? C'mon, it'll be fun. You might even be able to have cake by the ocean."

"Tori, trust me, I've had the equivalent of a dessert party by the ocean."

She draws back, her lips drawn up to her nose as though she's smelling something unpleasant. "Ew. Poor taste. TMI. Overcompensating."

The apples of my cheeks warm. This woman will keep my ego in check for sure. And she'd fit in just fine with the rest of my family. I can picture Tori squeezed between my sisters on my parents' couch as they razz me about something. The image should make me shudder. But the idea of adding Tori to my family peanut gallery takes up residence in my brain and refuses to move out.

She scoots her chair closer to mine, dragging her drink along with her. She brings the glass to her lips. Rather than take a sip from it, though, she swings the drink away from her face. "There," she says with a mischievous glint in her eyes. "Do you see that woman at the bar? She's been checking you out for a while now."

I follow the trajectory of her swing and glance at the subject of our conversation.

"It's like she's trying to figure out if she knows you," Tori continues.

The hairs on my arms rise. It's nothing. Well, I *hope* it's nothing. No, I *pray* it's nothing. But given my current state of dishevelment, it's probably something. Since I can't just run out on dinner, my best option is to go talk to the woman and find out what she knows. "Okay, I'll humor you. What advice would you give me?"

Tori leans into me, a few strands of her long, curly hair brushing my shoulder. "Don't use a line. Be yourself. She's going to wonder why you're talking to her when just a few seconds ago, you were talking to me. Explain that we're friends. And if she seems to be slipping away, hit her with"—her voice drops to a whisper as though she's revealing a secret—"the eyes."

"The eyes?"

"Yes, Carter, your eyes. Unless you're truly clueless, you know they're one of your best features. Give her 'the smolder,' and she'll be yours."

I stare at her for several seconds more than necessary, practicing "the smolder." Her gaze is transfixed on mine. I glance at her lips, and she parts them—unconsciously, I'm sure—and then she snaps them shut. With her face averted, she leans back and stretches her arms above her head as though she's bored.

I shake my head in disappointment. "See? I think you're overestimating their allure."

But then she blows out a slow breath. Maybe she's not unaffected by me after all. Even if that's true, though, I'm committed to not doing anything about it.

"Just take my advice and run with it, Carter. You'll thank me later." She gestures for the bill and shoos me with a smile and a thumbs-up.

I make my way across the patio, unsure how we got here. Tori's encouraging me to flirt with another woman, when all I want to do is spend time with her. But right now, the bigger question rattling in my brain is this: Does this woman recognize me? If she does, I'll beg her to keep quiet about it, making noise about my privacy. And if she doesn't, I'll give Tori enough of a show to make her think I tried—and failed—to pick up my admirer.

As I approach, the woman swivels in her seat as she pokes the ice in her cocktail with a straw.

I claim the stool next to her and gesture for Damon's attention.

He furrows his brows for a few seconds, but then he slips into his professional bartender demeanor. "What can I get you, pal?"

"A Coronado."

He nods. Less than a minute later, he returns and places a bottle in front of me.

The woman doesn't turn my way, but I catch a small smile before she takes a sip of her cocktail.

I turn my head and glance at Tori, who nods her encouragement.

"Lovely night, isn't it?" I say to the woman.

"It is," she says.

I offer her my hand. "Carter."

She places her small hand in mine. "Janine."

Then I lean into her. "Janine, I'm going to be frank with you."

The half smile is now a half frown. "Okay."

"Did you happen to notice that I was just sitting next to a woman?"

"I did." Her eyes go round as saucers. "Oh God. I'm so embarrassed. I was staring, wasn't I? I didn't mean to make you uncomfortable. It's just that you look so familiar to me. But then I figured it's true what they say—that everyone has a twin."

"I get that a lot. One day I'll have to figure out which celebrity I favor."

She nods. "Well, anyway, please tell her I don't have designs on her man or anything."

"Oh, no, it's nothing like that. You see, she thinks I need help in the dating department. What she doesn't realize yet is that I'm very interested in her."

Janine sighs and her eyes brighten. "That's *so* romantic. But why don't you just tell her you're interested? Honesty's always the best policy and all that."

I turn back and glance at Tori. She's shaking her head and motioning for me to abandon my pickup attempt. That's precisely what I'm doing—for my own reasons—but I make a mental note to ask her later why she wanted to call it off.

My arm brushes against Janine's side when I swivel the stool in her direction. "Well, she broke up with her boyfriend recently, and she's not interested in dating anyone. I'll tell her when the time's right. If it's okay with you, I'll just say that, much to my disappointment, you told me you have a boyfriend."

Before Janine can respond, a shadow blankets the table and a thunderous voice coming from behind me says, "Her boyfriend's right here, asshole."

Oh shit.

Chapter Eight

Tori

THE BEEFY GUY standing behind Carter clenches his fists and stretches his thick, tattooed neck. Are all bullies taught to signal their willingness to fight in this way? I tried to warn Carter that the man had been looming in the background, but Carter's incapable of reading a signal. Since I got him into this mess, I suppose I should help him out.

When I reach the table, the Hulk appears to be one button way from busting out of his shirt.

"That's not what I asked, dipshit," he says to Carter. "Why are you sniffing around my woman?"

The woman rolls her eyes at her boyfriend. "Greg, stop being a jerk."

Greg places his hands on his chest. "Oh, *I'm* the jerk? Some guy's trying to pick up my girlfriend, and *I'm* the jerk? That's classic, Janine."

Greg pounces on Carter, grabs him by his shirt, and pulls him close. "As for you, I should kick your ass."

A few chairs scrape across the patio floor as other guests move out of the way.

"Do you mean that literally? Because if you do, I should tell you that my ass is indestructible. It's like a superhero's ass." Carter says this last bit under his breath. Or tries to.

The guy tightens his hold on Carter's shirt, because Carter is just as incapable of muttering under his breath as he is incapable of heeding a signal. "Is this a joke to you?"

I wedge my arm between their chests and separate them. "Whoa, whoa, whoa, big guy. Settle down. He's with me."

"Then what's he doing trying to pick up my girlfriend?"

I shove Carter behind me while the guy waits for my explanation. "Well, you see, um…my boyfriend and I have this thing we do. Um…we pretend to be single and pick up other people." My heart is racing. And damn, this is embarrassing. Carter owes me big-time. "We like watching the other flirt with someone else." I reach back and clasp one of Carter's hands. "Don't ask me why, but it turns us on to pretend that way."

"It's a shit thing to do," the Hulk—rather, Greg—says.

With a vigorous nod of my head, I agree with him. "Yes, you're so right. I…I mean, we see that now, and we're going to put this game to bed. Right, Carter?"

"Right," Carter says behind me with laughter in his voice.

I will kill him if he's smiling. Of course, when I turn around, I see that he is. My sandal-clad foot "mistakenly" connects with his shin, and the smile disappears.

"Okay, again, we're sorry about this," I say to Greg and his girlfriend as I pull Carter away. "Have a nice evening."

"Yeah, right," Greg says.

"Have a nice evening, you two," his girlfriend chimes in, a cheesy grin on her face.

"Thanks for the save," Carter says as we walk back to the opposite end of the bar. "I would have been fine, but having a fight in Aruba is not my idea of a relaxing vacation."

It hits me then. Carter lives in an alternate universe where skinny men overpower guys twice their size simply by force of will. The guy continues to stare at us despite his girlfriend's efforts to engage him in conversation, until she grabs him by the chin to redirect his gaze toward her. But seconds later, when I peek behind Carter, Greg's again preoccupied by Carter and me, likely wondering if we've tricked him out of a fight he clearly wanted to have.

"So that didn't go as planned," Carter continues.

"Carter, be serious for a minute. That guy's going to be on you the entire vacation if you don't convince him you truly had no designs on his girlfriend."

"Well, I didn't."

"Yes, you did, and he's looking for a reason to make you pay for it."

"And what do you suppose I do about that?"

I'm going to regret this. It's a bad idea, yes, but I don't want the remaining two days of my supposedly stress-free vacation to be affected by the Hulk. And I don't want Carter's mug pulverized. It's a nice face, and it's growing on me. "Kiss me."

Carter shakes his head as though the idea is ludicrous. "What?"

Oh, for God's sake. "Kiss me, Carter." I jab my finger into his chest. "And make it look like you can't get enough of me. Our audience is watching."

Carter's gaze darts to my mouth, and then he peers at me as he bites his bottom lip. After he puffs out a harsh breath, he asks, "You sure about this?"

"Just do it already," I say through clenched teeth.

After a moment's hesitation, Carter springs into action, closing the space between us and sliding his hand around my waist so that we're chest to chest. He reaches under my hair and cups my neck, his fingers gently coaxing me to tilt my head upward. The tenderness with which he's approaching this charade roots me to the spot. My brain, on the other hand, is running like a turbocharged engine. Will a single peck be enough? Should I touch him? If I moan, will Greg and his girlfriend hear me?

None of this contemplation matters, though, because I float away into a dream state when Carter presses his lips to mine. Oh, they're *so* soft. And warm. Oh God, they're fuzzy-socks-on-a-frigid-day warm. And I've never kissed a man with a beard. The brush of it against my cheek makes me think of frantic sex, the kind where neither person takes the time to remove their clothes completely. I gasp against his mouth, and he slips his tongue inside, the contact that much more startling because he's simultaneously drawing small circles against the nape of my neck with a single finger. A random thought penetrates the haze: Greg can't see Carter's finger. Oh, but I can *feel* it, so it must be just for me.

My arms hang at my sides. I make several attempts to place my hands somewhere on Carter's body as he presses butterfly kisses against my lips and jawline, but nothing feels right. "Did you know the average person will spend more than twenty thousand minutes kissing during their life?" I squeeze my eyes shut after I share that fun fact. Dammit, when did I become this awkward?

Carter smiles against my neck. "That's a lot of kissing."

I scan the area around us. We're in a dark corner, a few feet shy of the bar, but people are milling around everywhere. And we must be attracting attention, so I should stop him, right? But then the pads of his thumbs land on the sensitive spots behind my ears, and oh, that's nice. *Really* nice.

Carter nudges my chin up and dips his face into the crook of my neck. "Stop thinking so much, Tori." His voice rumbles against my throat, and I raise my face to the sky in answer. "Just enjoy this for what it is." He takes my hands in his and guides them to his waist. When I take hold of his sides, he releases me with a squeeze and slides his hands under my hair, bringing his mouth to mine again.

Just enjoy this? What *is* this, exactly? Oh, I know. It's too much, too soon, and for the wrong reason. Still, I can sense a good kiss when I experience one, and this one rivals all the kisses before it. Except I'm not an active participant, not in the way I'd like to be, and I want so much to correct that.

I lift my hand from his waist and thread my fingers through the hair at the nape of his neck. Carter smiles against my lips, and a burst of electricity slams against my belly, as if someone lit a sparkler inside my stomach. He widens his stance, pulling me deeper into his space, making it ours, and I collapse into him. With his lips still close, and his breath floating over my face, he asks, "Was that enough?"

I drop my head to avoid his questioning gaze. "Can't really say," I mumble at his chest. "Maybe a little more to be sure?"

"Yeah," Carter breathes. "That's a good plan."

Desperate to get his mouth back on mine, I take the lead this time, drawing up on my toes and pulling him down to me. Carter groans his approval. Another man might have been inclined to whisper dirty thoughts in my ear, but the guttural sound of Carter's desire is significantly more effective.

I *like* this man's hands on me. I *like* the way he swirls his tongue with mine, a light touch that gives me the confidence to take him deeper into my mouth. He slides his hands down my back and caresses my ass, pulling me flush against him, and oh my, he's so happy to see me he's damn near delirious. I *like* that the most.

After our mouths separate, he cups my face and swipes a thumb across my tender lips. "Was that okay?" His voice, sure and inviting, massages me like strong hands kneading sore muscles. I want to groan in relief, but I manage to hold myself together while I consider what just happened between us.

Okay? That was way more than okay. So okay that I want to burrow into him while I catch my breath and then continue the kiss in private. You know what? An island fling might not be such a bad idea after all. Carter would—

Somewhere behind the bar counter a glass shatters, serving as the proverbial sound of sense being beaten into me.

Mason.

I haven't even talked to Mason.

And I'm kissing a man I met just two days ago.

I pull back and search Carter's face, noting his dilated pupils and labored breathing. He's as dazed as I am.

Afraid to acknowledge the explosive nature of the kiss, I downplay its significance instead. "Wow, Carter. That was an Academy Award–winning performance." I clap enthusiastically. "Bravo."

Carter's face pales as he rubs his lips with two fingers. Is he still thinking about the kiss? Regretting it? Wanting more?

Remembering the reason for the kiss, I step around him and search for our audience. I spot the couple walking by the other end of the bar, leaving for parts unknown. And when I turn to tell Carter the good news, I see nothing but his retreating form—because he's leaving, too.

Chapter Nine

_____

Carter

I'M HIDING IN the shadows of the hotel's courtyard, unsure what to do next and trying to understand Tori's appeal.

I've done some stupid shit in my life.

Kissing Tori was *not* one of them.

Not telling her who I am before I kissed her, however? Dumbest shit yet.

Let me explain.

When I was twelve, I told my parents I wanted to be an actor. They smiled and shipped me off to a summer talent camp in Upstate New York, figuring the combination of being away from home for six weeks and attending nothing but acting workshops would cure me of my pie-in-the-sky dreams. Contrary to their plan, I returned from camp with a four-year action plan for achieving my career goal.

One of the workshops at the camp focused on emotions and how to make them believable in a scene. The teacher's point was simple: If a scene calls for a specific emotion, the actor should draw on personal experiences to bring that emotion to life. It's a fundamental technique for people who practice method acting, and those who apply it well are said to have "emotional range."

Years later, I auditioned for a made-for-television movie pitched as a dark and sexy thriller about a rookie detective whose objectivity is compromised by his growing obsession with a key witness. Unfortunately, my audition, like my parents' plan to steer me away from acting, was a bust. The actress and I had zero chemistry, and I couldn't conjure a single emotion to mimic the state of being consumed by someone. At the time, not even acting had consumed me in the way the role demanded. I simply had no frame of reference.

Well, I have one now—after *the kiss*.

Don't misunderstand me, I'm no stranger to lust, but what just happened between Tori and me falls outside my range of experience. The minute her lips touched mine, I wanted from her what I'd never wanted from anyone else: anything and everything she was willing to give me. And it's freaking me the fuck out.

I've been in the business since I was sixteen. Aside from my family, most of the people I interact with daily know me only as actor Carter Stone. I have plenty of acquaintances but few friends—by design.

Julian's my best friend for many reasons, but chief among them is that I trust my relationship with him isn't about what I can do for him. He knew me well before I became Carter Stone, and although he does a kick-ass job as my agent, he does it grudgingly, not because he hates it but *precisely because* he doesn't want to blur the lines.

And now there's Tori. She has no agenda. Yes, it's because she doesn't know who I am, but the effect is still the same. For the first time in my adult life, a woman I'm attracted to wants to hang out simply because she enjoys being with me.

It's a heady experience, and I want more of it. But I can't explore my feelings for Tori if she doesn't know I'm Carter Stone. See? I'm screwed.

So I'm going to be smart about this and tell her who I am. That's what I should have done from the beginning. I'll explain that I was wary of introducing myself as Carter Stone because I'm supposed to be incognito for the duration of this trip. I'll explain that I hadn't anticipated going any further than enjoying her company while I was here. I'll explain that I want to explore our friendship and figure out if we could have more.

Still, I suspect I'm going to need a shitload of luck to get her to understand why I concealed such an important aspect of my life.

I plod back to the restaurant bar and survey the area. My heart slows when I realize Tori's no longer there. But then a flash of yellow whirs past a few tables, and I spot Tori ducking into the ladies' room. I relax my tense shoulders and claim a stool at the bar, angling my body in the direction of the restroom entrance.

A middle-aged man wearing a navy blazer and jeans drops into the stool next to mine, blocking the view of Tori I'd hoped to have when she reappears.

He greets me with a nod and raises his finger to get the bartender's attention.

Damon ambles over. "Hey, Carter. Need anything?"

"I'm good, thanks."

While the man orders, my phone pings, alerting me to a text. It's from Jewel.

Hey, Carter. Received a strange call today. I accidentally mentioned you're still in Aruba. Maybe it's nothing but ... give me a ring when you're free.

I'll call her in the morning. Right now, my mind is focused on making things right with Tori.

Damon sets a beer bottle in front of the guy.

"This is a great place, isn't it?" the man beside me asks.

"Yeah."

"You here for some R & R?"

I turn and give him a once-over. "Yeah, something like that."

I'm not in the mood to talk to anyone except Tori, but this guy doesn't appear to be going anywhere soon.

He eyes me over the rim of his bottle. "That's quite a beard you've got there."

I laugh at his observation. It's a pain in the ass, and I want it gone yesterday. "That's putting it kindly, I'd say."

He leans into me, and I rear back. Is this guy making a move on me?

"You don't like it?" he asks as he wiggles his brows.

"I like it fine. It just takes a little getting used to." My monotone voice should give him an indication that I don't want to be bothered, but he continues to stare at me. He reminds me of Skeevy. "Look, I'm not trying to be rude, but I'm waiting for someone, and I don't want to be distracted by"—I point a finger between us—"whatever this is."

He takes a swig of his beer and sets the bottle on the counter. He again leans in close. "I'm going to be up-front with you. I know you're Carter Stone."

Shit. My jaw clenches. What the hell is the point of the beard if it doesn't keep a slimeball like this one away from me? "Listen, I'm not sure who you think I am, but I'm sorry to disappoint you. I'm no one."

"No ones don't have someone else change their hotel reservations at a moment's notice."

Well, there's no big mystery there: My freaking driver ratted me out. And Jewel mistakenly confirmed I was here.

"We can make this easy," the guy continues. "Or you can make this hard. I'm just trying to make a little money for my family, okay? Just one pic and I'll be out of your hair."

"This is ridiculous," I say through gritted teeth. "You're harassing me."

A pop of yellow registers in my peripheral vision, alerting me that Tori's headed over. My stomach knots, and I blow out a few breaths to calm my nerves. *Do not hit the guy, Carter. Do not hit the guy.* "C'mon, man, give me a break here. How about you come back another day? This shit isn't cool."

"Have it your way," the guy says.

Then he pulls out a professional camera and snaps a photo, but I cover my face to mar his shot.

"Give me one shot, Mr. Stone, and I'll be out of your hair. What's the harm?"

Dammit, I can't think straight, but I know I don't want Tori to find out about me like this. Unfortunately, this is an instance when I'm not going to get what I want.

Chapter Ten

Tori

THE MIRROR NEVER lies: Carter slayed me with that kiss.

But my glossy eyes and flushed cheeks tell only part of the story. I'm light-headed, and my nipples tingle every time the fabric of my romper shifts against them. If I wasn't in the resort restroom, I'd slip my fingers in my panties and take care of the ache between my legs. Instead, I dampen a paper towel and swipe it across my forehead. It's not an adequate substitute—at all.

Squaring my shoulders, I give myself a mental pep talk: *Yes, you're attracted to Carter. No, you didn't expect to do anything about it. But hiding in the restroom isn't a mature response to those facts. Get out there and talk to him.*

After exiting the bathroom, I spot Carter at the bar.

Except he's not alone.

Instead, he's engaged in a heated discussion with the man next to him, and judging by the glare Carter's directing the man's way, they're not talking about the weather. I march down the lit path toward them, ready to intercede if necessary, my heart pounding against my chest. As I get closer, the man pulls out a large black camera and tries to snap Carter's photo.

"C'mon, Mr. Stone. Give me one shot, and I'll be out of your hair. What's the harm?"

Carter blocks his face from view and jumps up from his stool while Damon and a resort security guard descend on the man. I slow my steps as I try to comprehend what's unfolding. A few guests gawk at the commotion and gasp in surprise.

The man yelps when Damon twists his hand behind his back.

"You're trespassing," Damon says against the man's ears. "You can't come here and harass our guests."

"C'mon, Mr. Stone's used to this. Smiling for the camera is his job." The man throws his body forward, trying to escape Damon's hold, and yells at the guard, "If you break my equipment, I'll break your neck."

Smiling for cameras is his job? Mr. Stone?

The guard ignores the man while he and Damon switch places, and then the guard pushes him toward the walkway leading to the hotel lobby.

Carter has his back to me as he paces and rubs his neck. When he turns around, his eyes plead with me to understand. And I do. Oh yes, I really do.

Carter *Williamson* is Carter *Stone*.

Carter *Stone* is Carter *Williamson*.

My stomach quivers, and my chest tightens. He's an actor. *A well-known actor.* And for the past three days, I've made an ass of myself as he pretended to be a regular guy who…how did he describe it? Oh, right, a guy who works on studio sets.

I can't even begin to process all of this, but I do know that I can't stay here any longer. I turn and sprint through the courtyard, refusing to acknowledge Carter's choked voice as he shouts my name.

Within seconds of entering my hotel room, I have my phone at my ear, and I'm waiting to speak with an airline customer service representative, because this vacation sucks, and I want it to end.

Puñeta.

I ESCAPE ARUBA on the first flight back to Philadelphia the next morning. The guy in the seat next to me attempts to manspread, but I shut it down with a pointed look and a shake of my head. He wisely snaps his knees together.

I'm extra pissy because I had to pay a flight-change fee, making this already expensive trip more unafford-able. I can hear my credit card crying now. Not good circumstances under which to process, but process I shall.

I dissect every conversation for clues to Carter's identity. How much did he hide? Or had I just been obtuse? He told me he was a Hollywood insider who worked on studio sets. I'm guessing from his perspective, that's technically true. In my mind, he was being annoyingly and purposefully vague. And did I really ask him to share gossip about Hollywood celebrities? Shit. My face flames when I recall that exchange.

A flight attendant taking drink orders hovers in the vicinity. I pull down my tray table and ask him for a cup of coffee. When he's gone, disparate thoughts crash into my head like a tsunami. I got Carter drunk. I goaded him into a situation that could have resulted in serious bodily harm. *The dogs.* Okay, the dogs were hilarious. But wait a minute. He let me buy him drinks, *the bastard.* The least he could have done was offer to pay for his own damn liquor.

The main takeaway? He's a *celebrity*, whose company I enjoyed under false pretenses, and we shared one of the best kisses of my life. Sadly, I'll compare any future kiss to that one.

I squeeze my eyes shut. *No, don't do this to yourself, Tori.* You know from experience that overthinking a bad situation only worsens it.

After taking a sip of the terrible coffee, I throw on my headphones and listen to my favorite playlist for times like these. I tap my thighs as I listen to Destiny Child's "Survivor." The lyrics remind me that I'm being overdramatic about the situation.

I don't have to *survive* Carter. I just need to move on.

AFTER PAYING MY short-term parking fee, I drive to my apartment in the city's Fairmount section. Because it's Saturday, I zip through traffic and get to my place in less than thirty minutes.

With one hand on the carry-on handle and the other hand holding my keys, I kick the door to the apartment closed. I'm not sure if it's the apartment or me, but something has changed. It feels empty, or maybe I'm empty. I just don't know. I take a deep breath and drop my keys into the bowl in the foyer. Abandoning my suitcase at the door, I sort through the mail that came in while I was gone.

Eva's melodious voice drifts through the apartment, which means it's cleaning day. She's singing to the tune of "I Feel Pretty" from *West Side Story*, except this is Eva, so she changes the lyrics—typically, to fit her mood.

I feel petty,
Oh so petty,
I feel petty, and bitchy, and right
And I pity
Anyone who fucks with me tonight
Lalalalalalala

Oh, I'm returning to grumpy Eva. Fantastic.

My roommate breezes through the living room with a duster in her hands. She halts when she sees me. "What are you doing home? I expected you to come back tomorrow."

I'm not ready to debrief her on my vacation—not yet—so I shrug. "Change of plans."

She tilts her head and surveys my face. "Spill it. And don't be cute about it, because today's not the day. What happened?"

Eva rounds our teal sofa, drops onto it, and sets the duster by her feet. She adjusts the neckline of her black tank top, looks up at me expectantly, and pats the seat cushion.

I blow out a harsh breath and flop onto the faux fur armchair across from her. "I met someone."

Her dark eyes brighten, and she claps. "Please tell me you had copious amounts of cake by the ocean."

"I did not. But he was nice. And I enjoyed his company. And I kissed him."

Eva purses her lips. "None of that sounds like a reason to come home early."

"And he neglected to tell me he's a minor celebrity."

She sits up, her eyes glowing and alert. "Who is he? Someone I'd know?"

I nod. "I think so. Carter Stone."

Eva widens her eyes and leans forward. "The TV actor? From *Man on Third*?"

That's not how I think of him, but yes, that's exactly who he is. "Yep, that's him."

"Ooh, he's hot." Then she shakes her head and frowns. "But how could you *not* know it was him?"

"He's lost some weight. A lot of weight, now that I think about it. And he was sporting a beard. I'm telling you, Eva, you wouldn't have made the connection, either."

"Right," she says with a dubious glint in her eye. "So how'd you find out he was Carter Stone?"

I give her a play-by-play of my last evening in Aruba. Afterward, she regards me with a bemused expression. "You left without talking to him?"

"Yes," I say, drawing out the word. "What the hell would we talk about?"

"You could have asked him to explain why he never mentioned his true career. When you ask questions, you get answers. You should try it sometime."

"I ask questions all the time," I say.

"No, you really don't," she says with a laugh. "May I remind you that you left the country to escape a confrontation with Mason? Who, by the way, has stopped by twice in three days."

"Oh, Eva. I'm sorry. I didn't mean to leave you to clean up my mess. Is that what's got you grumpy?"

"I'm not grumpy because of Mason. I'm skilled at showing men the door." She sweeps a demonstrative hand up and down her body. "This less-than-bubbly mood is courtesy of my dad."

Eva's parents separated when she was ten, and her father took primary responsibility for her care after that. Unfortunately for Eva, he reminds her of his martyrdom any chance he gets. "What'd your father do now?"

"I told him I was studying to get my personal training certification, and he was not impressed." She mumbles something to herself. "Told me to stop futzing around." She runs her fingers through her hair—this week it's styled in a pixie cut—and rests her fingers at the nape of her neck. "Anyway, you're trying to change the subject. So what happens now?"

"What do you mean?"

"With Carter Stone?"

There's not much to think about here. "Nothing. Nothing happens now with Carter Stone. He's off to Hollywood, and I'm off to bed for a nap."

She rises from the couch and pulls me out of the chair. "I'm glad you got home safely," she says as she wraps me in her arms. "And I'm sorry Stone disappointed you. But consider the bright side: You kissed a celebrity, and you and Mason are history."

Well, Carter and I are history, too.

And for some annoying reason, that fact doesn't comfort me in the way I know it should.

Chapter Eleven

Carter

I RETURN FROM Aruba to the Philly condo I'm still renting for another few weeks. A day later, Julian visits me, and his appearance forces me to stop thinking about the many ways I screwed up any chances I might have had with Tori.

"What's up?" I ask after closing the door.

Wordlessly, with a thick letter-size envelope under his arm, he glides past me and enters the living area.

I plod after him, scratching my ass through my sweats and not giving a shit that I haven't showered or tackled my beard today.

Julian faces the wall of windows, an imposing dark-suited figure with impeccable posture. When we were younger, we'd wrestle each other to the ground, giving each other noogies and wet willies. Even the occasional wedgie was part of our bond. I wonder if he remembers that as well as I do, or if he chooses to stuff it away in some part of his brain he refuses to access when he's in agent mode.

I'm reaching for the remote on the coffee table when he rounds on me.

"Is there something wrong with your phone?" he asks.

"Nope."

His eyes diminish into narrow slits. "So you're intentionally ignoring my calls?"

"I needed a little space."

"I'm not your girlfriend, Carter. I'm your agent—"

"Friend," I say, my voice rising to match his. "Don't forget you're my friend, too."

He takes a deep breath. "If you want me to be your agent, you have to pick up the phone when I call. I can't do my job otherwise. I half expected the doorman to tell me you wouldn't see me."

"Sorry, it won't happen again. Did you have a chance to talk to Ashley?"

He drops his head and pinches the bridge of his nose. "She's fine. But can we talk about that later?"

As usual, Julian approaches our discussion like a Venn diagram: agent business in one circle, personal business in the other, and any overlapping is limited to transition sentences. Taking in the bags under his eyes, I resist giving him shit for it. "Okay, what's so important that you got on a plane to see me?"

"I was here for other business. Thought I'd stop to check in on you, since you're so hard to get ahold of."

What business does Julian have in Philadelphia? Sure, he has other clients, several of them to keep him busy when I'm not, but they're all in LA or New York. "Other business, huh? You cheating on me again?" I say with a laugh.

Julian's face reveals nothing. "It's only cheating if we're exclusive. And we're not. I'd hardly be able to make a living otherwise." He circles the couch, sits on it, and motions for me to do the same. Satisfying my need to be contrary, I take the single seat to his left and prop my feet on the coffee table.

Julian shakes his head and pitches the envelope onto my lap.

"What's this?" I ask as I lift the flap and pull out a stack of papers.

"That's the partial script for *Swan Song*. They want you to read for the lead."

My gaze shoots up to his. "Seriously?"

Julian nods, a hint of a smile softening the hard lines of his face. "Seriously."

Getting a lead in *Swan Song* would be huge. Career-defining. The film adaptation of the best-selling book by the same name is still in development, but it's already the subject of a lot of buzz. Gwen Styles is rumored to be in talks to play a fifty-something divorcée and cancer patient who falls in love with a soldier twenty-five years her junior.

I cover my mouth and blow into my hand. "They want me to read for Alex's part?"

Julian again nods. "I wouldn't have bothered coming here if it was a minor part. But remember, it's just a read.

And before they make a final decision, they'll want you to do a read-through with Styles."

"Where and when's the first read?"

"New York. May fourteenth."

Holy shit. That's two days from now. "Location shooting?"

"New York and Denver."

"You think this is the right move?"

Julian furrows his brows. "It's what you wanted, isn't it?"

"But maybe I'm reaching. Playing a cantankerous soldier who falls in love with his pen pal isn't exactly what my fans expect of me."

"The question is, what do you expect of yourself?"

I expect to be perceived as more than a handsome face or a well-timed joke. *I want my work to matter.* Losing forty pounds for my cameo in *Hard Times* was my first attempt at making that happen. A featured role in *Swan Song* would cement it. "Point taken."

"So you'll do it?" Julian asks.

This time there's no hesitation. "Hell, yes."

"Congrats."

I flip through the pages, my hands already itching to read and highlight my parts. "Thanks, J."

Julian and I discuss a few issues about my contract renewal for *Man on Third.*

Twenty minutes later, he asks, "Anything else? Are we done here?"

"Yes."

He removes his jacket, folds it in half lengthwise, and places it over the back of the couch. Then he turns back to me. "Okay, now that we've got the business out of the way, why don't you tell me what bug crawled up your ass."

I collapse in the chair. "No bug. A woman."

"Didn't know you rolled like that," he says, his face deadpan. "Figured you for missionary all the way." When I don't hit him with a snappy comeback, he leans back and surveys my face. "Back the hell up. A woman's got you twisted?"

That's not what's going on. It's just...I can't shake the memory of Tori's face when the paparazzo ambushed me at the resort. She'd been ready to charge into the fray in my defense, until she'd undoubtedly heard his question and figured out I'd been less than forthcoming with her. She'd furrowed her brows as her run had turned into a trot, and then she'd stopped altogether.

With the photographer's camera flashing in my eyes and chaos surrounding me, she'd become my beacon, and I couldn't take my eyes off her. I'd expected her to be livid. Wouldn't have been surprised if she'd clocked me. Instead, she'd taken a visible breath and dropped her shoulders before she turned away in the direction of the resort's courtyard.

"I met someone on vacation."

Julian motions for me to continue, his eyes impatient. "Do tell."

"And I liked her."

He again motions for me to continue, this time wearing a grimace. "But?"

"But I didn't tell her I'm Carter Stone, and when she discovered that small detail, she bolted."

Julian's face relaxes. "Ah, she's a challenge."

He's wrong. Well, maybe there's a kernel of truth in there somewhere, but it isn't as simple as he's making it out to be. "It's more complicated than that. At first, she didn't know who I was, and she liked me anyway."

"Given that you look like shit, I question this woman's taste."

"Fuck you, Julian. My point is, we hung out, just as friends, and I think she liked me. It was nice."

"Nice? It was nice? Who the hell are you?"

I rise from the chair and chuck the remote onto the couch. "Screw it. Forget I said anything. It's neither here nor there anyway. She obviously wants nothing to do with me. The end."

Julian slouches and falls back against the couch, a million personalities away from the guy in the suit who arrived thirty minutes ago. "I'm not trying to be a dick, man. If there's something there, why not explore it?"

Because I misled her.

Because I'm sure she thinks I was toying with her.

"Because it's pointless," is what I tell him. Then I recount my run-in with the paparazzo.

"Did you tell her your compelling reasons for withholding critical information about your identity?"

"It's scary how those words just roll off your tongue." The observation reminds me of the jab Tori made at me at the bar. "Are you sure you aren't a robot, J?"

He ignores my question. "What did you tell her?"

Needing something to do with my hands, I swipe a pillow off the couch and toss it in the air. "I didn't tell her anything because she never gave me a chance to explain. She left the next morning."

Julian considers me for a moment. "Ah. Then what you need is closure."

"C'mon, man, it's not like we were dating."

"No, but you're feeling guilty, and you want to be absolved of your sins. Can you locate her?"

I nod. "She manages a fitness center here in Philly."

Julian jumps to his feet and slips back into his jacket. "Then find her and apologize. You're trying to get the acting role of your dreams. This isn't the time for you to be distracted."

He's right. I need to make peace with Tori, so I can be in the proper mind-set to prepare for auditions. But I want more than that, too. I want a chance to experience that sliver of magic I felt in Aruba.

I walk Julian to the door. He surveys the kitchen and living areas as he slips into his jacket. "Nice digs. How long you plan on staying here?"

"I have the place for a few more weeks, but I think I'm going to ask Jewel to negotiate a lease through the end of the summer. I'm in no rush to go anywhere. I'll check in with you after the read."

"You do that," he says.

After I close the door, I lean my head against it and realize Julian never fully answered my question about Ashley.

And I still don't know what other business he had in Philadelphia. That sneaky bastard. I'll hound his ass later.

For now, though, I'm focused on Tori. Tomorrow I'll find her and apologize. Maybe then I'll be able to concentrate on preparing for the audition that could make or stall my career.

Hard Core Daily Motivation

Watch Out for Fitness Saboteurs

Posted 5/13/2017 by Tori Alvarez | <u>Leave a comment</u>

Hey, everyone! This month's motivational tips will focus on "Fitness Saboteurs," the people in your lives who undermine your fitness goals. We'll talk about family members, coworkers, and, yes, the person in the mirror. Today we're tackling a group of saboteurs who may be under your radar: celebrities. We covet their bodies and envy their ability to eat junk food and maintain six-pack abs. How many times have you seen a photo of a perky celebrity carrying a yoga mat, her skin dewy and her ponytail perfectly in place? Did that photo warm your insides? Be honest. Look, it's fine to admire a fit body, but if you're comparing your body with a celebrity's, you're also setting yourself up for disappointment. Many celebrities, or at least those celebrities who are photographed with yoga mats under their arms, get paid to sell us an image. Their bodies are part of their brands, commodities to be shaped and reshaped to meet consumer demands—or their latest role.

Some celebrities spend hours exercising, hire celebrity chefs to plan their meals, and enhance their natural assets. *cough* And I say more power to them, but unless you're similarly situated, bemoaning your ability to attain a celebrity body will sabotage your fitness goals. Studies show that people who commit to a regular exercise routine because they want to improve their health outcomes are more likely to stick to it than people who do so for aesthetic reasons. So throw out that celebrity rag mag and head outside for a brisk walk—or better yet, come visit us at HARD CORE. Your body (and mind) will thank you.

Chapter Twelve

Tori

AFTER TWEETING A link to Hard Core's daily motivation tip, I roll back my chair and stand in front of the trainers' desk in the corner of the gym. My first client won't arrive for another hour, but I've been away from the gym for almost a week, and I'm eager to get back to my regular routine. Also, I *need* to be busy. *Idle hands are Google's best friends.*

I print several copies of the gym's group fitness schedule and post them on the glass doors to each of the three studios. After pinning the last one to the corkboard above the water fountain, I turn around—and gasp.

"Tori."

"Mason."

He's wearing vintage Mason. The ensemble consists of a light gray suit that's purposefully snug around the widest part of his muscular thighs, a bright white shirt, and a red silk tie. He wants to project confidence and power, but he's always been woefully unimaginative about it.

"What are you doing here?" I ask through gritted teeth.

His smile falters at my icy tone. "Figured this would be the only way to get you to talk to me. You haven't answered any of my calls. And Eva wouldn't tell me where you were."

I stride past him and stand behind the trainers' desk. "I've been out of town."

He visibly relaxes, picks up the orange on the desk, and tosses it in the air.

I want to smack him for touching my morning snack.

"Where'd you go? Anywhere fun?" he asks.

Is he kidding? The man announces he's single and available in a radio interview and we're supposed to chit-chat as though nothing happened? Not in this lifetime. Plus, why does he have his hands on my orange? "See-ing as I'm not *anyone special in your life*, I don't imagine that's any of your concern."

He stops tossing my orange and blows out a breath that puffs his cheeks.

I snatch my fruit back and motion for him to follow me to the staff room.

"You listened to the show," he observes behind me.

I give him an of-course-I-did-you-nitwit sneer. "You *asked* me to, Mason, so I did. And it was an eye-opener."

When the door to the staff room closes, he reaches for my hand. "It's not what you think, baby. For whatever reason, people in this town are interested in who I'm dating. I know you hate that part of our relationship, so I was trying to throw them off your scent, so to speak."

After sidestepping his attempt to touch me, I stare him down. He claims not to know why the local press is interested in his exploits, but he cultivates that interest with the skill of a ten-person public relations firm. Mason's political aspirations go well beyond his current position as a Philadelphia councilman, a fact I wish I'd known before I began dating him seriously. "So you pretended not to be dating anyone to protect me?"

"Exactly. No need for me to claim you if you hate everything about being claimed."

Claimed? ¡Mira este hijo de la Gran Puta! Sorry. I'm caught up in the moment. He's a son of a bitch, is the gist of the point here. The man should come with a warning label: "Manufactured in a facility that processes nuts. May contain traces of asshole." The more he talks the angrier I am with myself for dating him. How could I have disregarded the obvious? Mason's career will always come first. "Look, I can't begin to understand why you thought that was a good idea. Only you know that. But I do know that listening to you dismiss our relationship on air made me realize we're going nowhere and it's time for us to move on."

He licks his pretty lips and massages his neck. "Tori, there's something here. I *know* it. We just have to work at it a little, that's all."

"And by *we*, you mean *I* need to work at it, right? Because for this to work, *I* should be more comfortable in the public eye." I use my fingers to tick off the list of helpful suggestions he's made in the time we've dated, which weren't helpful at all and which I now realize were largely aimed at making me a more marketable version of myself. "For this to work, *I* should go back to school and get a degree in nutrition counseling. For this to work, *I* should spend more time than I already do performing community service, preferably with organizations that *you* care about."

I'm riled up now, thanks to him. I open my locker and slap my orange on the top shelf. After slamming the door shut, I spin around. "Oh, and let's not forget that for this to work, *I* should be able to converse with your constituents about local politics and—"

"Okay, okay. I can see you're worked up about this in a way I didn't anticipate."

I blink at him. "You *expected* me to be worked up about this?"

He dons a contrite expression. "I was hoping the possibility of losing me would spark something in you, make you want to be with me. Realize what's at stake if you don't make more of an effort to grow our relationship."

This should hurt more, shouldn't it? I want to be angry, but I'm too tired to care. I'm simply not invested enough in us as a couple to expend any more emotional energy on him. And *oh damn, oh damn, oh damn*, a small part of my spirit shrivels when I realize Carter's lie of omission hurt me more than Mason's machinations. "Mason, you can't manipulate me into staying with you. You know that's not how a relationship works."

I've always known Mason wasn't my great love. I didn't expect to be with him forever. But he was funny and ambitious and okay, yes, good in bed. And although I was *in his life*, I was never really *a part of it*, if that makes any sense. I see now that I approached our relationship like a mediocre book I'd borrowed at the library: I enjoyed it as much as I could before its due date and was willing to return it unfinished without harboring any regrets.

"I think we got caught up in the idea of us," I tell him.

He laughs, although his eyes are sad. "It's a great story."

Holy shit. Look at me. Breaking up with the guy like a boss. "Great idea. Poor execution." I cover his hand with mine. "It was passable while it lasted, huh?"

Mason throws his head back and laughs. "I'd tell you not to change, but somehow I don't think that's necessary. You'll make the right guy very lucky someday."

I take his hand and squeeze it. "Take care of yourself."

"You do the same, Tori."

He pivots and strolls away, stopping a few times to shake the hands of gym members who recognize him. With Mason, everything's a performance. Before he descends the stairs, he meets my gaze and gives me a warm smile. As he disappears from view, I take a long, cleansing breath, the weight of our tenuous relationship no longer bringing me down. Unfortunately, Mason's departure frees me to think about other things, other *people*.

One person, specifically.

The computer looms in my peripheral vision. I can almost hear it calling me. *Tori, come play with me. You know you want to.*

It's post-Aruba day three, and I repeat the mantra that has kept me sane thus far. I will not Google him. I will not Google him. I will *not* Google him.

But I'm weak. So annoyingly weak. And I can't help myself. I scramble back to the desk and type in his name. My jaw drops at the images that appear with each click. The man staring back at me is not the man I met in Aruba. Well, he is and he isn't. Now that I know who he is, I can see that this is a different version of the man who sat next to me on the plane.

I don't care what Eva thinks. There are a million reasons why I wouldn't have made the connection. This guy's hair is fuller, his cheeks are clean-shaven, and he's about forty pounds heavier.

Take someone out of their natural environment and they're bound to look different. Happens all the time. Like those optical illusions where a guy playing a banjo is hidden in an elderly woman's face. At least for me the hidden image is only obvious after someone points it out. Now that I know Carter's secret, I can see that he's Carter Stone through and through.

Someone clears his throat, and I look up to find none other than the man whose thumbnail-sized images cover the computer screen like wallpaper. Oh my God. Can't I get a break today?

ACTING ON IMPULSE 133

He's still sporting a beard, but it's neatly trimmed, and he's thinned out his mustache. His eyes, although as arresting as ever, continue to be surrounded by a supporting cast of dark circles. The royal blue baseball cap he wore on the plane sits atop his head, a small section of hair escaping its hold and falling over his right eye.

Memories from our time in Aruba flash in my head, a montage of funny, ridiculous, and sexy moments that make me long for Carter Williamson's return. Where's *that* guy?

I really don't know what to do. There's no guide for dealing with someone who befriended you on vacation and neglected to tell you that he's a major Hollywood actor. Carter doesn't owe me anything. The human condition doesn't guarantee that every person you encounter will be straight with you. But I assumed he was—being straight with me, that is—and knowing I was wrong about that hurts.

And if I'm being honest with myself, I felt small and insignificant, someone he'd decided he could play around with because he had nothing better to do. I don't know how I'll react or what I'll say. I guess I'll just see how this goes.

"Tori," he says in a low voice.

"How'd you get in here, Mr. Stone? This is a members-only area."

Apparently, my brain has decided to activate my all-business mode.

His eyes widen when I greet him by his stage name. "I told them I was interested in touring the facility. Ditched my tour guide in the bathroom, so I don't have a lot of time. Tori, if I could just have a few minutes?"

I lean to the left, looking beyond him, and am relieved to see my ten o'clock appointment, Maureen Dowling. "Sorry, Mr. Stone. You've caught me at a bad time. I have a client to train."

"Another time, then. I need to explain. And I'd like to try to convince you to give me a second chance."

I stand and motion for Maureen to begin her warm-up on the treadmill, and then I gather the internal strength to resist him. "Carter...Mr. Stone, there's nothing we really need to say to each other, so don't bother. We had a fun time in Aruba up until...Anyway, I think it's best if we leave it at that. We're good. Really." I give him a full smile to prove my point, but it gets weaker the longer he stares at it.

"Just like that?" he says.

He asked the same question on the beach when I told him I'd get over Mason. Yes, it must be *just like that*, because if being with my ex was a crash course in dating in the public eye, doing *anything* with Carter would be like embarking on a PhD in an even more demanding field.

Carter Williamson would have had a shot. Carter Stone most certainly does not. "Yeah, it's just like that. Like I said, *Siempre pa'lante. Nunca patras.*"

He swallows hard, as though he's preparing his vocal cords to speak, but he doesn't say anything.

His tour guide, a teenager we hired to swipe IDs at the front desk for the summer, skids to a halt by the trainers' desk. "Mr. Williamson," he says between pants. "Thought I lost you there."

Williamson. Is that even his real name? Or is it a fictitious name he uses with unsuspecting women he meets on vacation? It's a potent reminder that I have no idea what his end game was, and given who he is, I really don't care to be enlightened.

This man belongs in my past.

"Mr. *Williamson* was just leaving, Darryl."

Carter tilts his head at me and presses his lips together before saying, "Take care of yourself, Tori."

"Yeah," is all I'm able to muster in response.

Brilliant, Tori. Just brilliant.

What I should have said was, "*Have a nice life, Carter, and please, please, please stay out of mine.*"

Chapter Thirteen

Carter

"MR. STONE, CAN I get you anything? Is there something you *desire?*"

The receptionist's sultry voice pricks the bubble of self-pity surrounding me. *C'mon, man, snap the hell out of it. Don't let Tori's rejection throw you off your A game. That was yesterday. Today you can change the course of your career.*

I sit up in the chair and scan the waiting area of casting director Samantha Bell's office. Unlike jobs I've pitched in the past, this audition doesn't require that I sit among thirty other hopefuls sizing up the competition before we're each called in. I'm alone with Bell's receptionist, who lowered the neckline of her top when I walked in and who bent over to pick up several dropped items in the short time since I arrived.

"Water would be great," I tell her.

She drops her shoulders and then hitches them up again. "Right." She rises from her seat, sashays to the small fridge in the corner, and retrieves a bottled water. With a wink and a smile, she hands me an Evian. "There you go."

I say thank you at the same moment the intercom buzzes.

"Hannah, let Mr. Stone know we're going to need a little more time," a raspy voice says.

"Sure," she replies.

I nod at Hannah to let her know I'm aware of the delay.

Samantha Bell's reputation precedes her like gym stench. A former actress herself, she delights in crushing people's dreams. She's making me wait on purpose. Because power games are very much a thing in the business.

I sigh and pull out the partial script for *Swan Song*. The story is layered and brutally honest about the flaws of each of its main characters. I would play Alex, a marine stationed in Al-Taqaddum, Iraq, who struggles to set aside his prejudices as he trains Iraqi soldiers for their continuing fight against militant groups. While there, he strikes up a friendship and ultimately falls in love with a widow who sends him letters as part of a military pen-pal program. But she never tells him that she's twenty-five years his senior or that she's battling cancer, and the latter half of the film explores their relationship after Alex returns to the United States and as they try to come to grips with their true selves. It's not a feel-good movie by any stretch of the imagination, but it's a meaty role that will help me escape the rom-com jail in which I'm imprisoned.

Minutes later, after a long buzz from the intercom, Hannah escorts me to the entrance of the audition room.

When I walk in, Samantha lowers her glasses to the bridge of her nose and scans my body. "Mr. Stone, it's great to meet you. I'm a fan."

Everyone's a fan in this business. Just once I'd love for someone to tell me they hate my work and don't understand why I get paid $50,000 an episode. That shit would be refreshing. "It's good to meet you, too."

I set my messenger bag on a chair by the door and wait in the center of the room, a drab gray curtain serving as my background.

Samantha's sitting at a long steel table. To her left, a man is positioned behind a video camera, while a woman, presumably the casting director's assistant, is standing next to the cameraman as she peers at the monitor that will display the audition feed. I don't approach anyone for a handshake because Samantha's already jotting down notes.

"Did you get the new sides?" she says with her eyes still on the papers on the table.

She changed the lines they expect me to read? Dammit. More games. "I didn't."

She turns to her assistant. "Jess, why don't you get Mr. Stone a copy of the new sides?"

"Sure." Jess lifts a set of stapled pages off the top of a stack and hands it to me.

"Take a minute to look that over, and then we'll have Jess read with you," Samantha says.

"Okay, great."

Samantha picks up her phone and swipes left so quickly she reminds me of a character in *The Matrix*.

In the scene she's selected, Alex, wearing civilian clothing, arrives at Pam's doorstep after returning from Iraq. It captures the moment Alex meets Pam in person and discovers that she's ill and that she failed to disclose this to him during their months of correspondence. An image of Tori during our final night together in Aruba flashes through my mind, but I force myself to read the words and get into my character's head.

After a few minutes, I look up and tell Samantha I'm done reading.

"Do you have any questions about the role or the scene?" she asks.

I lick my lips and tamp down the urge to pace. "No, I think I'd prefer to just get to it."

She nods, and Jess approaches with her copy of the lines. The advice my first acting coach gave me plays in a loop in my brain: "The papers in your hands should be your only prop. Use the sides to steady your nerves. Tighten your movement to account for the camera taping your audition. Don't let the reader's monotonous voice throw you."

"Ready when you are," Samantha says.

Jess pretends to open a door. "May I help you?"

I pretend to remove a cap from my head. "Yes, ma'am. I'm looking for Pam Larsen."

"That's me," Jess says with hesitation in her voice.

The rest of the scene takes another three minutes to complete. Samantha asks me to read a few lines at various spots in the script. When I'm done, she writes furiously and ends her note taking by underlining something in hard strokes.

"Thank you, Carter. Let me ask you this. You've done pretty well for yourself as a situation comedy actor. Why the switch?"

I retrieve an image of my former agent, Simon Cage, from my mental file drawers. He can be found in the file marked "J for Jackass." Cage tried to convince me that my best assets were my abs and a wicked sense of comedic timing. He's wrong on both counts—my ass is killer when I'm properly conditioned, and I can handle more challenging roles just as well as the so-called serious actors in film. I just need the right vehicle to show it, and *Swan Song* could be it.

"I don't think of it as a switch, so much as a progression. All actors need to grow. It improves their craft. A role like this has the potential to take my career to the next level, and most importantly, I think I can handle it."

Samantha angles her head and again scans me from head to toe. "Let's dispense with the formalities. You're in the running for the part, and we'd like you to read with Gwen Styles. But there's a catch."

There always is.

"I appreciate the effort you made to meet the physical demands of your latest role, but we're interested in casting the Carter Stone who's amassed a following among women. *Swan Song* is a drama, but that doesn't mean we're not going to include several strategic body shots. Think Alex running on the base in the morning. A bare-chested Alex in bed reading one of Pam's letters. So we'll need you to come here with the right look. Think you can regain the weight in a month?"

"Probably not. It took me three months to lose it."

"I can give you six weeks to show us you're on the right track."

"All right. I'll do what I can."

Samantha nods, a small smile playing across a face that's been expressionless so far. "I'm not asking for too much, am I?"

She is, and she knows it. "My only option is to try."

"Great. I'll be in touch with your agent about the details. Thanks for coming."

I'm stunned by her relatively cordial behavior. Although she gave me a semihard time, she's not the bar-racuda I expected her to be. Other actors have shared stories of dismal auditions in which Samantha made them cry. I roll up the sides and slap the pages against my thigh. "Thanks for the opportunity."

With my shoulders high and a smidge of swagger in my step, I stride out of the audition room. I grab another bottle of water from the reception desk and guzzle it.

"How'd it go?" Hannah whispers, leaning forward so there's no way I miss her impressive cleavage.

"I think I did all right. We'll see."

Something's missing, though. I spin around, hoping to jog my brain. Shit. I left my messenger bag. Careful not to make too much noise, I walk down the hall and approach the door to the audition room—and stumble on the conversation inside.

"I wouldn't have cared if he'd read the phone book," Samantha says. "That man is so fucking sexy."

"But he really needs to add on weight," Jess says.

"Nothing a few hamburgers couldn't fix. But that monologue about progression and bettering his craft was pitiful."

The ensuing laughter hits me like barbs. Who the fuck cares what they think? If I get the part, I'll show them how wrong they are. Before I re-enter the room, I knock on the door and peek in. "Hey, sorry about this. Forgot my bag."

Samantha's gaze darts to her assistant, and then she straightens. "Not a problem at all."

I grab my bag and get the hell out of dodge, dismissing their petty conversation because that's just how the industry is. The important part is that they're still considering me for the role. But hell, they're giving me only six weeks to bulk up.

Tori and her gym immediately come to mind as a potential solution. In Philadelphia, I'll be less susceptible to distractions. Plus, I have no doubt Tori would take the assignment seriously. And maybe we could start over, with no lies between us. It's a brilliant idea.

Now all I need to do is convince her to train me.

AFTER A QUICK call with Julian about the audition, I slip into a booth at a random diner in midtown Manhattan and order a cup of coffee and a slab of blueberry pie. I hum in approval when I take my first bite, the crumbs of the buttery, flaky crust spilling onto my shirt. I'm impersonating a toddler, and I don't care. The rest I consume like it's my last dessert ever. After today, there'll be no more sweets for me for the next six weeks.

I sip the coffee while I look up Tori's gym on my phone.

The home page displays a semitranslucent image of the gym and a generic welcome message. A daily motivational tip sits in its own box on the right side of the page.

Aha, Tori recently posted an entry. Coincidently enough, it discusses celebrities—*in less than flattering terms*. I'm not so egotistical as to assume I'm the reason she's down on Hollywood types, but meeting me couldn't have helped. There are no comments, and a quick scroll through the other blog entries shows they're not shared often.

I click the icon to share the link with my followers. To ensure I have Tori's attention, I find her Twitter handle and tag her:

Check out this motivational tip from @torialvarezTR of @HardCoreFitness. So simple even a celebrity could handle it. ;)

Despite Tori's initial impression of me, I'm not a creeper. If she doesn't respond, I'll abandon my plan to hire her as my trainer.

Dozens of my devoted fans immediately retweet my post. A few fans reply, too.

Replying to @cwstone: Is that how you got your fantastic body?
Replying to @cwstone: I'd work out with you anytime!
Replying to @cwstone: Sounds like she doesn't like celebrities!?!
Replying to @cwstone: I guess you two won't be friends, huh?

Wanting to shut down the conversation before it goes sideways, I send another tweet.

Re: last RT: A little harsh on celebrities but advice is good just the same. Running and weights for me.

Then I swipe through the camera roll on my phone and stop at the only photo I took my last morning there: a pic of the divi-divi tree on the beach near our hotel. My fans would appreciate this photo, so I share it on Twitter with a few hashtags: #Aruba #dividivi #fascinating. This, too, gets dozens of likes and retweets.

Twitter can be a mind suck, so I exit the app and call Jewel.

"Hi, Carter," she says in a professional tone I've never heard before. "What can I do for you?"

Something's wrong. Jewel doesn't ever answer my calls politely. "What happened, Jewel? Everything okay?"

"Everything's fine, Carter. Were your travel arrangements to New York acceptable?"

"Okay, Jewel, now you're scaring me."

She sighs on the other end. "I'm trying to do my job, Carter. I don't always do it well."

I flip through my mental Rolodex, trying to figure out what's provoked her sullen mood. Oh, I know what this is about. She's still feeling guilty about confirming my whereabouts to the paparazzo in Aruba. "Jewel, am I perfect?"

She chuckles. "Hardly."

"So why would I expect you to be perfect, huh? The guy was underhanded, and you *inadvertently* confirmed that I was still on the island."

"It's my *job* to handle those types of calls, but my conniving-jackass radar wasn't working properly. I'm so, so, sorry."

"It's fine, Jewel. Please. As much of a pain as you sometimes are, I *need* you to be you. Just like I need Julian to be Julian, as cantankerous as he can be most times. Be real, okay? I need that in my life. You have no idea how much I appreciate the hard time you take so much pleasure in giving me. And don't blame yourself."

"Okay," she whispers. Then she clears her throat. "What can I do for you, Your Majesty?"

I'm grinning like an idiot. "That's more like it. I called because I'm thinking about staying in Philadelphia for the summer. Can we talk about arrangements?"

The click-clack of her nails tells me we're back on track. "An entire summer without my boss afoot? This should be good."

Twenty minutes later, Jewel and I have mapped out a plan for the major commitments I've made in the next two months.

"Good to hear your voice, Jewel."

"You too, Carter."

After hanging up, I glance at my phone's home screen and see that I missed more than a dozen Twitter notifications. Well, well. The Hard Core account responded to my tweet. It says:

Glad you liked our tip. Doubt you could handle Hard Core, though. #notready

This is progress. At least she's willing to engage with me. And then I focus on the opportunity presented by her tweet. Ah, Tori-not-short-for-Victoria, didn't anyone tell you it's not wise to issue a challenge when it can't be retracted? My response is swift and succinct:

Challenge accepted. #bringit

My Twitter mentions blow up within seconds.

Whoa. Maybe I shouldn't have done that.

Remember when I said my biggest mistake yet was not telling Tori who I really was? My Spidey sense tells me *this* mistake might rival that one.

@celebritywatch: RT @cwstone: Hmm. Is this a friendly challenge, or are actor Carter Stone and @torialvarezTR feuding on Twitter? #curious

Challenge accepted. #bringit

Chapter Fourteen

Tori

WHAT. IS. GOING. ON?

A small crowd greets me in Hard Core's reception area this morning. It's not an unusual sight—getting everyone's ID through the scanners can cause a logjam during high-usage times—but I can tell from the camera in one of the loiterer's hands that this is a different situation.

"Tori! Tori!" they yell.

"What's your relationship with Carter Stone?" a woman with a small recorder in her hand asks.

"Are you and Carter feuding?" asks another.

As I'm bombarded with questions, I fish in my purse for my club card, my mind struggling to make sense of what's prompted this frenzy.

Darryl takes my ID in a rush, his fingers fumbling to fit the card in the slot so he can swipe it.

"They've been here all morning?" I ask him.

"Yes," he says. He rubs the back of his neck and glances at the journalists, although I suspect that term might be more generous than they deserve.

"Do you have any idea what this is about?"

"Not sure. Something about Carter Stone retweeting you?"

Oh, for goodness' sake. So what if Carter Stone retweeted me? I can't believe there are journos chasing this nonstory down. Must be a very slow news day in Philly.

Then again, *The Philadelphia Inquirer* once reported that a film actor had slapped the butt of a San Antonio Spurs player at a Sixers game. My reaction then was: *And this is news why?* I suppose this explains the commotion I'm dealing with now. Philly is a city that craves celebrity gossip even though there are hardly any celebrities making news here. Yay, me.

"Should I call someone?" Darryl asks.

"Is Nate around? He'll know how to handle it."

Darryl nods and picks up the phone.

I turn back to the three gossip peddlers still asking me questions. "I'm not sure what this is about, folks. Carter Stone and I aren't feuding. Period."

My announcement snuffs out their collective energy, and one of them stamps his foot in annoyance. I wave good-bye and pass through the turnstile.

One of Hard Core's owners, Ben, greets me at the stairs. "You've gotta be fucking kidding me." He chuckles to himself. "You know Carter Stone?"

I take the stairs two steps at a time with Ben at my side. "I don't know him, Ben. Just a silly thing on Twitter, apparently."

"That's not what Darryl says," he singsongs. "He says he walked up on a heated exchange between you two a couple of days ago."

Technically, Ben's my boss, but he's not adept at maintaining clear boundaries. Says he's not into "labels." That works for me, too. Hence, this conversation.

"I checked out that Twitter beef," Ben continues.

I halt midstep and turn around. "What Twitter beef?"

Ben shakes his head in confusion. "The Twitter exchange yesterday. Am I missing something?"

A simple retweet does not a Twitter beef make. "I think I'm missing something, too," I mutter to myself. After I meet with Ben and Nate, I'll check the Internet and try to figure out what's going on.

Ben follows me into the staff room and surveys me as I take items out of my gym bag and place them in my locker. "So how do you know Carter Stone?"

He's not going to let this go. Dammit. I throw my head back. "Okay, fine. I met him on vacation. We chatted for like two seconds." To emphasize my point, I hold up two fingers. "I didn't know he was Carter Stone. He never told me, either. That's the story. End of." Yes, I know it's not exactly how it all went down, but what happened in Aruba is none of Ben's business.

"The bastard," Ben says as though this information has scandalized him. Ben is a muscle-bound giant, his light brown hair styled in a crew cut that makes him look like he recently completed a stint in the armed forces. The idea that he'd be scandalized by anything is laughable.

I slam the locker closed with more force than necessary. "It wasn't that deep, Ben."

He precedes me into the gym's small conference room, where Nate, my other boss, is fussing with the high-tech coffee and tea machine that Ben insisted was a "must-buy."

Nate's muttering is more pronounced than usual. "You know," he says over his shoulder, "you have to be alert to operate this machine, but I can't be alert if I don't have my coffee. Do you see the problem here?"

Ben bumps Nate out of the way, his hands flying over the buttons. After one last flick of a switch and a pointed glare at Nate, Ben walks away with the resulting sound of brewing coffee serving as his "screw you."

Just a typical day in our workplace.

Four years ago, Ben and Nate opened this tiny gym with a combination of savings, borrowed funds, and wild dreams. Six months after that, they brought me on as an employee, and I took on a management position two years later. Since then, they've expanded the gym to two floors and we've settled on a distribution of labor that works for us: Ben uses his business acumen to keep the books straight, Nate uses his excellent interpersonal skills to handle staff issues, and I focus on running the gym's day-to-day operations.

We also needle each other at every opportunity.

I grab one of the stapled packets in the center of the table. "Children, can we get on with it? Nate has a staff meeting at ten."

Nate furrows his brows, twists his lips to one side, and rubs his brown, bald head. "Ah, damn, I forgot. You're indispensable, Tori."

"This is true," I reply with a broad smile.

Ben, the informal leader of our three-person management team, scoots his chair in and flips through the pages in front of him. "Okay, let's get to it. The first item is just a heads-up. I'm working on renegotiating our lease—"

"Before we get to that," Nate says—he takes a sip of his coffee—"can we talk about actor Carter Stone and that helluva fortuitous Twitter exchange?"

I groan. "*What* Twitter exchange?"

Nate waggles his brows. "Stone and I had a bit of a conversation after he tweeted a link to your daily motivational tip."

Nate on Twitter? This I must see. I point to his laptop. "Show me, please."

Ben chimes in, too. "Yeah, Nate, what have you been up to?"

Nate opens the Twitter app and scrolls through the gym's tweets until he finds the exchange. "Here, take a look."

I angle his screen in my and Ben's direction. Oh my God. Why, why, why is this happening? I pin Nate with a murderous glare. "This makes it seem like *I* was responding to Carter."

Nate frowns and repositions the laptop in front of him. "Does it? I said 'our tip,' not 'my tip.'" He peers at the screen as though he's contemplating his own question. "Why does that matter?"

"They have history," Ben tells him.

I jab Ben in the side. "We do *not* have history. We met on my vacation."

"That's even better," Nate says with a self-satisfied grin on his face. "We can capitalize on that."

"No, no, we cannot capitalize on that. We'll pretend this never happened and go about our regular business. *¿Mi intiendes?*"

Nate shakes his head. "No, I *don't* understand. It's an opportunity, Tori."

Ben nods.

"How so?" I ask.

"The guy practically challenged you to train him," Ben says. "Do you know how impressive it would be to snag him as a client?"

"The guy practically challenged *Nate* to train him. That wasn't me flirting in one hundred and forty characters." I point an accusing finger at Nate. "That was *you*."

"In any case, we could get a lot of marketing mileage out of this," Nate explains. "People who've never heard of the gym might be curious to check us out. And if the training's a success, which I know it would be, we could promote that everywhere."

"Why can't one of you do it?" I ask.

"You have fewer clients," Ben says. "It'll be easier to rework your schedule."

Huh. Interesting. For weeks, I've been lobbying them to roll out a new class geared to people at any level of fitness. They claimed my schedule was too full given my management and personal training responsibilities. "So let me get this straight. There's enough time in my schedule to train Carter Stone, but not enough time for me to teach a class on a trial basis?"

Nate and Ben glance at each other.

What is it with these two?

Nate clears his throat. "We just don't think the class fits with the gym's brand, Tori. We're selling gym membership, equipment, locker rooms. Your class says all that's unnecessary."

"So you've been giving me the runaround and hoping I'd just forget about it?"

"It's not like that, To—"

"No, it's fine. I get it." I give them a dismissive wave. "I just wish you would have said this when I first proposed it." I've been holding the class at a community center in my old neighborhood, hoping to get the guys on board and move it here soon. I guess it's time to find a permanent home for it elsewhere.

"We should have said something sooner," Ben says as he glances at Nate.

Given the pinched expression on Ben's face, I'll bet Nate was tasked with telling me and never got around to it. He's a forgetful man.

"Getting back to Carter Stone," Nate says. "It's not a big deal. Now that I've reeled him in, all you'll have to do is get him in shape. He won't be able to deny the fantastic job we've done for him, and then we can exploit that everywhere."

I chew on my lip as I contemplate what's a very big deal to me. I mean, there's so much wrong with this scenario

I don't even know where to begin. It's all a jumbled mess in my head.

The idea that I'd have to work with Carter for the gym's benefit and for what likely amounts to shits and giggles for him literally makes my skin hot. If his latest weight loss is any guide, he takes his apparently healthy body for granted, taxing it unnecessarily to fit whatever role he's playing. *Oh, and hey, there, Grudge. I see you haven't gone away yet.* Yes, I'm still annoyed about what happened in Aruba. He did all the things to make me like him except disclose the one fact that would have stopped me from doing so. And I won't even venture into an analysis of the implications of that kiss. We'd be here forever. I sigh loudly. "It's not a bad idea."

Nate pumps his fist. "I'm glad you—"

"It's a *terrible* idea," I say. "No way. N. O."

Ben huffs. "Why the hell not? This is pure marketing gold."

"I don't *like* the guy."

Which is technically true. I liked the guy I met in Aruba, when he was just Carter Williamson. Carter Stone is an unknown. "That Twitter exchange was a blip in the social media universe. You're trying to make something out of nothing. Let's forget about trying to capitalize on my *brief* acquaintance with Carter Stone and focus on the kind of marketing that will bring in new clients."

"Too late," Nate says. "Things kind of escalated overnight."

My stomach drops. Leave it to impulsive Nate to do something without consulting us first. "What did you do?"

He gives me a wide smile, waggles his eyebrows, and turns his laptop to face me. The screen shows the gym's Twitter account. *Dammit, dammit, dammit.* He responded to Carter's #bringit missive last night. The tweet said:

Show up or shut up. We're open seven days a week. #notscared

I turn to Ben. "We need to disable his access to the Twitter account."

Nate laughs. "Oh, c'mon. I thought I was flexing my social media skills. Isn't that what the account is for? You're always saying I should run the account sometimes, so I did. Plus, I didn't know then that you two have"—he makes air quotes—"history."

Ben blows out a long breath. "Listen, we're talking in circles. If this guy wants to hire us, we'll make it happen, okay? We'd be crazy not to. We'll worry about the whos and why-nots if and when we need to."

I'm sure my pout is super attractive. "Fine."

Nate smiles. "Okay, then. Besides, Stone was probably bluffing."

Ben straightens the sheets of paper in his hands. "Getting back to the lease—"

The speakerphone in the middle of the table beeps.

"What's up, Darryl?" Nate asks.

Darryl's disembodied voice fills the room. "Mr. Carter Stone is here to speak with a member of our personal training department."

Ben and Nate grin at each other.

I drop my chin to my chest and let out a weary sigh. I'm done, I tell you. Done.

Chapter Fifteen

Carter

TORI AND TWO men stride through the gym like they're Marvel superheroes. One of the men reminds me of John Cena, and the other looks like Taye Diggs, only taller and sturdier. Tori's in the middle, her gaze trained on me as she approaches.

Given how she teased me on Twitter, I expected her mouth to be curved in a smirk. Instead, she's wearing a wry expression.

The Taye Diggs look-alike reaches out to shake my hand. "Mr. Stone, it's great to meet you. Nate Warner. I'm a fan."

"Thanks, man," I say.

Nate points at the other guy. "And this is Ben. You know Tori, of course."

Ben nods, a warm smile softening his rugged face. The phrase *C'mere, you big lug* was custom-made for this guy.

Nate claps his hands together and rubs them. "So, are you here to accept my challenge?"

His challenge? My body tenses, and my mouth falls open. Dammit. I've miscalculated the situation. No wonder the cold is surrounding Tori like a dry-ice cloud. She never encouraged me to come here. "*You* tweeted that stuff at me?" I ask Nate.

Ben reaches around Tori and pokes Nate in the arm. "We enjoyed that bit of fun on Twitter, but we weren't issuing a challenge. Right, Nate?"

Nate folds his arms over his chest. "Right."

"Glad to hear it," I manage to say as I recalibrate my expectations. "I'm not a very competitive person."

Tori snorts, and we all look at her.

"Sorry," she says with a reluctant smile. "Continue."

Okay, so she's not completely frostbitten. That's a relief. I clear my throat. "Anyway, I'm looking for a personal trainer for the next six weeks."

"Well, you're looking at two of our best trainers right here," Ben says. "Can't go wrong with either one of them." Ben puffs out his chest as though he's personally responsible for the state of Tori's and Nate's bodies.

I peer at Tori. "Ms. Alvarez's motivational tips drew me in. I'm interested in her viewpoint on training."

"He's interested in something all right," Ben says under his breath.

Tori narrows her eyes at Ben and flares her nose. Then she turns to me with a customer service smile. "Mr.

Stone, you're probably accustomed to a certain amount of privacy while exercising, and I'm afraid our gym isn't equipped to offer you that luxury."

"What if we made arrangements to conduct parts of the training somewhere else?" I ask. "I'd be willing to pay a premium for that kind of accommodation."

Tori shakes her head. "I don't think—"

"That's a great idea," Ben says. "If the gym becomes invasive in any way, we can find an alternative location for you. We have colleagues at cooperating gyms who would be able to loan us private space."

"Excellent," I say.

Tori jumps in. "Mr. Stone—"

"Carter."

"Right. Carter, would you excuse us for a minute? I need to speak with Ben and Nate about something."

"Sure, no problem. Mind if I take a spin around the club again?"

"No problem," Ben tells me.

The trio walks to an unoccupied corner of the gym. As they talk, I roam the exercise floor, glancing at them from time to time. There's a lot of head shaking and frowning going on. Mostly on Tori's part. A minute later, they return to their original places, and I saunter over to them.

Nate pats my arm twice. "We're going to leave you in Tori's capable hands. After we get a better idea of what you're looking for, Ben will send you an estimate. If there's anything else we can do for you, just let us know."

"Give me a day or two to work out something with an alternative location," Ben says. Then he salutes me with two fingers, and the two men walk away, leaving Tori and me alone.

For several seconds, we do nothing more than stare at each other. And those tense moments sum up what's going on between us. We're in a state of emotional limbo, unsure where we stand with one another. It's an excruciating experience, mostly because I know what it's like when Tori enjoys my company, and this in no way resembles that.

Now's not the time to play games, Carter. Be straight with her. "I thought it was you. The tweets. Otherwise, I wouldn't have come."

Her brows lift in surprise, and then her face falls. "I appreciate that, but it doesn't matter. You need our help, and my bosses want me to do the helping."

"But you don't?"

She expels a deep breath through her nose. "Can I be honest and say I'm not sure?"

"That's fair."

"What are you doing here, Carter? Really."

"I wasn't lying when I said I need training. I've got about six weeks to get in shape for a role."

She tilts her chin up as though she's calculating what's physically possible. "What are your goals?"

"Gain muscle and thirty pounds."

A vigorous shake of her head tells me I'm overreaching.

"Can't be done," she says. "Not without major damage to your lean tissue."

"What can I do in that time, then?"

"You're young, and you've got muscle memory. Gaining twenty pounds in that time is aggressive but doable. It won't be pure muscle mass, though."

As I suspected, she knows her field, and it only makes her more attractive to me. "Okay, you're the expert."

"Speaking of…why me?"

"I've got a short-term lease at the Mayburn through the summer, so I can stay in Philly for the duration of the training. I think you know what you're doing…and I trust that you'll be honest with me about my limitations."

"You value honesty, huh?"

She might as well have slapped me. The sting wouldn't have been any worse than this. "We should talk about that."

"No, we shouldn't. Let's treat this like the business arrangement it's meant to be."

A gym member brushes against me on her way to the water fountain, and I'm suddenly self-conscious about having this conversation in the middle of a gym. I gesture to the trainers' area. "Can we…?"

Tori straightens and scans the space around us. "Yes."

I follow her to the other end of the gym. "I know you want to act like none of this happened. I bet you'd erase any memories of Aruba if you could. But you can't, and I won't. So I need to say this." Shit, this is hard, because it's all on me. "I'm sorry I didn't tell you about my alter ego."

She draws back, her brows nearly kissing. "Is that how you think about your profession?"

I grasp onto the back of my neck. "In a way, yes."

"Why didn't you tell me?"

Her words come out like they've been wrenched from her lips. She doesn't want to have this conversation, but she's toughing it out anyway. And considering even the little I know about her, her willingness to ask the question is no small thing.

"I just wanted to be Carter Williamson for a bit. I didn't want the pressure of being that guy. And I figured nothing would happen between us, so there'd be no harm. I was wrong. But I wasn't trying to trick you. I think I was trying to trick myself into thinking I could meet someone without having to unload the baggage that comes along with being me. Again, I'm sorry."

"Okay. I appreciate your honesty *now*."

I hold out my hand. "Friends?"

She ignores my question—and my hand. "Let's focus on your training. If we're going to do this, we'll have to set a few ground rules."

"Of course. Go for it."

"I have the final say on your training program."

"Meaning?"

"Meaning I'll design your training program and you'll follow it, no complaints."

She might as well know at the outset that I'm going to be a pain in the ass. It's in my nature. "I'm an actor, Tori. Complaining is as crucial to my existence as air."

She shakes her head. "Fine. You can complain all you want, preferably under your breath, but you must follow the program anyway. The minute you don't, the arrangement is over."

I stroke my chin as I consider her. Plenty of women dig that move. Judging by the bored expression on her face, however, she's not one of them. "What if something is dangerous?"

"I promise to keep your safety in mind at all times."

"Deal." I stretch my arm out. "Shall we shake on it?"

She steps backward and places her hands behind her back. "Ah, ah, ah. We're not done with the rules yet."

"Okay, what else?"

"You'll do your best to spare me from being drawn into any media crap."

"Tori, I'd like to be out of the limelight as much as you apparently do."

"Really? I'd always assumed publicity was one of three pillars holding up a celebrity's career, with talent and ego being the others."

"You're right, but I can live without the publicity for now. All bets are off when we're done, though. I'll want to show off the results of my training."

She rolls her eyes. "Of course you will, but that'll have nothing to do with me. So we're on the same page?"

"Yes, we are. I'm at your mercy."

Her eyes brighten, and she dazzles me with a playful smile. "Yes. Yes, you are."

Damn, that's hot. Let's hope she's having dirty thoughts about us. "So when do we begin?"

"Tomorrow. We start with Zumba right here."

"What's Zumba?"

"It's a fitness class. High-intensity movements."

"Like intervals, you mean?"

She hiccups on a laugh. "No, Carter, it's not like intervals. It's a fitness class, with high-energy movements, and usually lots of women."

"So far, so good. What's the catch?"

"Lots of Latin dance. Salsa, merengue, samba."

"Limbo, too?"

"No, no limbo, you smart-ass. Although given your experience in Aruba, I'd think you would be happy about that." She grimaces, probably regretting the reference to our time on the island. "Anyway, sometimes hip-hop is mixed in. Forty-five minutes, including the warm-up and cooldown."

"You want me to take a dance class?"

"It's an effective way to build your endurance."

"Is this one of those classes where the women sneak peeks at the men and laugh at them?"

"That's about right."

"Let me think about it." Several seconds pass as I pretend to contemplate her proposal. "I've thought about it. No, no, and *hell* no."

She shakes her head. "Saying no is not an option. It's my way or no way. That's the deal. Plus, if you don't go, you'll miss out on the opportunity to see your classmates in skimpy shorts and bra tops. And we'll be shaking and shimmying all over the dance studio."

"Well, that's a different proposition. Why didn't you lead with that?"

She treats it as a rhetorical question. Smart woman.

"Will I be the only guy?" I continue.

"Probably not. Recall the skimpy shorts and bra tops I just mentioned."

"I'm there. What time?"

"Ten o'clock."

"It's a date."

She gives me a face that could freeze the sun. "No, it's not."

I deflate under the force of her stare. "I didn't mean it that way."

She waves away my explanation. "Forget it. Before you leave today, you'll need to fill out a health questionnaire. You can leave it with Darryl at the front desk."

"Will do. Anything else?"

She hesitates and mumbles something to herself.

I lean forward and cup my ear. "Sorry?"

"I should take your measurements, but if you'd prefer to wait until tomorrow—"

"Now works, too."

"Let's do this in the office, then," she says. "Most clients prefer the privacy."

I peer at her. "Be straight with me, Tori. If you want to have your way with me, just say so. No need to invite me to the office under the guise of *taking my measurements*."

She levels me with a glare that makes my balls snug up to the base of my dick. They sense the danger, too.

"You don't get to make that type of joke."

I straighten. "Too soon?" After pouting for a few seconds, I shrug. "Okay, got it. I'll try again next week."

She tries to convey her annoyance, her hands settling on her hips and her breath expelling in a huff, but she's also holding back a smile. My heart falls into that thump-and-a-catch pattern I experienced when I first saw her on the plane. Then my brain goes to that place I know it shouldn't: *Someday I'm going to marry the woman sitting in 12D.*

"Carter?"

I shake my head to clear it. "Yeah?"

"I asked you to come with me."

I gesture for her to lead the way, and then I follow her down a long narrow hall with athletics-themed stock photos lining its walls. We enter a small office with two desks and a round wood table. Tori reaches inside one of the desks and pulls out a tape measure and a notepad.

She stands in front of me and purses her lips.

"Would it be easier if I take off my T-shirt?" I ask.

"No," she blurts out. Her gaze darts to the ceiling and returns to me. "That's not necessary. I'll just get a general sense of where you're at. Could you put your arms out to the sides?"

"Sure."

I do as I'm told, and she wraps the measuring tape around my biceps, her gaze trained on the wall behind me. She glances at the number and jots it down on the notepad on the desk. Next, she measures my chest and shoulders like she's a tailor sizing me for a suit, her movements quick and efficient. Then she loops the tape around my waist, and now her face is hovering inches from my chest. From here, I can see the strands of gold threaded in her brown hair. I make fists to stop myself from sliding my fingers through the mass to grip her scalp and raise her face.

I shift and arch my back. "Sorry. I just need to stretch a bit."

Her breathing quickens, and then she turns away to jot down the measurements. With her back to me, she says, "Stand with your feet hip-width apart."

"You got it."

She kneels and slips her arm through my legs to fasten the measure around my thigh. There's no way I'm going to make it through six weeks of this. I squeeze my eyes shut. Shit. How could I forget why I'm here? I'm here to further my career, and I've hired her to do a job. *Her job.* She's been in this position with other men, and they've probably acted like assholes, too. Unless she wants me to act on this attraction, I'll suppress it.

Don't be a douche, Carter.

"What should I do about my diet?" I ask.

"I'll set you up with a local nutritionist. She's excellent. Until then, stock up on bananas, whole milk, brown rice, and lots of protein." She stands and turns away to write down the last measurements. "I'll also give you a plan for working out at home. Nothing too strenuous, though. Your muscles will need time to recover." Then she holds out a sheet of paper. "Feel free to stay here while you fill out the intake form."

I take it from her. "Okay."

"Don't forget to leave it with Darryl on your way out. Plan to show up a half hour early tomorrow to fill out your remaining paperwork. We'll weigh you then, too. I'll see you in the morning."

She glances at me and rushes out, closing the door behind her. I didn't even get the chance to thank her. Hoping to catch her before she's out of sight, I twist the doorknob. To my surprise, Tori tumbles into me with a yelp, and my hands fly up to hold her upright. *Well, that's one way to catch her.*

"Sorry!" she says.

"Not a problem," I say, my arms still wrapped around her shoulders. "Were you coming back in?"

She closes her eyes and shakes her head as she steps out of my embrace. "No, I was just gathering my thoughts. See you tomorrow."

I reach for her hand and stop her. "Wait a sec, Tori."

"Yeah?" she says, her eyes shiny and bright.

"I just wanted to say thank you. For accepting my apology. For working with me. For everything."

"You're welcome, Carter. But don't thank me too soon. I'm your trainer now, and I'm going to work you hard."

In a movie, this would be the point where my character would turn his head and stare into the camera with his eyes wide. Because seriously? She's going to work me hard?

Have mercy.

Chapter Sixteen

Tori

I'M GOING TO crush his soul. And he has no idea.

Carter wants me to train him? Okay, sure. But I don't have to make it easy on him. My *job* entails getting Carter physically conditioned for his next film. So as I see it, I can torture him at my discretion and still help him reach his objectives. Why should I be the only one suffering?

Yes, yes, that's it. He'll pay for making me want him—in sweat and tears.

"Tori, are you listening to me?" Eva asks.

"What? Go with the red."

"Red? I'm choosing foundation, not lipstick, which you'd know if you were paying attention."

I snap my head up. "Sorry. What are the options again?"

Eva and I are headed to my parents' restaurant in North Philly—*eventually*—but she won't stop gushing about her makeup's "amazing" ability to transform her skin's inner luminosity, and I'm the enabler who drove her to the mall after work so she could buy it.

"It comes in a range of colors, Tori," she says. "Even ones for our brown skin tones, and it feels buttery soft on your skin."

The smile-free beauty consultant nods approvingly at Eva's description of the product's benefits.

I turn over the dispenser and read the price tag. "Holy shit, Eva. That's expensive." It's called Peau Lumineuse. "The name's unfortunate, too. Makes me think of luminous urine."

She snatches the bottle from me. "It's my holy grail foundation, *chica*. Don't knock it until you try it." Eva takes my hand and swipes a streak of foundation on it. "And if you think about it, a hundred and thirty-eight dollars isn't all that much to spend on a foundation that will last you six months, give or take a few weeks."

The beauty consultant hands me a few samples. "Peau Lumineuse promises to improve the quality of your skin while providing essential SPF protection."

I stuff the freebies in my purse. "With that price tag, will it also promise to give me orgasms on command, too? If not, I'll pass."

"You're hopeless," Eva says.

The beauty consultant nods in agreement.

"Please pay for whatever you're getting so we can go," I tell Eva. "My ten-dollar drugstore foundation and I will wait for you over there."

She shakes her head in disgust. "Okay, woman, damn."

Before Eva decided to join me, my plan to visit the restaurant had been simple. In the blessedly solitary confines of my car, I would belt out a few songs from the *Hamilton* musical—*yes, I'm obsessed*—and *try* to forget that I'll be working with Carter for the next six weeks. But Eva's obsession with obscure makeup brands is rivaled only by her love of my mother's cooking, so she invited herself to tag along and convinced me to make this "quick" out-of-the-way pit stop.

After making her purchase, she loops her arm through mine, a small gold shopping bag in her other hand. "What's the matter? Is being a celebrity's crush getting to you?"

I separate our arms and push her away. "I'm not his crush, and my mood has nothing to do with him."

She stares at me in horror and shrieks. "Oh my God."

"What? What? What is it?" I ask as I brush away the hair on my face. "A bug?"

She points at me. "No, it's your nose," she says in a high-pitched voice. "It's growing as we speak. Because. You. Are. A. Liar."

I walk ahead of her and say over my shoulder, "Someone seems to have forgotten their lack of transportation."

She catches up with me and throws her arm over my shoulder. "I'm just kidding, *mama*."

I take her waist as we exit the mall and walk to my car. "I know, and I'm sorry if I'm being moody."

"*If?* Oh, honey, there's no *if* about it. You're in a mood, for sure. And I think I know why."

"Feel free to keep your thoughts to yourself. They're more interesting that way."

I unlock the car, and she places her bag in the backseat, giving me glorious side-eye as she does.

"Seat belt, Eva."

"Hang on, I need to grab my notes." She twists in her seat and reaches for the huge red binder containing her study materials for her personal training certification. After she's secure, I drive out of the mall and follow the signs to take the interstate toward North Philadelphia.

"How's the studying coming along?" I ask her.

"It's good. The course I took last weekend helped a lot."

"I'm glad."

"I'm still salty I missed out on a trip to Aruba, though."

"There's no way Ben and Nate would have let us both take time off at the last minute."

Eva flips through the pages, or maybe *attacks* the pages would be a better description. "There's no way Nate would facilitate anything remotely fun for me, so you're right about that."

I hazard a sideways glance. "What's going on with you two anyway?"

"To be honest, I'm not sure. He's been snippy with me lately, and I can't figure out why."

I make a mental note to ask Nate about it.

Eva studies while I hum along to the *Hamilton* soundtrack.

Twenty minutes into the drive, Eva drops the binder onto her lap and stretches.

I can feel her gaze on me. "What?"

"Nothing."

She picks up the binder again and flips through the pages. "Aha. Found it. I came across a practice question that was really thought-provoking."

I know my friend, and this is a setup if ever there was one. "And you're going to read it to me, right?"

She turns to me and gives me a cheesy grin. "Right." After clearing her throat, she speaks in a stiff and authoritative voice: "Which of the following is an appropriate activity under the Guidelines for Professional Conduct? (a) counseling your client on their personal relationships, (b) devising a calorie-restricted diet plan for your client, (c) referring your client to experts for diagnostic care, (d) straddling your client as he bench presses, or (e) all of the above."

Eyes still on the road, I laugh. "It doesn't say anything about straddling your client. What does it say really?"

"Okay, it asks about massaging your client. Just wanted to make your choices more colorful."

"The only one that's appropriate is referring your clients to experts for diagnostic issues."

She nods. "But you're missing my point."

"I missed it because you didn't make one, Eva."

"If you *do* find yourself tempted enough to straddle a client, make sure you're circumspect about it."

I pull up in front of Mi Casita and pin Eva with my best no-way-in-hell stare. "I won't find myself tempted."

She pinches her index finger and thumb together. "Not even a little?"

I grip the steering wheel. "I'd be a fool to do anything with Carter."

"Why?" she asks as she climbs out of the car.

I climb out, too, and stare at her over the car top between us. "Why? I'll tell you why." I'm unable to keep the exasperation out of my voice. "Does Mason ring a bell? If I couldn't handle his theatrics, what makes you think I'd handle Carter's? And let's not forget he's my client. I can picture the snide comments on Page Six already. *Carter Stone gets worked over by his personal trainer.* And when he's long gone, that bit of gossip will haunt me forever, always one click away on the Internet. No thanks."

"Maybe he's not Mason."

I round the car, and we walk to the restaurant's entrance. "Maybe. But I'll never know. And I'm okay with that. So, no. There will be no kissing, straddling, humping, or sucking of any kind with a client, especially Carter Stone."

"You sure about that?"

"Absolutely."

Well, probably.

Okay, sort of.

MI CASITA SITS between a flower shop and a *bodega* on a tree-lined street in North Philadelphia. The trees are artificial royal palms, a project of the city's revitalization plan and an homage to the Puerto Rican ancestry of most of the neighborhood's residents. Every time I walk into the restaurant, I'm transported to my grandmother's kitchen on the island. A mural of Puerto Rican symbols—the flag, the tiny tree frog, and conga drums—covers an entire wall.

There are no white table linens here. Instead, my sister, Bianca, decorated the place with function in mind: wood tables and chairs in neat rows, dark linoleum floors, and a long luncheon counter for the people who come here to have a quick meal or drink my mother's *café con leche*.

When my sister sees us, she lifts her elbows off the counter and straightens to her full height. "Close the door, please. We don't want any flies in here."

Bianca can't even be bothered to say hello. *Madre de Dios*, give me strength.

Standing behind me, Eva whispers in my ear, "If you need me to, I will cut a bitch."

I drag Eva into the restaurant and steer her to a table in the back. "*Don't* call my sister a bitch," I try to say without smiling. "Only I get to call her that. Now sit here and don't say a word. If you don't follow those simple directions, there will be no free food for you."

"Fine." She pouts and places her clasped hands on the table. As I walk away, she sings, "*I feel petty. Oh, so petty…*"

I'm laughing when I claim one of the red-top swivel seats and face Bianca. She grimaces, and I'm thinking the counter between us is serving a useful purpose: protection—although it's not clear which one of us needs it. "Hey."

"Hey. What brings you to this side of town?"

Bianca and I have never been close. She's always treated me like an interloper. I'm virtually certain she hated me at first sight when my parents brought me home from the hospital when I was a baby, and her opinion of me hasn't changed since then. Take now for instance. I come here when I can—admittedly, not as often as I used to—yet she always treats me like a visitor passing through the area.

I ignore her sour attitude. "How's it going? Busy?"

"Steady. Why do you ask? Planning to put on an apron and help?"

Maybe I will take Eva up on her offer to cut my sister. Nothing dangerous, just a superficial wound that won't require stitches. "Help? Ha. Like you'd let me."

We both know that would never happen. This is Bianca's domain, the place where she and my mom share their mutual love of cooking. She'd rather chew off her own arm than let me help with the restaurant in any way.

Eva's chatting with a patron who's about twenty years her senior. She glances at me and raises the butter knife from her place setting and points it at Bianca. I shake my head.

"Where's Mami?"

"*Fue a la iglesia.* She'll be back soon."

My mother visits her church when she can, sometimes before the evening rush, when the restaurant isn't busy. She lights candles for her deceased parents, for her children, and for many other people and causes.

A friend is sick? Light a candle.

The world's gone mad? Light a candle.

The restaurant's deep freeze is acting up? Light a candle.

El poder de Dios—the power of God—heals all.

And after more than one occasion in which I witnessed a bad situation improve after my mother lit a candle, I believe.

That's why I'm sure she's never lit a candle to mend my relationship with my sister. This shit is broken—and I have no idea why.

"Can I get back there and put something together for Eva?"

Bianca gives me a dismissive wave as though she couldn't care less what I do. "Whatever." Still, her eagle-eyed gaze follows me as I move behind the counter.

After washing my hands, I lift the silver chafing dishes containing today's menu options. I know what Eva likes, so I heap large amounts of *arroz blanco, carne guisada,* and *platanos* on her plate.

"Don't forget the *relleno de papa*," Eva yells from her seat at the table.

"Got it," I yell back.

The *relleno de papa* is basically a fried ball of mashed potato stuffed with seasoned beef. It's one of a dozen fried items that sit under hot lamps near Mi Casita's storefront window. My father once dined on *cuchifritos* daily; he loved them, but they did *not* love him back.

The bell above the restaurant's door chimes, and my mother walks in. "*Mija*, you're here," she says to me from the entryway. Several people shuffle in behind her, and Bianca motions for them to follow her to a table.

Mom gives me a kiss on the cheek and smiles at the plate in my hand. "You're eating?"

"No, this is for Eva."

The brightness in her eyes dims. I suspect she thinks I'm rejecting her, not just declining her food. It's a balancing act, and sometimes I'm off-kilter.

I bump her with my shoulder. "I'm not hungry, but I'll take a to-go plate, okay?"

She gives me a reluctant smile. "*Bueno.* I've got to get back into the kitchen before the dinner rush. Can you stay?"

I shake my head. "Not long. Eva's meeting her dad, and I have to drive her back. Where's Papi?"

"Your father's helping one of his friends with an engine."

My father fixes cars on the weekend, a hobby he's had for decades. After he experienced a stroke last year, he spent most of his days on the couch watching the news. I'm glad to hear he's not holed up in the house. "He's never around when I'm here."

My mother peers at me. "Sometimes I think you prefer it that way."

I avert my gaze and swallow the lump in my throat. "That's not true. Why would I?"

She shakes her head. "I don't know. You tell me."

Eva clears her throat, sending the bat signal for her food, and I'm quick to answer it. Anything to get me away from this conversation. "Excuse me, Mami. *La reina quiere su comida.*"

My mother walks with me to Eva's table, and I set the plate in front of my friend. "Your food, my queen."

"Thank you, ma'am," Eva says as she unfolds a paper napkin and places it on her lap. She closes her eyes in appreciation after eating a forkful of the *carne guisada*.

My mother claps, and then she squeezes Eva's chin. *"Te gusta la comida?"*

"Como siempre," Eva replies, still chewing.

My friend learned enough Spanish to tell my mother she likes her food—"as always." The woman is resourceful.

My mother glances at me, and then she shuffles away, eventually disappearing through the swinging doors that lead to the kitchen.

"Be right back," I tell Eva.

She digs her fork into the food. "No rush. I'm happily occupied."

The kitchen is small and clean, and my mother, who's short and sturdy, fills the space with her energy. Dolores, my mother's kitchen helper, stands in the corner chopping vegetables for the dishes they'll make this evening.

"Hola, Dolores."

"Hola, Tori."

I shadow my mother as she moves about the room. "So has Daddy been eating okay?"

My mother's nose flares. "He's been eating fine." She spins away from me and pulls items from the fridge.

"No *cuchifritos*, right?" I ask.

She freezes at the open fridge. Several seconds of silence pass before she turns around with a stick of butter in her hand. "Every once in a while, yes."

This is what I was afraid of. My father has no self-control, and my mother has no control over my father.

He can't afford to slide back into his old bad habits. "Ma, remember what the doctor said."

"Yes, *mija*, I remember what the doctor said, but your father's a grown man, and if he wants an *acalpurria* from time to time, I'm going to let him have it." She raises her chin as if she's daring me to object.

I should have known better than to broach the subject. The wall of indignation that rises when I question her about Papi's diet is getting too steep to climb. If I keep pushing, eventually it'll be insurmountable. *Just let it go, Tori.*

Bianca enters the kitchen and stands shoulder to shoulder with her. "Everything okay in here?"

"I was just asking her about Papi's diet."

Bianca's face hardens. "You don't get to march in here whenever you want and act like a food inspector. Everything's under control."

"Bianca, please," my mother says.

I take a deep breath. "It's fine, Mami."

My sister and I can't even find common ground about our father's health. There was a moment when I thought that wouldn't be the case: the day my father had his second stroke. It was the first time in our adult lives that Bianca and I hugged. Between taking turns consoling our mother, we'd clung to each other, both distraught and unsure whether our father would survive. I'd never felt so helpless, and my sister's embrace was the support I hadn't known I needed. Sometimes I feel like I'm the only one who remembers that day.

Although I know everything's not under control as Bianca claims, if I push too hard on this, I'll push them away, too. "Okay, I'm glad to hear everything's okay. I'm going to head out soon. Tell Papi I'll see him next weekend."

I kiss my mother's forehead, and she squeezes my hand.

"Bye, *mija*," she says. "Take care of yourself."

I know she means that literally, but in my head, I hear it differently: *Take care of yourself—and don't worry about taking care of us.*

Eva and I don't talk much during the ride back to Center City. There's nothing I can do about my family's resistance to my advice. It's just how they are, and I don't want to alienate them by pressing for changes they're not ready to make. So I'm going to focus on what I can control—namely, my life and the people I allow into it.

When Eva and I get home, she pulls me into a hug as soon as we close the apartment door. "Cheer up, *chica*, and get some rest. You have a big day tomorrow."

I pull back and give her a blank look. "I do?"

She gives me a knowing smile in return. "Yes, you do. Operation Resist Carter Stone begins tomorrow morning."

"No, sweetie, you've got it all wrong. Tomorrow I begin Operation *Crush* Carter Stone."

Picturing him in Eva's Advanced Zumba class, I squint and press my steepled fingers against my lips like a villain.

"Damn, you're evil, Tori," she says on a laugh.

I wink at her. *"Mwahaha."*

Chapter Seventeen

Carter

HELLO? 911? MY emergency is this: I'm fucking dying.

I'm gasping for air as I try to follow the Zumba instructor's choreography. I need water, preferably gallons of it. But I didn't bring a water bottle—because I'm a dumb ass. Maybe sucking the sweat above my upper lip will do the trick.

Tori neglected to tell me that Zumba is a cult, and its followers are insane. No, these women are sadists, and Eva, the instructor, is their mistress, cracking her whip at everyone—especially me. She keeps referring to me as "Mr. Tall Drink of Water," and she's watching my ill-fated moves like a vulture with her sights on roadkill.

Beside me, Tori's enjoying my torment. She's a sadist like the rest of them. I don't understand how they can move their feet this quickly, while their arms do something altogether different. Just when I think I've gotten the hang of a move, they switch to another one. Plus, my hips don't move like that. They just don't.

"How you doing over there, Carter?" Tori asks.

My eyebrows are pinched in concentration as I count out the beats for the next combination. "Can't talk right now, Ms. Alvarez, but it's not as bad as I expected it to be." I'm trying to keep my voice even, but the words sound like they're being forced out my lungs. My pulse is racing. It's not the exertion. It's the pressure of having to remember all the steps. Stop laughing; it's true.

Tori smiles, not a sheen of perspiration on any visible part of her body. She's not breathing hard, either. "*Bien, bien.* Glad to hear it."

I must admit the music's great. Lots of drums and horns and a thumping base. We're doing an easier combination now—just three hops, a slide, and a pumped fist in the air—and I'm smiling for the first time.

"Now, switch," the instructor shouts at us.

Apparently, I'm the only one in the class who's struggling because when I look up thirty-plus sets of eyes are on me. Yes, the entire class is facing me. I might as well be naked. The shame is real, people.

Tori's eyes twinkle, and her lips are compressed. She's trying hard not to laugh, and I welcome her reaction, even if it's at my expense. It means we might be able to get beyond my initial stupidity. Maybe, just maybe, I can prove to her that I'm a decent guy who made a mistake.

Another twenty minutes of abuse later, Eva the Tyrant talks us through the cooldown period as she meanders around the room, occasionally correcting someone's form. I tense when she approaches me. Perhaps if I don't blink she'll move on without commenting on my stretches. But of course, she slows and plants her hands on her hips. "Goodness, you're a flexible one, aren't you? It's not often that a man in my class can touch his toes like that."

Tori stretches her arms over her head and falls to her side, glancing at me before she drops her head. "Time to wrap this up, Eva."

Eva straightens and smiles. "Right."

After a few more stretches, Eva thanks everyone for coming, and her students, myself included, clap and cheer. As people trickle out, a few members make eye contact with me, and one of the guys in the class extends his hand to shake it. I give him a fist bump instead and then grab a towel to dry my wet face.

Tori sidles next to me and sips on her water bottle, nowhere near resembling someone who just completed a forty-five-minute fitness class. "What did you think?"

I'm wheezing as I respond. "That was great. I wouldn't mind doing it again."

She drops her shoulders, and her bright smile fades to black.

Now why would that be? Didn't she want me to enjoy Zumba?

"No complaints?" she prods.

Ah, I get it. She must think I'll reconsider the arrangement if I hate her training plan, and she's trying to break me. Well, let's have some fun with this, shall we?

"So, Tori, the first day of training has got me hyped for more. What's on the schedule for tomorrow?"

She gives me a smile that makes the hairs on the back of my arms stand. "We're not done for today. But to answer your question, tomorrow is hot yoga."

Fuck. That doesn't sound cool.

I EASE MY aching body into the tub. Tori kicked my ass today, employing a regimen of weightlifting and muscle-building exercises that pushed me beyond any training I'd ever done before. For the next six weeks, I'll be alternating between sessions for my chest, biceps, triceps, legs, and abs. And after an hour-long meeting with a nutritionist, I have a diet plan that consists mostly of eggs, chicken, beef, avocado, and nuts.

I'll be taxing my body, yes, but this is a small price to pay for the chance to land a career-defining role. Plus, I get to spend time with Tori. If I play this right, I'll warm the cold shoulder she's been throwing at me since I reappeared in her life. But first a soak, eight hours of sleep—Tori's orders—and finally hot yoga.

After my bath, I throw on a T-shirt and boxers and call my sister Ashley. Although there's a hot yoga studio on every corner in LA, I've never ventured inside one. I figure Ashley might be able to give me some tips so I don't make an ass of myself in front of Tori.

Ashley picks up after the first ring. "Hey, bro. Everything okay?"

"Everything's fine. What about you?"

"Oh, you know, I almost smacked a passenger on yes-terday's flight, and my supervisor thinks I pour too much Dr. Pepper during beverage service, but other than that, life's great."

Ashley's a bit of a rolling stone—it's been years since she's settled in one place—so you'd think being a flight attendant would be the perfect gig for her. Spoiler alert: *It's not.* "Why'd you almost smack a passenger?"

Ashley growls. "She kept stretching her feet out in the aisle and made me trip twice. When I asked her—*nicely,* I might add—to keep the aisle clear, she sucked her teeth."

Oh no. Not teeth sucking. That's Ashley's pet peeve. "I'm guessing she didn't comply."

"She did after the beverage cart *accidentally* clipped her ankles."

"Well done, sis. Well done."

"So what do you need, Carter?"

"I'm looking for tips. What do you know about hot yoga?"

"It's yoga, and there's lots of sweat involved, and because there's sweat involved that's the extent of my knowledge. Ashley doesn't do perspiration. Not that kind, at least."

"First, stop talking about yourself in the third per-son. You're not an actor. Second, even a hint of sexual activity on your part is strictly forbidden during our conversations."

"Okay, fine. *Ashley* was going to tell you about her ini-tiation into the mile-high club, but never mind."

"You're a brat."

"And that's among the many reasons why you love me."

"I'm confused. You were all psyched about kickboxing six months ago."

"You're so behind it's sad. Carter, I was psyched about kickboxing six months ago because I was interested in my instructor. He had zero skills in bed. So no more kickboxing."

"I'll let that breach of our agreement pass. But you should have stuck with the instructor. Johnny Doche was not an improvement."

"*Au contraire, mon frère*. He *was* an improvement, but not in the way you'd want to hear about, so let's leave it at that."

"Yes, let's." In fact, I'd gladly allow someone to snatch this conversation from my memory if they were so inclined.

"Wait. Why are you doing hot yoga?"

"I'm training."

"But…hot yoga. Why?"

"I'm not sure, but I have a theory."

"Which is?"

"My trainer's playing me."

Ashley laughs. "Is your trainer a woman?"

"Yep."

"Does yoga relate in any way to the role you're preparing for?"

"Nope."

"Oh, you're definitely being played. I wish I could be there to see it. What's the woman's name?"

"Tori-not-short-for-Victoria."

"What?"

"Nothing. It's Tori."

"Are you interested in her?"

Interested is an underwhelming word in this context, but I can't explain this to Ashley without opening myself to all kinds of sisterly abuse. "I'm definitely interested."

"And she wants you to take a hot yoga class? Carter… you've met your match."

"You may be right."

"Why does she feel the need to play you?"

"I have a theory about that, too. She's not interested in dating someone in the public eye."

"Oh, she's a keeper, Carter. Do you know what you have to do?"

Tell me. Tell me what to do. Please. "What?"

"Be Carter Williamson."

I move the phone away from my ear and frown at it. "I *am* Carter Williamson," I say in a loud voice.

"Yes, yes, I know that, but to her, you're Carter Stone. In her mind, he represents a life she doesn't want. But that Williamson guy is a different proposition. He's the one she could fall for."

"She needs to accept all of me if we're going to make it work."

"Baby steps, Carter. Baby steps."

"Okay, thanks for the advice," I say on a yawn.

"Am I boring you?"

"No, Ash. I'm exhausted. Anyway, when will I see your pretty face?"

"Not sure, Carter. I don't have my schedule for the next few weeks yet. I'll get it soon and let you know. But I'm doing fine. No need to worry about me, okay?"

Which reminds me…"Did you see Julian when you were in LA last week?"

"Yeah."

Static fills my ear, and then Ashley's talking to someone on her end.

"Gotta go, Carter. We'll catch up soon."

WHEN I ARRIVE at Hard Core the next morning, the kid at the front desk hands me a temporary ID and several sheets of paper.

"What do we have here?" I ask him.

"That's your temporary gym card, sir, and that's the waiver form for hot yoga. Tori left them for you."

A waiver? That's never comforting. Plus, where the hell is Tori? For someone who claims to be my personal trainer, she's being noticeably impersonal now.

The club provides its members with a swank lounging area that belongs in a dance club rather than a gym. Situated twenty feet beyond the reception desk, a large-screen television, tuned to ESPN, dominates the space and is flanked by two large velvet couches. To the right, two staffers prepare smoothies at a health drink bar where members in athletic clothes flex their well-earned muscles. One guy's pecs are particularly distracting. He plainly never heard the rule that your tank top must be big enough to cover your nipples. If I doubted his ability to kick my ass, I'd tweak them.

Pen in hand, I claim a space at one end of the couch and drape the waiver over the tufted arm. Hmm, let's see. It begins by setting out the relevant parties: the gym and me. Then it gets cutthroat. The waiver states that by signing it I acknowledge:

"The room in which the ninety-minute class will be conducted will be maintained at a temperature of 104 degrees and at a humidity level of 40 percent." *In other words, I'm taking a class on the surface of the sun.*

"Proper hydration is an essential component of the hot yoga experience. Hard Core urges the participant to hydrate before, during, and after the class." *Okay, cool. This time I remembered my water bottle, so that shouldn't be a problem.*

"If the participant experiences dizziness, shortness of breath, heart palpitations, or any other unusual signs of physical distress, the participant will immediately advise the instructor so that medical attention may be sought if necessary." *Damn, is Tori trying to kill me?*

"Participant has read and understands the risks associated with participating in the class and agrees to hold Hard Core harmless for any injuries associated with such participation." *So let's see if I've got this right: If Tori is trying to kill me, which seems more probable now than ever, I agree not to sue her?*

Despite my reservations, I sign the waiver and hand it back to the kid. His name tag says Darryl.

He removes his headphones. "Enjoy your class."

Although I've signed the waiver, I'm not enthusiastic about it. I'm tempted to ditch hot yoga, but I'm sure

Tori would love to claim that I'm violating the spirit of our agreement, and I *refuse* to give her the satisfaction. Besides, how bad could this class possibly be?

Twenty minutes later, the verdict is in: It's bad. *Very bad.* By this point, my body temperature has adjusted to its new normal, and the poses have moved beyond the Mountain Pose and Downward Dog. The instructor assures everyone that we should go at our own pace, demonstrating modifications for those with less flexibility.

Still, no accommodation will make a difference when I'm sweating profusely and sucking water from my bottle like a dog lapping at his bowl. My body is so hot I'm itchy, and my shorts and T-shirt are drenched in perspiration. At this point, I'm not doing much of anything. If there's a dazed yoga pose, that's what I'm attempting.

Next to me, Tori bends in ways that make my own muscles protest in pain. While on her knees, she bows her back and touches her forehead to her knees as though she's presenting her ass as a gift. I don't want to think of the obvious benefits of such a position in bed, but my fuzzy brain goes there anyway. Damn, it's fucking hot in here.

"Carter, breathe," she whispers. "It's not as hot as your brain thinks it is."

"It's not my brain, Tori," I say between ragged breaths. "It's my pits, my ass, even the soles of my feet. And I don't mean to be crude here, but my man parts are sizzling. This is supposed to help with stress?"

"It does help."

"Then I'll suck it up because I definitely need stress relief."

Her head jerks up. "What do you have to be stressed about?"

"I'm trying to land an important role, and it's annoying as hell that getting it probably hinges on whether I'm in shape to the filmmakers' liking. It's crass."

"So why do it?"

"Because I want the part, and sometimes you have to accept the realities of a fucked-up situation to get what you want."

"This really matters to you."

She says this as though it's surprising. Like she thought I was goofing around about needing to regain the weight.

A woman near us grumbles, probably pissed that we're messing with her concentration.

Tori unfolds from the kneeling position. "C'mere. Sit down and face me."

I crawl over and sit across from her. "Now what?"

"Now widen your legs in a V." She does the same. "We're going to help each other stretch, okay? All you have to do is hold my wrists and pull me forward."

She's giving me permission to touch her? I'd skinny-dip in a volcano for a chance like this. So I grasp her wrists gently and pull her toward me, and she flattens her back, her nose nearly touching the floor.

"Hold for seven," she says. Then she straightens to an upright position. "Now you."

She circles my forearms with her soft fingers and pulls me. My nose gets nowhere near the floor, though.

"Relax into it," she says in a calm voice. "Don't worry about how far down you go. Just soften your body."

The muscles in my back lengthen and release, and I moan as she counts for seven seconds. "Oh, that feels *so* good, Tori. So, so good."

Above me, I hear a small noise. Like a yelp. No, no, like a whimper.

"Sit up," she says.

We both straighten. She refuses to meet my gaze, and her face is flushed. Did hot yoga put that color in her cheeks? Did I?

She jumps up from the floor and helps me stand. But I don't have my bearings. Seconds later, I've lost all sense of place and time. An angel hovers near my face.

"Carter," the vision says.

She waves a hand in front of me, and my body sways toward the welcome breeze caused by the movement. It's Tori. I blink several times and then shut my eyes to be sure. When I open them, she grabs my wrist and pulls me out of the room, waving at the instructor on her way out. The cool air outside the studio pricks my skin like a million needles.

"Come with me," she says in a voice that's devoid of emotion.

I follow her up the stairs and down a long hallway, until we reach the door to a room marked "Staff." She motions for me to enter.

The room is dim, and there's an entire wall of lockers. Two benches sit in the middle, and a couple of desks face each other near a single floor-to-ceiling window. Function over form, 100 percent. "What's going on, Tori?"

She blows out a breath and meets my gaze. "We need to talk."

Chapter Eighteen

Tori

THIS ISN'T GOING to work.

I pull several bottles of water from a small fridge in the corner of the break room and a stack of bright white towels from one of the lockers. With my gaze on the floor, I thrust two bottles into his hands. "Here. Drink them both."

As he guzzles the water, I do my best to ignore the long column of his neck and the tendons stretching there as he swallows. I drape a towel over his shoulder and hold the rest of the stack in my hands.

When Carter's done with both bottles, he tosses them in the recycling bin and uses the towel to wipe the sweat that's still pouring down his face.

"How are you feeling?" I ask.

My words are clipped, and judging by the way he narrows his eyes, Carter notices my frustrated tone. He's serious about preparing for this role, and I'm messing around with him like a vindictive child—and trivializing my own job in the process. And for what? Because I'm attracted to him, and I refuse to do anything about it? That isn't his fault. *Oh, Tori, how low can you go?*

"I'm feeling fine," he says. "You didn't have to pull me out of the class."

My head pounds, warning me of a migraine. I haven't had one of those in a long time. "Yes, I did."

"I would have handled it just fine. In fact, one of those poses was—"

"Carter, stop. You shouldn't have been in that class. It has nothing to do with your fitness goals. I let my lack of objectivity in this situation inform my training program. It's inexcusable, and I would understand if you didn't want to work with me anymore."

He draws back and gives me a dazed look. "Why?"

I look up at him then. "Why, what?"

"Why'd you have me take hot yoga when it has nothing to do with my training?"

I blow out a long breath and tilt my head to the ceiling. "I guess I was annoyed by everything. The fact that you insinuated yourself into my life. The fact that your presence here threatens the quiet existence I'd like to pursue. The fact that I'm…"

"What? The fact that you're what?" he asks with urgency in his voice.

"Nothing. Just...I'm sorry I let my personal issues affect my professional judgment."

He raises his hand slowly and caresses my cheek with two fingers. I lean into his touch, wanting forgiveness, wanting whatever he wants, but just as quickly I draw back and circle the bench so that it creates a barrier between us. After a pause, I open a locker and deposit the remaining towels inside.

"I'm sorry," he says.

With my back to him, I take a deep breath and lay a hand on top of the open locker door. After a pause, I turn around and tilt my head to the side. "Sorry? What for?"

His gaze is kind. "For not being honest with you when we met. I'm used to shielding myself from the prying eyes of strangers, but the minute I figured out I didn't want us to be strangers, I should have said something."

I drop my gaze to the floor and fiddle with my sports watch. "You've apologized already. You don't owe me anything."

"I apologized for not being honest. But I didn't apologize for the consequences of that dishonesty. You shared details about your life, and I didn't do the same. You thought you were getting to know Carter Williamson, while I knew Carter Stone wasn't far behind. I wish I could hit Rewind. I'd redo the day we met. But I can't."

This is too much. He's being too sweet, too good, too much of the person I want. I need space. I square my shoulders and lift my head, meeting his gaze full on. "Here's my suggestion."

"I'm listening."

"Ask Nate to train you. He's excellent, and you'll get the results you want."

"I don't want Nate to train me." He licks his lips and pierces me with a heated gaze. "I want you."

Yes, he wants me, and yes, I want him. But he's no good for me, and I don't want to be an accessory in his crazy life. Maybe he sees the hesitation in my eyes, or maybe he understands that chewing my lip raw means this isn't the right way to persuade me to change my mind.

Whatever it is, he continues to speak as though a switch has been flipped in him. "I'm trying to land the role of my career, Tori. It's important to me. This isn't some flighty distraction. Despite what you may think, I'm not being careless with my body or my health. When I learned I'd have to lose weight for the last film, I consulted a doctor to advise me on proper nutrition and to monitor my health as the pounds came off. He gave me advice, sure, but he also snapped pictures of me and sold them to a tabloid."

Oh, Carter. How awful. "That's terrible...and unethical...and just fucked up."

"I couldn't agree more, and I'm not looking for a repeat. So in my mind the best candidate for the position is the person who fled when she learned I was Carter Stone. You don't care about all that, and you have the expertise. This is going to be a grueling experience. Don't make me do it alone—or with Nate."

How can I say no to that? I can't, and I won't. After blowing out a long breath, I nod. "Okay."

At that moment, his demeanor transforms. Carter's smile is broad, and his eyes are brighter than I thought possible. "Great. Thank you."

"Let me check in with Ben about his efforts to set us up at another gym."

"Sounds good."

"Take the day off and get some rest. It's going to be really tough from here on out."

For the both of us.

BEN ARRANGES A deal with a CrossFit affiliate on Broad Street. Because the location has extended business hours, our only options are to train either very early in the day or late at night. Carter scoffed at the idea of getting up before sunrise, claiming he needed his "handsome rest," so we settle on a one-hour workout session six days a week from nine to ten in the evening. It's not ideal, but the circumstances are unusual, and the good news is that I'm not locked into this hellish schedule forever.

But I soon encounter an issue more serious than a scheduling inconvenience.

When Carter arrives for our first night of training under the new regime, I'm struck by the innate intimacy of our environment. We're alone in a gym, where I'm serving not only as his *personal* trainer, but also as his *private* instructor. Save for the occasional blaring of a car horn from the street below, we are the only sources of sound in the gym, and there are no people milling around as is typically the case when I'm working with clients. I'm hyperaware of him, and it's seriously messing with my brain.

Carter's undergone a bit of a transformation that doesn't help matters—namely, he's shaved his beard. Which means I can now see his square jaw and better appreciate his Cupid's bow lips. And upon further scrutiny, I discover he has a dimple in his chin. Damn you to hell, Carter.

After returning from a quick restroom detour, he stands in the middle of the gym floor waiting for my guidance. "Ready?"

"Sure. Let's get you on a treadmill for a five-minute warm-up, and then we'll work on stretches."

He jogs for the allotted time, and then we move to the floor in front of the floor-to-ceiling mirrors. I demonstrate the stretches I'd like him to complete before each workout, and all is well until we get to the supine bridge.

It's a mainstay of training programs for good reason. It prepares your body for squats, dead lifts, and the bench press, but as I lower myself to the ground, I'm mortified by what I'm about to do: It's essentially a hip thrust. Which must be held for fifteen seconds and repeated. With my back against the floor and my feet hip-width apart, I raise my knees at a ninety-degree angle and lift my ass off the ground. Thrust. Hold. Lower. Repeat. Thrust. Hold. Lower. Repeat.

Oh shit, oh shit, oh shit. Why didn't I think to put on music? Or would that be worse? Yes, *yes*, that would be worse. I've done this a million times. Why is it so difficult now? Because we're alone. That *must* be it.

Carter watches without saying a word, which makes me ten times more uncomfortable than I'd otherwise be. Okay, that demonstration should suffice. I scramble to my knees and jump up like someone stuck a firecracker up my butt. "Okay, you get the idea, right?"

"Right," Carter says in a strangled voice.

He sits on his rear and lowers his body in a reverse curl, and then he's thrusting, but his form is poor.

"Be sure to use your glutes to lift yourself off the ground, hold...and down."

This is *not* a good time to notice that Carter has nice legs. No, no, he doesn't. They're average. So damn average. And to make matters worse, my cheeks and forehead are burning. The flu maybe? Yes, it's May, but I'm sure it happens.

"Um, Tori?"

"What's wrong? You okay?"

"Yeah, I'm fine," he says as he continues to thrust, hold, and repeat. "It's just...I feel like you're coming on strong, this being only our third training session. It's a little more forward than I'd expected."

His face doesn't bear a hint of humor, but then he tilts his head and he's wearing a grin that spreads into a full-on *gotcha* smile. I cannot emphasize enough how dangerous a man with a sense of humor can be. And if his gaze pierces you when he does nothing more than make eye contact, take my advice: back the hell up and run.

Well, if there are valid reasons for you to resist temptation, that is.

Like, say for instance, the man is your client and a relationship with him would be inappropriate.

Or maybe it's that he's a celebrity and you'd rather smear your body with honey and run through a field overpopulated by bees than play out another relationship in the public eye.

One thing's for sure: Our arrangement was tailor-made to be complicated. Because Carter's a handsome man, whether he weighs 160 pounds or 200 pounds, and yes, a flutter tickles my belly every time I see him. And because the gods have cursed me, he's funny, and nice, and cares about my feelings. But if I'm to be competent at my job, I must resist him. And the injustice of it all is that I can't escape him, not for the next five-plus weeks at least. If I could, though, I'd scurry out of this gym and leave skid marks in my wake.

Instead, I'm watching him perform squats. If this were anyone else, I'd place a hand on his back and correct his form. But because he's Carter, I demonstrate the correct posture using my own body, not trusting myself to touch him. That's it. I'm a perv who deserves to have her training license revoked.

And because I think there's safety in talking, my next coping mechanism is to chatter. With my clipboard in hand, I jot down notes about the session and ask Carter questions about anything and everything when he's resting between sets.

"What was your childhood like? Did you have tutors?"

He scoffs at the idea. "No, nothing like that. My acting career didn't really take off until I moved to LA when I was nineteen. Before that, I did mostly commercial work in New York. I went to high school in my hometown, kissed girls under the bleachers, tortured my sisters, and went to prom. What about you? You were the popular girl in school, right?"

"From the outside, yes. I was loud and I knew how to hold people's attention in a group. So, sure, I was invited to parties. And I always sat with someone during lunch. But it was superficial like high school often is. I didn't have a bestie who had my back. And to be honest, I probably didn't give off vibes that I was looking for someone like that in my life. My strained relationship with my sister made me wary of getting close to anyone. I mean, if your own sister doesn't have your back, who else will? Meeting Eva changed all that. She has a way of breaking down your defenses before you even know you have them. But back then? Yeah, no one searched for me before the bell rang or called me to gossip. I was just…there. Like I used to imagine that if I failed to show up to school one morning no one would notice."

He bends and lifts two dumbbells from the rack. "If I had gone to your school and you didn't show up one day, I would have noticed."

I have no answer for his comment, partly because I'm transfixed by the kindness in his eyes. As I stare at him, the sweetness of his words pour into me, and now I have this ooey-gooey center that's making it even more difficult to resist him. I'm trying to build a wall, but Carter's standing behind me, pulling out individual bricks before I can slap on the mortar.

Note to self: *Don't talk to Carter.*

CARTER AND I settle into a comfortable training rhythm. In just one week, he's gained four pounds.

In that time, I've also learned he hates silence. Which means I must do the very thing I was trying to avoid: *talk* to him.

He tells me about his upcoming and final season of *My Life in Shambles*, a show I'm embarrassed to say I've never watched. I learn that he has a tepid relationship with Nina Blake, his costar, but they're cordial with each other, and that's enough for him. And his older sister, Kimberly, divorced her philandering husband when her kids were still in their diapers.

Carter also asks questions. So many questions.

Today, he opens with, "How'd you get into personal training?"

Together, we add weights to the bar for his bench press circuit. He's up to lifting an impressive 170 pounds.

He lowers himself to the bench, and I stand behind the bar to spot him. I don't notice his chest. *Not at all.*

"I wasn't particularly athletic as a kid. But in high school I started jogging as part of my phys ed class. And then I discovered a cardio kickboxing video and loved it. It was empowering. I'd never felt so in control of my own body. It gave me confidence to engage in different kinds of physical activities. Biking, swimming, even roller-skating. So when it came time to figure out my career, a guidance counselor steered me to Temple's degree in exercise and sports science."

Am I babbling? Yes, I am.

Do. *Not*. Judge.

"Let me know when you're ready," I tell him.

"Ready," he says.

"Do you want a lift off the rack?"

"Yeah."

I help him lift the bar off the rack and stand ready to grab it if necessary. His face reddens under the pressure of holding the load, but he breathes out and pushes through it. He completes three reps, and then I help him lift the bar back onto the rack.

"That's one set. Four more. Great job, Carter. We're resting for three minutes."

He nods and walks to the water fountain. After taking a sip of water, he straightens and winces.

"What's wrong?" I say from across the room.

He waves me off. "No big deal. A small bruise below my breastbone."

I meet him halfway. "Let me see."

He lifts his tank top, and I immediately regret asking to see anything as I try to scan the area with a clinical eye. It really is a small welt, and there's no reason for me to touch it, but those facts no longer matter now that this part of his body is exposed to me. There's so much texture. Smooth skin. Fine hairs. Hills and valleys marking the spots where muscles reside. I'd love to trace those points of interest with my fingers—or my mouth. My breath quickens, and my nipples tighten against my sports bra. The juncture between my thighs aches with need.

I step back as if I'm avoiding a snapping turtle. "That should be fine."

He furrows his brows and stares at me. "That's what I told you."

"Indeed, you did. I'm going to the restroom. Be right back."

As I walk away, I repeat this in my head: Five more weeks. Five more weeks. Five more weeks. I can maintain my professionalism during that period, right?

No te rías. It's not *that* funny.

EARLY IN THE following week, Carter appears sluggish and irritable during his workout. When we're finished for the evening, he goes to the restroom, and I wait for him by the door.

A few minutes later, he bounds down the hall with a scowl on his face.

"What's wrong?" I ask him.

"Nothing," he says.

"You look tired."

He rolls his eyes. "That's nice of you to say."

Oh my God. I can't believe he just hit me with the eye roll. I'm poised to tease him about it, but then his stomach grumbles, the sound reminding me of the scrape of heavy furniture being dragged across the floor when our upstairs neighbors decide to redecorate in the middle of the night.

Carter's eyes go wide, and then he turns a shade of pink so lovely Maybelline might want to replicate it.

I hold back the laughter as well as can be expected under the circumstances. Which is to say, tears are streaming down my eyes. "*¿Tienes hambre?*"

"Oh, that one I know," he says. "Yes, I'm hungry. *Starving*, in fact." He gives me a sheepish grin. "I don't even recognize myself."

I give him a saucy smile. "I know a place."

His nostrils flare. "Take me to your leader."

Ten minutes later, we're sliding into a booth at Broad Street Diner in South Philadelphia, one of the few places in the city open all night.

"I would have taken you to my mother's restaurant, but it's closed."

He perks up despite his desperate need for fuel. "Your mother owns a restaurant? What's it called?"

"Mi Casita. It's like a luncheonette. In North Philly."

"Will you take me someday?"

Would I? Should I take my client to my mother's restaurant? This is Carter, though, so it's a different proposition. I won't obsess about the reasons why. "I usually visit on Saturdays. Maybe I'll invite you along when your six weeks are up."

He winks at me. "I'll hold you to it."

When our server arrives, Carter orders an orange spritzer, a steak, and a sweet potato.

"Anything for you?" Carter asks.

"Nah, I ate before I came to the gym. Like I was supposed to."

"I won't make that mistake again, believe me."

The server spins around, but I stop her. "Actually, could I have a slice of that apple pie and a glass of milk?"

"Sure thing," she says.

When she's gone, Carter's mouth drops open. "Seriously?"

I nod. "Seriously."

"That's mean."

"It's not mean. You'll have to resist sweets if you want to bulk up quickly. Consider this part of your training."

The server returns with my milk and apple pie and Carter's drink.

He stares longingly at my dessert and groans. "This is the hardest part yet. Distract me. Tell me something I don't know about you."

"Hmm." I glance at the fizzy liquid in his cup. "I can tie a knot in a—"

Nope. Not something I should mention.

"What? Don't leave me hanging. What were you going to say?"

"Hang on a second. I need to slap myself."

Carter's eyes dance. "Oh, this is going to be good. Tell me, tell me."

"I can tie a knot in a cherry stem with my tongue."

Carter looks unimpressed. "Oh, that. Yeah, I can, too. I thought you were going to tell me something juicy."

I sit back and fold my arms over my chest. "Oh, yeah? Show me, then."

Carter smiles and plucks one of the two cherries from his glass, his eyes gleaming. He throws his head back, exposing his neck, and raises the cherry above him. Then he slowly lowers it into this mouth. He's performing, the shit. After he bites down on the cherry, he pulls the stem off and then chews the fruit. "Here's the stem. No knots, see?"

I nod. I don't think talking is an option.

He places the stem in his mouth and works his mouth and teeth on it. When he's done, he shows me his handi-work by sticking out his long tongue.

This is what you get for saying whatever comes to mind, Tori.

"Okay, let's see how you do it," he says, offering the other cherry gleefully.

"No," I croak. "It's not impressive anymore." I take a gulp of the milk. "I teach a class on Saturdays that I'm really excited about. I think of it as a come-as-you-are class."

"What?"

"Carter, keep up. I'm telling you something else you don't know about me."

"Changing the subject again?"

"Advancing the subject, actually."

He smirks at me. "Okay, tell me about this class."

"I've been working on this concept. People of all ages and sizes and abilities, all working out together in one place and using only their bodies. I'm trying to show that exercise doesn't have to be complicated. It doesn't require thousands of dollars in equipment. It can be accessible and fun."

"Sounds great. Maybe I'll check it out one day. If I can handle Zumba, I should be able to handle this class, too, right? Well, unless Eva's a co-instructor."

"Oh, no, it's not at the gym. I teach it at a community center in North Philly."

He furrows his brows. "Why not at Hard Core?"

I frown at the question. "Ben and Nate don't think it's on message." I don't want to talk about the class anymore, though. It's stirring my resentment. "Tell me why you're torturing your body for this role. Why is it so important to you?"

Carter settles into his seat and sips his water. "Okay, let's see. For years, I've gotten the same kinds of roles, most of them in made-for-TV romantic comedies. Light, fluffy portrayals that don't demonstrate my range. I want my work to command respect. I want people to take me seriously. The role I'm vying for would get the industry to think about me differently."

"There's nothing wrong with romantic comedies, though."

"Of course. It's just not…enough. I'm thinking about my legacy."

The guy's twenty-seven. Why is he thinking about his legacy already? Maybe he thinks his career will be short-lived? If he were a woman in Hollywood, I'd understand his preoccupation with making his mark at such a young age. But he'll still get parts when he's in his sixties—and his leading lady will be in her twenties. Sigh. "So the solution is a so-called serious movie?"

"Exactly."

"The world cannot live on humorless period dramas alone, you know."

He smiles at me, a genuine smile that I think means he agrees with my sentiment in principle. But I'm not so sure he sees how it applies to his situation. "My father had a stroke last year," I blurt out. "His second in five years."

Carter reaches across the table and covers my hand. It's warm and distracting. "I'm sorry, Tori."

I was making a point. What the hell was it? Oh, right. Value. "My dad's okay now. Well, he can no longer work as a bus driver because his peripheral vision is compromised, but he's walking, and he's…yeah, he's fine. Anyway, he spent a few days in the hospital then, and my mother, my sister, and I took turns staying with him. I hated everything about that place. It was cold. Machines were beeping all the time. And no amount of fresh paint could hide the death happening within its walls."

"Life was happening, too, though?"

"Yeah, I suppose babies were being born, but I couldn't see anything good about the place, not with my sleeping father propped up in a sterile bed with scratchy, bleached sheets. For hours, I stared at a motivational poster that hung in his room. 'Always forward, never backward,' it said."

He raises his chin. "Ah, that's where that came from."

"Yeah. And it was driving me nuts. The staring, the worrying, the everything. And Eva came in one day and dropped a set of books in my lap. Romance books. I devoured them. Couldn't have stayed by my father's bedside without them. And some people call those books light and fluffy. But to me, they're books about the most complicated and universal emotion. Love. They got me through one of the worst periods of my life. They're important, and they mean something to me. And I'll bet your acting has meant something to a lot of people, too."

He studies me with an unblinking gaze, his long fingers sliding over the perspiration on the outside of his glass. "I'm glad I met you, Tori."

I tilt my head. "Is this the part of the evening where we talk in non sequiturs?"

He leans forward and places his forearms on the weathered table, his gaze boring into mine. "Thank you for saying my work matters. I've never thought of it that way. I love hearing how you think about things." He again covers my hand with his. "Also, I'm glad I met you."

Unable to decipher the meaning behind his serious expression, I drop my gaze to our hands, his on top of mine. We shouldn't be this intimate with each other, not at all but especially not when someone could capture it on camera. Thankfully, the server arrives with Carter's meal, which gives me an excuse to break our physical connection. I draw back and pick up my fork. "Dig into that steak, buddy. You've earned it."

Note to self: *If you want to resist him, don't eat with Carter, either.*

Chapter Nineteen

Carter

My BODY IS a temple—in ruins.

When Tori's done with me, I might very well be in the best shape of my life, but I'm seriously questioning my ability to live long enough to see the results. Everything is tender to the touch. There's soreness in places I'd rather not think about. My ass hurts, for fuck's sake.

This is after week two. Week. Two.

Today I'm going to reward myself and chill. I'll sit on my sore butt and read the script for the first episode of *Man on Third*'s new season. Maybe I'll order takeout. That's it. A day of respite.

But then the intercom buzzes. It never does, so I approach it as if it's a glowing orb that might release an army of mutants when I press it. Eventually, I gather the courage to hit the push-to-talk switch. "Yes?"

"Mr. Williamson, this is Bill, the doorman. I have a few guests who say they're related to you. They wanted to surprise you, but I told them I couldn't permit them to enter the building unannounced."

"What do I look like?" a strong voice with a dash of attitude asks in the background. "A murderer?"

Folks, meet my mother. And if she's here, my dad's here, too.

I scrub a hand down my face. "Bill, how many?"

"Five, sir."

Shit. That's most of the clan.

"Send them up, Bill. And sorry for any abuse."

"No problem at all, sir."

A few minutes later, someone bangs against my door, because the doorbell's apparently too much of a hassle. I open the door, and the Williamsons rush in, my mother leading the brigade like a four-star general.

She pinches my cheeks and envelops me in a tight hug. "Randall, I told you he's not getting enough food," she says to my father, who grunts in response. She squeezes my upper arms and descends to my wrists. "What's going on? Are you ill?"

"I'm not sick. I told you I had to lose weight for a role. Hey, Dad."

After scanning the living room, my father plops onto the couch and commandeers the remote. "Hey, son." Within seconds, he's watching a baseball game on ESPN. My older sister, Kimberly, kisses me on the cheek and allows my niece and nephew to drag her to the kitchen, where they all begin rifling through the cabinets and fridge.

"You said you had to lose weight," my mother continues. "You didn't say anything about looking like a crackhead."

I can always count on my mother to deliver her fiery brand of unfiltered honesty. I wrap my arm around her. "I'm fine, and I'm working on gaining it all back."

"Please do." She sorts through the contents of her insulated thermos bag and places several containers on the table. "This new look does not suit you."

A high-pitched wail shatters the mother-son moment. Isabella, my sister's seven-year-old daughter, howls like an ambulance siren, her voice rising and falling at regular intervals. "I'm...hungry...so hungry." My mother hands me cartons of food, presumably so that I can put them in my fridge, and walks down the hallway as though her grandchild's distress is nothing new.

"Bathroom's to the left," I call after her.

"Perfectly capable of finding a bathroom on my own, dear," she calls back.

She's going to snoop, and my giving her directions undermines her plans.

"What are you guys doing here?" I ask no one in particular.

Kimberly yawns and enfolds my niece in a bear hug. "Mom woke up and decided a road trip would be a good idea. Said you were too close for us to pass up on a surprise visit, so we piled into the Range Rover and here we are. You'll have to put up with us for one night."

"Did you drive?"

Kimberly quirks an eyebrow as though the question is ridiculous. My dad is prone to sleep at the wheel, and my mother hates to drive, so she has a point.

"You must be exhausted, then," I tell her.

"I am, but more than that, I'm famished. Can we order something before these kids kill each other?"

My nephew, Donovan, puts his little sister in a head-lock. I beam at him with pride. The kid's got good big-brother genes.

"Mom," I call out. "You all right back there?"

"I'm fine, Carter," she says from somewhere at the back of the condo that is *not* the bathroom.

They must go. Immediately. "I've got an even better idea. Let me take you somewhere for lunch."

Kimberly's eyes widen in horror. "With these two?" She points at the angel-devils stamping at each other's feet.

Tori once described her parents' restaurant as a very casual place. It makes sense to take them there. No ulterior motives whatsoever. Besides, I don't know that she'll be there anyway. She didn't say she visits *every* Saturday.

"Where'd you park the Ranger?"

"I persuaded the doorman to let us use the building lot," Kimberly says. "Why?"

"We're going to North Philly."

"So long as there's food, I'm game."

My mother emerges from the back of the condo with a few dirty cups in her hands. "Not as bad as I thought it would be."

"I have a cleaning service," I say.

"Ah, that explains it. What's this about heading to North Philadelphia?"

"I want to take you to a place owned by my friend's parents. A Puerto Rican restaurant."

My mother knits her brows and purses her lips in confusion. "But I have containers of food. A lovely chicken salad. Some couscous, too."

"The kids aren't going to eat that, Mom," Kimberly says.

Mom rolls her eyes. "They need to eat what they get."

I suspect there's a simple way to get her to relent. "Mom, the friend whose parents own the restaurant? She's a woman."

My mother's blank face would make the perfect photo for a gag Christmas card. She shakes her head as though she's dislodging a pebble that's settled in her brain. "A woman?"

"Yes."

"Do you like her?"

"A lot."

That pronouncement even gets the attention of my dad, who sits up and hits the power button on the remote.

"Well, let's go, then," my mother says as she packs up her purse. "Randall, use the bathroom, please. We're heading to North Philadelphia to eat."

I SPEND TWENTY minutes searching for a parking space. When we pass through Mi Casita's threshold, Isabella's whimpering and my father's stomach is gurgling.

Surveying the space over my shoulder, my father clucks his tongue. "We're the only white people here," he observes.

"Hush," my mother scolds. "That means the food will be good."

It's a legitimate conclusion. A Mexican-American crew member on the set of *My Life in Shambles* shared a tip along these lines when I joined the show. "If you go to a Mexican restaurant and there are no Mexican Americans eating there, turn around and find another place," he told me. My stomach deeply regrets the two times I failed to heed his advice.

A young woman who bears a striking resemblance to Tori greets us with a warm smile. She's shorter and rounder than Tori but just as pretty. "Good afternoon, everyone. Joining us for lunch today?"

"We are. Do you have room for six?"

She grabs several laminated menus. "Plenty of room. Two kids' menus?"

Kimberly nods. "Yes, thank you."

The group shuffles to our table, and when we get there, we play an inevitable game of musical chairs as we figure out where everyone should sit. Because I'm Isabella's favorite uncle—technically, I'm her only uncle, but if she had more than one, I'd be her favorite—I sit between her and my mother.

The woman I'm assuming is Tori's sister explains that most of the food is prepared in advance and takes our drink orders. The kids' meals are made-to-order, so

Kimberly wastes no time in ordering chicken nuggets and fries for Isabella and Donovan.

With a pair of reading glasses perched on the edge of her nose, my mother scans the menu. "That's not her, I take it?"

"That's her sister, I think," I reply.

She lifts her chin. "Ah."

Pen and pad in hand, the young woman returns to take our orders. "Do you have any questions about the menu? Need any suggestions?"

The menu, which is written in both Spanish and English, includes mouthwatering descriptions, and I want it all. Figuring I'm in gain-weight mode anyway, I order enough food for two people. My mother and Kimberly agree to share an order of shrimp with garlic sauce, and my father's all over the fried pork chops with rice and beans.

This woman who might be Tori's sister taps her pen against the pad and stares at me. "I feel like I know you from somewhere."

"He's an actor on TV," my mother says proudly. "*My Life in Shambles* and *Man on Second*."

She never gets that right. "Third, Mom. It's *Man on Third*."

Our server straightens, and her eyes sparkle. "That's right. Oh my goodness, you're Carter Stone. It's great to have you here. I'm Bianca. Maybe we can take your picture before you go, huh? Put it on the wall or something."

"Sure, sure."

She rushes off to the kitchen, and I glare at my mother.

"What?" she asks, her eyes falling to the juice in her glass as she takes a sip.

As we wait for our food, I entertain the kids with tricks. I scrunch up the paper covering my straw and let a drop of water from the tip of the straw fall onto the paper. The piece of paper unfurls like an inchworm, and the kids momentarily forget their hunger as they watch with wide eyes.

Isabella claps vigorously, and then she throws her arms around my neck. I lift her onto my lap, and she twists her body so she can ruffle my hair. When Bianca approaches with the kids' meals, Isabella scrambles off me and dives onto her chair. We won't be hearing anything but humming from Isabella and Donovan for the next fifteen minutes or so.

The bell above the door chimes, and I turn my head to see who's coming in. Tori stands at the threshold with her mouth open. She's wearing a top made of soft material and a matching skirt, and she's holding a duffel bag in her left hand. I know my heart was beating before she arrived, but now it's thumping against my chest like a bird that doesn't want to be caged. I want to meet her at the door and give her the kind of kiss that would land us on a best-kiss list, but we're not together—yet—and my family's here.

Our gazes lock, and she lifts her brows in question.

Her sister's voice distracts her from witnessing my sheepish smile.

"Close the door, Tori."

Tori shakes her head and stumbles into the restaurant. She and her sister exchange a few words before she disappears into the kitchen.

My mother leans toward me. "*That's* her."

"Yeah."

She covers my hand with hers. "She's lovely."

I take a sip of my water to alleviate the sudden dryness in my throat. She's so much more than lovely. She's funny, sarcastic, smart, and ambitious. And sexy. I can't ever forget sexy.

"Don't take this the wrong way, son, but she looks like she could kick your ass," my mother continues.

The remark causes me to nearly choke with laughter, and the evil woman slaps my back.

A few minutes later, Tori emerges from the kitchen with two plates in her hands and heads to our table. Her sister intercepts her seconds before Tori gets to us. "What are you doing?"

"Helping," Tori says.

"I can handle this table," Bianca says, pointing to our group. She doesn't wait for Tori to respond and takes the plates from her.

"Here you go," Bianca says with a smile. "*Camarones al ajillo* to share." To my father, she says, "I'll be right back with your *chuletas guisadas*." Then she turns to me and winks. "And you, I'll need three hands for yours."

"Carter," Tori says. "This is a surprise."

Bianca's gaze swings between Tori and me. "You two know each other?"

"She's my personal trainer," I tell her.

You don't have to be a genius to know that Bianca and Tori don't get along well. But even an idiot could intuit that fact watching Bianca's response to my pronounce-ment. She purses her lips and draws a silent breath. The flared nostrils are an added touch. "Of course she is. I'll leave you to catch up," she says. Then she walks away without a backward glance.

I've made a tactical error coming here. Tori's perplexed by my appearance, and my presence has heightened the tension between the two sisters. She didn't invite me to this part of her life, but I dropped in unannounced anyway. One day, I'll learn to control my impulses, but today is not that day. In the meantime, I hope I can save the situation.

My mother reaches behind her and pulls another chair to the table. "Come join us, Tori. I'm Susan. Carter's told us almost *nothing* about you."

I'm fucking toast.

Tori laughs as she takes a seat. "Nice to meet you, Mrs. Williamson."

"Susan."

"Susan," Tori repeats.

My mother takes on her hostess role. "This is Randall, my hubby of thirty-four years. Kimberly, Carter's older sister. And these two cuties are Kim's kids, Donovan and Isabella."

"It's great to meet everyone," Tori says with a cheerful smile.

Maybe coming here wasn't a terrible idea after all. The woman I like is meeting my parents under circumstances that won't induce stress. Years from now, Tori will thank me for being forward-thinking.

"Tori, would you like to hear embarrassing stories about Carter's childhood? I've been waiting ages for the opportunity to share them."

Tori's eyes crinkle, and her gaze darts to mine. "Oh, that would be great. Then I can share a few embarrassing stories about Carter's adulthood."

My mother chortles while she pats Tori's arm. "Ah, my dear. You're a delight."

They're cute together, just as I imagined, but I'm not letting them swap stories about me this early in their relationship. "The restaurant's great, Tori. Has a real homey feel to it."

Future wife peers at me with a smirk on her face. "So what brings you to Mi Casita? I can't imagine you just happened to be in the neighborhood."

My mother shimmies in her seat and claps her hands. It's her patented I've-got-a-secret-and-I'm-about-to-share-it move. "Carter said he—"

"Well, look at that," I say to my dad as Bianca places his plate in front of him. "Those pork chops look fantastic."

Another woman, this one older than Bianca, places my plates on the table. I rub my hands together and unwrap the paper napkin surrounding my utensils.

"Carter, you're *not* going to eat all of that," Tori says.

Judging by the surprise in her voice, the correct answer is no.

Kimberly leans forward and snickers. "Busted."

Tori's stern expression clears. "Can I speak with you in private? It'll only take a sec."

I rise from my seat. "Sure. Lead the way."

As I follow her, the kids chant, "Carter's in trouble. Carter's in trouble."

They don't know the half of it. I've been in trouble since the day I met her.

Chapter Twenty

Tori

ONE DAY. ALL I wanted was *one* day to regroup from expending so much energy resisting Carter. Instead, he's here, in my parents' restaurant, with his family and a trough of food that will undermine his training goals faster than I can say *jackass*.

Jackass.

Okay, maybe it'll take longer than that.

I want to be annoyed, but I also can't deny the warmth that spread through me when I first saw him sitting at the table. How does he *do* that? How does he affect me simply by being in my presence?

I stride through the hall to the storage area past Mi Casita's restroom. I scan the space to make sure we're alone, and then I whirl around. "What are you doing?"

He scratches his temple, bringing his freakishly long fingers into view. Images of those digits curling around my thighs and squeezing them tightly flash through my brain. *Madre de Dios*, I'm in trouble.

Carter drops his hand. "Um, I'm eating. Is that a problem?"

"Carter, you know you shouldn't be eating like that while you're training."

"But if gaining weight is the goal, I can at least indulge in this from time to time, right?"

I make the sound of a buzzer for several seconds. "Wrong."

Carter slaps his hand against the wall, leans over, and laughs. "I can't believe you just did that."

My lips quirk up at the corners. I can't help being a little silly around him. "But seriously, do you have any idea how hard it is to gain muscle in six weeks?"

"I have a clue, but I'm sure you're going to tell me anyway."

"That's right. It requires discipline. It requires forgoing fatty foods. It requires your commitment to working your ass off to reach that goal, which, may I remind you, is *your* goal, not mine."

He threads his fingers through his hair, and then he rubs his neck. "Okay, okay. But here's the thing. I can't go back to the table and not eat. My mother's stressed out about my skinny frame as it is. So what if I put in an extra session tomorrow? You can punish me for indulging."

I cross my arms over my chest. "Fine."

With a twinkle in his eyes, he mimics my stance. "Good."

I drop my arms. "You're such a pain."

He stuffs his hands in the front pockets of his cargo shorts and bumps my shoulder with his. "Admit it," he says as he dips his head to get me to look at him. "You're starting to like me."

It's a flippant comment, not unlike the others he's made, but I absorb it differently this time—because it's the truth. Damn, damn, damn. He's right. I *like* him. But that's as far as my admiration will go. Anything more would be foolish. "C'mon, let me introduce you to my mother."

He smooths his hair and runs his index fingers over his eyebrows. "Do I look okay? This is a big deal, meeting your mother."

"You look fine, and it's no big deal."

"Does she know who I am? Will she be impressed?"

"Unless you're a star in one of her *telenovelas*, Denzel Washington, or an anchor on NBC10, she won't know who you are. No worries there, believe me."

He frowns. "Well, that's disappointing."

"Guess you'll just have to rely on your sparkling personality to charm her."

His smile returns with a vengeance. "That I can definitely do."

We walk into the kitchen, and the first thing I see is my father in the corner chomping on *frituras*. My mother's slicing onions as Bianca chats with her. The energy in here is happy, but my disappointment in my father threatens to ruin the atmosphere. He can make his own choices. Enjoying my mother's food in moderation won't kill him. I try to talk myself out of calling him out, but in the end, he's my father, and I'd rather have him around and annoyed with me than not have him with me at all. "Papi, what are you doing?"

My father spots me and drops the plantain chip in his hand onto his plate. After wiping his mouth with a napkin, he gives me a pleading expression and pinches his thumb and forefinger together. "I just wanted a little taste."

"It's never a *little* taste with you." Then I face my mother and Bianca. "Why are you letting him do this?"

My mother suspends the knife in midair and stands next to my father. "Do...what?"

"Letting him eat whatever he wants," I answer.

"Here we go," Bianca says with a roll of her eyes.

They all stare at me as if I'm hysterical, but I *know* I'm not. We almost lost my father, not once, but twice. Still, they refuse to learn from those hellish experiences. I could rant about how Papi's cholesterol numbers haven't improved. I could question him about his high blood pressure. But I'm forced to skirt around one of the issues that might make a difference in his health. So I can't tell them he should lay off my mother's cooking.

Not when this food has been passed on to us from generation to generation.

Not when this food is the staple of my mother's restaurant, her life's work.

Not when this food is the way my mother communicates her love to us.

It's such a central part of who we are that if I tell my father he shouldn't eat it, they'd perceive it as a rejection of our culture, my mother's love, and her sacrifices. But it hurts like hell to hold this inside.

I take an audible breath while I clench my fists at my side.

Behind me, a hand reaches for mine and squeezes.

Carter.

It's a small gesture, a show of support, but it means so much to me because I'm not standing on the other side of the divide alone. Somehow, he knows I need him. Deciding to disrupt the strained moment, I squeeze back and pull him next to me. "This is Carter. He's an actor, and I'm training him." I turn my head and meet his gaze. "He's a really good guy."

Visibly relieved, my mother and father speak at once, both saying hello and welcoming him to the restaurant. Mami even invites him to my father's upcoming birthday party.

"I'd love to," Carter tells her, glancing at me with a smile as he does.

Bianca speaks to my parents in Spanish. *"Él es una persona famosa."*

A hushed conversation ensues between them. They have questions, and she has answers, and wow, she knows a lot about Carter's career.

I study Carter, who stands still under their inspection. "Sorry. They're speaking Spanish so they can talk about you. It's a thing. Don't worry, though. Bianca's report is flattering."

Carter preens. "I'm picking up a few words here and there."

Finally, Papi uses his cane to stand and grips Carter's hand in a firm handshake.

"Mucho gusto," Carter says.

My father straightens, and his eyes go wide. *"El gusto es mío."* His smile is broad and welcoming, and I'm struck by how handsome my father is. He wears his age well, his salt-and-pepper hair curling a lot like mine, and he's got scarily perfect teeth. We almost lost him. Twice. And I don't want to lose him ever.

"I have to go," I say in a quavering voice. After grabbing my duffel bag off the floor, I rush out of the kitchen, shutting out the sound of my parents' voices as I make my escape. I don't cry often, the day of my father's stroke being the last time I've done it in recent memory. But the tears are welling under my lids now, and I bow my head to avoid the questioning eyes of anyone who might see my face.

As I pass Carter's family, I mumble, "It was great to meet you," and dash out the door.

Outside, my vision is hazy as I rifle through my bag for my car keys.

"Tori."

Carter stands next to me, his hands hanging from the pockets of his cargo shorts.

"I'm okay," I say, wincing when my voice snags on the second word. I clear my throat and give him an "I'm fine but not really" smile. "I have to teach a class in an hour, but I'll see you tomorrow, okay?"

"Do you need me to take you?"

"No, I've got my car over there."

He raises his face to the sky and closes his eyes, the long column of his neck exposed to the sun. Would it be weird if I bit him there? What am I asking? Of course it would. What is even happening to me?

"Tori, I can spot an actress a mile away."

I try to laugh, but my voice isn't cooperating, and a sigh emerges from my lips instead. He tugs my hand and pulls me close, bending his knees to meet my glistening gaze. Before I can stop him, he swipes his thumbs under my eyes and wipes my tears. "Can I ditch my family and join you?"

There's so much in my head it might burst. My father. My family. Carter. I know he means well, but I wish he'd stop being so fucking nice. *Don't be sweet*, I want to scream. *Don't disarm me by showing you care.* And I feel wretched for it. Because who thinks this way?

I shake my head. "Wouldn't your family be offended if you leave them?"

"Their bellies are stuffed, and they've been riding in a car for three and a half hours. They'll be napping in my condo within the hour. Don't make me listen to my father's snoring. Please."

I wrinkle my itchy nose and clear my throat. "Okay, I'm teaching at Open Arms Community Center. It's at…Carter, quit staring, break out your phone, and take this down."

He jerks to life. "Right." He pulls his phone out of his back pocket and jots down the address I give him.

"Don't call attention to yourself, and wear a hat."

"Why would you want to stifle all this gorgeousness?"

I shake my head. "The class starts at two."

"I'll be there."

"Don't be late. The instructor gets cranky when some-one's tardy."

His mouth curves into a delicious smile. "I have an easy time picturing that."

I clip him on the shoulder, and he rubs the spot, pre-tending that I've hurt him.

"Don't worry. I'll be on time."

He spins around to head back in, but I grab the back of his shirt and stop him. His eyebrows lift in surprise.

"Thank you," I say.

His face softens in understanding, and all I want to do is hug him.

He squeezes my hand again. "It's no big deal."

And as I watch him slip back inside, I realize he's wrong. The way he shows he cares? It's a big deal to me.

Chapter Twenty-One

Carter

NOW THAT THE family is settled in my condo, for equal parts napping and snooping, I take a Lyft ride to Open Arms Community Center. I know nothing about this area of the city, but my driver, who says he's familiar with the street, gets me there with five minutes to spare.

The community center's brick walls are covered in peeling pastel-green paint, and the row homes beside and across from it are similarly painted in light colors. It's like the Easter Bunny ate every candy in the world and vomited on the block.

There's no reception desk, so I follow the people in workout clothes down a long hall and up a short flight of stairs that leads to a large room doubling as both a gymnasium and auditorium. Stacks of aluminum folding chairs are propped against the walls, and I spy a separate wheelchair-accessible entrance. By my estimation, approximately fifty people of all ages, sizes, shapes, colors, and ranges of mobility have shown up in the middle of a Saturday afternoon to take Tori's class. That alone impresses me.

Skirting the clusters of people chatting before the class begins, I stroll in and claim a spot by the double doors at the back of the room.

Tori walks in, and it's like the office boss is making the rounds unannounced. The chatter diminishes to a murmur, and people disperse to take their places around the room. A woman pushes a young man in a wheelchair to the center of the floor, and in that moment, I suspect I understand why Tori is driven to make this program a success. It brings people together in a way I've not seen in any of the gyms I've been to: young, old, differently abled—they're all here.

A laugh on the left side of the room snags my attention. A handsome guy with dark hair, dark eyes, and brown skin is talking to Tori as she adjusts the knobs of the stereo system and positions her wireless headset. He maintains a respectful distance for a few seconds, but when she joins in his laughter, he seizes the opportunity to reach out and place his hand on her arm.

She moves away from him and claps her hands, signaling the start of the class. "Hi, everyone. Thanks for joining me. My name's Tori Alvarez, and I'm going to make you sweat today. Do we have any newcomers?"

Several people raise their hands.

"Welcome," she says. "Chat among yourselves while I come around and greet the newbies."

Tori stops to talk to each of the individuals who raised their hands. When she gets to me, she tilts her head and scans my body. "Where are your workout clothes?"

"I'm resting today, remember? I'll just be observing."

"Right," she says, drawing the word out as though she's skeptical about my intentions. "You're just going to stand here?"

I hold up my phone. "And check my email. Maybe make a few calls. The stuff I can't do with my family around."

"Right," she says again. After casting a sideways glance my way, she spins around and strides to the head of the class. "For the new folks, I have three helpers. Assistants, come on up."

An elderly gentleman and a middle-aged woman weave their way to the front of the room, and the young man in the wheelchair joins them as well.

"This class is all about doing what you can and knowing that's enough. I don't focus on fitness levels here. It's all about moving your body and getting your heart rate up. I've worked with each of my assistants to modify the exercises to fit their comfort level. Follow whichever person—including me—who matches your personal comfort level, and bear in mind that you don't have to stick with just one person for the duration of the class. Any questions?"

She claps her hands together and clicks the small remote in her hand. "All right, let's go." After she places the remote on the floor, she jumps up. "One more thing. From time to time, you might hear a Spanish word or two. *Sigue asi. Vamanos. Muy bien.* Just know it's all encouragement, and I'm telling you to keep going, okay?"

Several people nod and smile. The positive energy reverberates through the room.

"Okay, *vamanos*," she shouts.

Tori leads a medium-paced class that tests everyone's coordination and stamina. Her assistants know exactly what move follows the current one, and many of her students switch between comfort levels with ease. The music is a mix of hip-hop, pop, and Latin sounds, and some of the members sing along to the more popular songs. They're having fun.

Tori has a gift for motivating people. And judging by her wide smile and bright eyes, she's embracing that gift to the fullest. I'd love to capture her happiness in this moment. When my phone vibrates in my hand, I'm reminded that I can. With a few clicks and a swipe, I open my phone's video camera and begin recording the class. I'm sure Tori would love to see the class from this perspective.

Soon after, the group transitions into a five-minute cooldown, and then the class ends to another round of applause.

The guy who monopolized Tori's time earlier seeks her out. She nods at whatever he's telling her, but her face loses all the brightness that kept everyone going through the class.

Tori repositions her headset and asks for her students' attention. "Bad news, folks. Open Arms has special events over the next three weeks, so we're not going to be able to use the room."

Their loud groans cut through the music still playing in the background.

"If I can come up with an alternate space," she continues, "I'll let Antonio know. If not, I'll see you next month."

I want Tori to know how impressed I am with the class, but *Antonio* is hovering around her like a miniature drone. Fuck it. I'm not above interrupting. I slide my phone into the back pocket of my shorts and sidle over to her and her friend. "Great class."

So fucking original, Carter.

"Why, thank you, Carter. Maybe next time you can participate?"

"Maybe."

The drone shoots his hand out. "I'm Antonio, Tori's friend and the director of Open Arms."

I give his hand a firm shake. "I'm Carter, also Tori's friend. I'm an actor. Prime-time television."

Antonio furrows his eyebrows. "Uh, right."

Tori, meanwhile, shakes her head as she stares at the gym ceiling. "He's also the kind of guy who refuses to do as he's been asked."

"Yes, well, not all of us come fully trained."

She gives me a reluctant smile, just the edges of her mouth tipping up, but it's enough for me.

"Can I talk to you a sec before I head out?" I ask.

"Sure. Excuse us, Antonio."

He waves us off, and she pulls me into the hall.

"What part of 'don't call attention to yourself' did you not understand?"

I shrug. "Most of it."

She sighs.

"No one here cares about me. Do you think Antonio's going to snap a picture of us and spin a tale about us being illicit lovers?"

Her cheeks bloom with color. "No, I guess not."

"Okay, look. I'm going to head back to my place before my family ransacks my room. But before I go, I just wanted to tell you I think you're doing an incredible thing here. This is your purpose. To motivate people." I want her to understand what I'm saying is truly heartfelt, so I take her hand and squeeze it.

Her mouth falls open, just a touch, and her gaze darts to her hand on mine. "Thank you, Carter."

Because I'm not above flirting, I give her *the eyes*. "You're welcome."

And whoa. Wait a minute. She shivers. This is exactly the kind of progress I've been hoping for. We've finally reached the point when it's almost impossible for her to mask her physical attraction to me.

So now my mission is clear. It's time to break her resolve.

Chapter Twenty-Two

Tori

DURING THE THIRD week of his training, Carter attacks the program with a renewed sense of urgency. Apart from the occasional joke, he says very little, which has the unfortunate effect of making me hyperfocused on his actions. When he bends, thrusts, grunts, or stretches, my mind travels along Dirty Imagination Boulevard—and it's a *long* stretch of pavement. He does appear to be lifting his T-shirt and licking his lips more often than usual, as though he's engaging in subliminal foreplay, but given the inappropriate direction of my thoughts these days, I'm probably projecting here. Still, I'm strung tight, and if Carter so much as breathes on me, I'll unravel.

When Carter walks into the gym Thursday evening, my senses are on high alert.

He's wearing red high-top sneakers and black athletic shorts that end above his knees. That's it. No shirt, people. No fucking shirt. I know this isn't a recipe for disaster. No, it's a recipe for lust: Mix one sexy man with one horny woman and this is what you get. Go ahead, take a sniff: Those are my pheromones in the air.

"Where's your shirt?" I ask.

He points to the nylon bag strapped to his back. "In there. I decided to jog over tonight. The shirt was messing with my flow."

A streak of warmth passes over my cheeks. "Do you want a minute to put your shirt on?"

Please say yes, please say yes.

"No, I'm good. Let me make a quick pit stop, and then we can get going."

"Sure."

As he passes me on the way to the restroom, he pulls the straps of his bag off his shoulders and arches his back. My gaze zeroes in on the muscles on display. Nothing wrong with that, right? It's my *job* to ensure he's meeting his fitness goals.

While he's gone, I flip on the lights in the gym. All of them. Dim lighting and Carter's sweaty chest will not coexist today.

Carter exits the restroom, pulls out his water bottle, and tosses his bag on the rubber tile floor. "Damn, I'm still hot."

"Want me to turn up the air-conditioning?"

"Nah. I'll just cool myself off with some water."

I'm not sure what he means, but then he raises the water bottle over his head and squirts it on his head and chest, running his hands through his hair to slick it back.

The fucker. When did the gym become the set of a J-Lo music video? Whatever game he's playing, I'll beat him at it, and I'll start by ignoring his antics. "Let's get going." I glance at my clipboard. "We're working legs today, so let's start with squats, hip circles, and lunges."

He winks at me and gets into position. "I've been thinking about your fitness class at the community center."

That draws me out of my shell. "You have?"

"Yep. Have you thought about getting a permanent location for the class? Your own exercise studio, maybe? You could have multiple classes per day. That way, you'd reach more people. And you won't have to worry about scheduling conflicts at the center."

I've toyed with this idea before. But owning an exercise studio is a big endeavor, and it requires money. Lots and lots of money. Even leasing a space is beyond my current cash flow. "I've thought about this, too, Carter, but I don't have the funds."

"Investors?"

"I tried that a few months ago, when Ben and Nate were giving me the runaround about teaching a class at the gym. Only one group expressed interest, and they ultimately rejected me."

He swings his arms in circles before he drops to the floor. "But there are more investment groups out there, right? And what about a bank? I don't know. I'm just thinking out loud…and I…"

My head snaps up. "What?"

He lowers himself into a full-seated squat. "I think you're talented. It would be a waste not to share it with as many people as you can."

There he goes again. Being nice. And thoughtful. And almost irresistible. "Thanks," I murmur. "I'll think about it." I take a deep breath. "Okay, let's start with leg presses."

Carter wrinkles his nose, and one of his eyebrows disappears under his forelock. "Shouldn't you check my weight and measurements first?"

The answer per Personal Training 101 is yes. Weight and body measurements should always be assessed pre-workout, before the muscles are engorged with blood and appear larger. But the answer per horny Tori is most definitely no. In my mind, I'm stamping my feet like a two-year-old: *I don't want to. Don't make me do it.* To him, however, I say, "Yes, let's get you over to the scale."

Carter precedes me to the far end of the gym, where the scale and the trainer's desk sit in a corner. His back is more defined than it was just two weeks ago. It's coming along nicely, thanks to me.

Whistling, he steps onto the scale and slides the counterweight to 150 and nudges the small scale to the right until it balances at 173 pounds.

"Good work, Carter. That's another four pounds."

"Excellent." He waggles his eyebrows. "I have a great trainer."

We smile at each other, and then we're left with nothing but silence.

Do something, Tori.

Which leads us to the moment I've been dreading: measurement time. Carter hops off the scale and dutifully stands in front of me. I swipe the tape measure off the desk and wrap it around his waist. We're inches apart, our torsos almost touching.

Carter lowers his head. He's so close, I can sense his breathing everywhere, in the slow rise of his chest, in the puffs of air near my ear, in the expansion and contraction of his oblique muscles.

"Here, let me get this out of your way," he says.

He slides his fingers across his waistband and lowers his shorts to reveal his happy trail, the action pulling the fabric away from his body so that I catch a glimpse of the goodies beneath it. The urge to slip my hands inside and caress him, in the most intimate of places, forces me to bite down on my lower lip. The prick of pain reminds me that doing anything with Carter beyond training him will not serve my best interests.

My head falls forward as I read the measurement, and Carter pushes back a curl that's escaped my ponytail.

I stumble backward, and the tape measure falls to the floor. "Okay. We can do this later," I say as I pick it up. To be safe, I back up as I wind the measure.

"What's the measurement?" Carter asks, his voice low and breathy.

I shake my head at him. "What?"

"My waist size, Tori. What's my waist size?"

The honest answer? I have no idea. How am I supposed to function when the man is within arm's reach and his shorts are riding low on his hips? "It's...um. It's thirty-one inches."

"Is it?" he whispers.

He doesn't move, nor does he have to. Because his voice alone can summon kinetic activity apparently. How else to explain the way my feet step in his direction, without any prompting from me? "Yes. Closer to thirty-one and a half."

"Is that your final answer, Tori?"

There's a hint of humor in his voice. More troubling than that, the laughter's coupled with something else. Something I don't want any part of. "*Yes*, that's my final answer."

"I don't think you're right. Can you check again?"

He's testing me, and if I don't do well here, I will surely flunk the class. So I stomp back to him and wrap the tape measure around his waist, my eyes focusing on the wall behind him.

"You seem agitated," he says against my ear. "What's wrong?"

"Nothing's wrong. See? Thirty and a half inches."

"But you said I was thirty-one and a half."

"Did I? It's not a precise science."

Now I sound like a *pendeja*. It very much *is* a precise science.

I take a step back.

"Do you want to touch me, Tori?"

I take in a gulp of air. *Lie, lie, lie.* "What? No."

"That's a shame," he says. "Because I want you to touch me." He takes a step forward and crowds me, positioning his mouth near my ear. "So. Fucking. Much."

A strangled moan escapes my throat, but the pounding in my ears makes it hard to decipher how he'll receive it. Does it sound like an objection? An invitation? Maybe both?

He holds his hands out. "May I?"

God, yes.

No, no, I shouldn't. But I want to give in so badly. Just this once. I answer by giving him my hands.

He turns them palms up, raises them to his lips, and plants a soft kiss in each center.

"Carter…this isn't a good idea. We shouldn't do this."

Avoiding this kind of entanglement is critical to my professional and personal well-being. Getting involved with Carter was never part of the plan. At most, I thought I'd be able to whisper about him decades from now, perhaps telling my grandkids that I kissed him on vacation long before I married their grandfather. With guys like Carter, there's always an end and an after. I'd much prefer that he remain my "what-if."

His gaze pierces mine. He's trying to test the truth of my words. With nothing more than a look. I drop my head to hide my heart. We both know it's a lie. *This* I want. Very much. Everything else that goes along with it? Not at all.

He cradles the back of my head and guides it to his chest. We exhale at the same time, as if we both know that simple connection is a turning point for us. "What do you think will happen if you touch me? The sky won't fall, the earth will still spin, I promise."

Every inch of my body is taut, bending toward him, eager to give in to this attraction. But my hands, the last defense in this uneven battle, are fisted so tightly that my nails are digging into my palms.

Carter covers my hands with his, so now he's aware of the tension, too. "Relax, Tori." He slowly spreads my fingers, flattening them against my thighs. Then he leans against the wall and tugs me to him. "Can I tell you a secret?"

"Okay," I whisper. I don't trust myself to say anything else. A few more syllables and I'll be begging him to take me on the floor.

"I think about you all the time. When I'm getting dressed, when I'm taking a shower, when I'm eating—"

"Even when you're—"

"*Don't* kill the mood, Tori."

That's exactly what I'm trying to do. I don't want to hear this. He's rallying scores of troops while I huddle in a straw bunker with no weapons or reinforcements. It's an unfair battle.

His mouth sweeps across my forehead. "I think about you when I'm in bed, too."

"You do?" I ask, my voice more high-pitched than I'd like. Even though I should silence him, I'm desperate to hear what he'll say. "Tell me."

"In *explicit* detail?"

"*Everything.*"

He positions his mouth close to my ear. "I think about all the ways I could have you," he whispers. "I think about my tongue between your legs. I think about fucking you long and hard. I literally picture my dick plunging into your pussy. Then I think about pulling out and taking your wetness with me. Over and over. And the vision is so fucking hot I touch myself, Tori." He lifts one of my hands and slides it over his length. "My cock grows, thickens just like this. I get so hard it's painful. But it feels so fucking good, too, because in my mind, you're there with me. Pleasure. Torture. It's all there."

"Sorry, not sorry."

His mouth widens against my ear.

"Are you laughing at me?" I ask.

"Never. I'm enjoying you. So where was I?"

"You're so hard it's painful, but it feels good, too."

"Right. My entire body locks, and my brain is focused on relieving the pressure. Can I show you how I stroke myself?"

Am I hearing him correctly? When he masturbates, he thinks about having his tongue between my legs? And he wants to give me a demonstration? I won't survive this, but I raise the white flag anyway. Because how could I say no to that? This time, I brush my cheek against his chin. "Show me."

"Pull down my shorts."

This is wrong, wrong, wrong. And risky. And it will complicate my life in ways I can't even imagine. But my attraction for him, this cloying need in my gut, propels me to touch him. My fingers fumble at his waistband, but I manage to lower his shorts and boxer briefs to midthigh, and his cock springs out. It's long and thick and heavy.

He guides my hand up and down his erection. "I tease myself, too, because I don't want it to end. And I go slow, from root to tip, squeezing myself along the way."

I'm taking shallow breaths as I listen to him knock down every pillar holding up my rationale for avoiding this intimacy. Who needs common sense when a man can get you this turned on just from petting him? "You're killing me, Carter."

Slowly, he removes his hand, and it's just me stroking him. "I've been dying for a while now, Tori." His hooded gaze is fixed on mine, and I can't look away. I apply more pressure, and he drops his head back and hisses. "Yes, keep doing that," he urges.

I step closer. Carter does, too. And then he cups my jaw with both hands and pulls me forward for a searing kiss. Aruba was a taste, whereas this is a full meal, and we're both ravenous. He grabs my ass, and I drop my hands to the sides because there's no more room for them between us. His erection presses against my stomach, and he slides it up and down against me as he masters my mouth.

"I don't want our first time to be in a gym," he says when we come up for air. "Let me take you to my place."

Let me take you to my place.

Wait. What? *No.*

I pull back and cover my mouth with one hand.

His eyes are glazed over. His lips are swollen. He's a wall of sexy male sprinkled with lust and pixie dust, and he looks edible and utterly wanton. I want him so badly I'm shaking. But it's not going to happen. "We can't do this, Carter."

My sharp tone signals that I don't want to be persuaded otherwise, and Carter apparently gets it.

He pulls up his briefs and shorts slowly, as if he knows time is on his side, and then he threads his fingers through his hair. "Talk to me. What's going on?"

My laugh is anything but cheerful. "You can't be serious, Carter. I'm your *personal trainer.*"

He gives me a slow smile and sags against the wall. "Is that all? Well, there's an easy solution for that."

"There is?"

I cringe at the hopeful tremor in my voice.

"Yes, you're fired."

My jaw locks so hard my face aches. I fold my arms over my chest. "That's not funny."

"I didn't mean it to be. Nate can take over from here."

My eyes will pop from the strain I'm putting them under. "That's insulting, you jerk. Consider what you just said. You hire me for my expertise, but then you fire me because you want to sleep with me? I should drop-kick your ass into next week for thinking that's appropriate."

He closes his eyes and pinches the bridge of his noise. "Sorry. That was a dick thing to say. I'm just so fucking frustrated because I want you, and I don't know how to convince you that we could work. And I don't *just* want to sleep with you, as you put it. This isn't a game for me, Tori. I want you in my life. And when you want something badly, you sometimes say and do stupid shit. So can we pretend that never came out of my mouth?"

I watch him warily, my gaze narrowed on his face. "You get one pass. Is this how you want to use it?"

"Yes. I will never screw up like this again. But tell me why you don't want me." His eyes plead with me for understanding. "Is there something else you're not telling me?"

He looks so earnest with his hands against his chest and that ridiculous lock of hair sweeping over his forehead. I can't offer him anything but the truth. "I want you. I won't pretend about that. But I don't want everything that goes along with *being* with you. I dated someone who desperately wanted to be in the limelight, and it didn't end well for me. He's a city councilman, and Philadelphia's notoriously light on celebrity gossip. It wasn't fun. What would that say about me if I put myself in the same situation?"

"Always forward, never backward."

Thank goodness, he gets it. I'm relieved he does. "Yes."

He shakes his head. "But I'm not your ex-boyfriend."

No, he isn't—and that doesn't work in his favor. "Don't you see? The risks are even *greater* with you. I don't want to go down in the annals of history as someone you slept with. That doesn't ever go away. What happens when I try to secure investors? Is that the first thing they'll see about me when they search Google? And when we fizzle, what happens then? With Mason, I learned about my breakup on a local radio show. With you, I'll hit the big time. And I just don't want to swim in the fishbowl you live in. So you're right. It's not the same situation. You're Mason times ten."

He stares at me for several beats before he speaks. "Mason. He's your ex?"

"Yes."

He grabs the back of his neck and gives me a bitter smile. "I hate him."

"No you don't."

"I hate how he's affecting my life, then."

"Fair enough."

I'm thinking about Mason differently now. Maybe I was meant to go through that experience with him so I could avoid going through one on a grander scale with Carter. Maybe the universe was preparing me for Carter?

I lean against the wall, claiming a spot beside him. "So you understand?"

Still leaning against the wall, he turns to his side, and I do the same.

The fiery determination in his eyes is my first clue that he's not fully ready to accept defeat.

"Yeah, I understand," he says. "You should know this, though. I will *always* take no for an answer, but the minute you say otherwise, you're mine, and I won't hold anything back."

That's the second clue.

Philly Water Cooler

6/3/2017
Heard Around Town
By Maisie Hunt | Leave a comment

Remember Tori Alvarez, the badass fitness instructor who snagged Mason King by challenging him to a push-up contest? Well, the plot thickens. *Celebrity Watch Online* is reporting that she and TV actor Carter Stone are an item. HGL traces the relationship back to a trip to Aruba, where both Alvarez and Stone traveled in May, according to separate tweets from their Twitter accounts. They followed the trip with a cute exchange on Twitter, in which Alvarez said Stone couldn't handle her fitness regimen, and Stone jokingly responded that her challenge had been accepted. A photographer then spotted them entering the same gym, which interestingly, is not the gym where Alvarez works. And it was *after hours*. And they couldn't hide their affection for each other in front of Mi Casita, a North Philadelphia restaurant owned by Alvarez's parents: A photographer for *CWO* snapped a pic of Carter pressing a kiss to Alvarez's forehead. Swoon.

Chapter Twenty-Three

Tori

It's EARLY AFTERNOON, and Ben and Nate have summoned me to the gym on my day off. I'm in front of my computer staring at the reason why. Last night, while I was telling Carter I *didn't* want to date him, an entertainment blog reported that I *am* dating him.

Eva nudges me to make space for her and reads the story over my shoulder.

With a carton of ice cream and a spoon in her hands, she draws back and pins me with a confused gaze. "When did he kiss you on the forehead?"

"He didn't. That was the day he brought his family to the restaurant. I was upset about my dad, and he was wiping away my tears."

"And they placed you in Aruba at the same time."

I smack my forehead at that one. "I stupidly posted a photo of the beach on Twitter. Apparently, he'd done the same."

Eva shakes her head and puts a spoonful of ice cream in her mouth. "Nate's going to kill you," she says with her mouth full.

"Yes, Mr. Stickler for Personnel Issues probably will. It's his job after all."

She jams the spoon into the carton and gives my shoulder a squeeze. "Want me to come with you?"

"No, I'll be fine."

"Well, all you have to do is explain how this was all taken out of context, right?"

"Yes," I say in a soft voice.

Eva's eyes narrow. "Right?"

I drop my head onto the keyboard.

"Oh my God," she shrieks. "You had sex with him?"

"I did not." I cover my mouth. Under my breath, I say, "But I might have given him an abbreviated hand job."

She leans in and cups her ear. "Say again? What's that now? You gave him a blow job?"

I push her away from me. "A hand job."

"Oh, well, that's qualitatively different for these purposes."

I stand with all the feigned outrage I can muster. "I will not stand here and listen to this drivel." Then I wave the ends of my robe like a matador and flounce to my bedroom.

Behind me, Eva laughs. "I love you, woman. Don't change. And don't be ashamed of that hand action."

With the carton still in her hands, she follows me into the bedroom and drops onto my bed while I pull out clothes from my dresser. "Remember when you said you wouldn't be tempted by Carter because you didn't want to end up on Page Six?"

I turn to her with several articles of clothing in my hands. "Yes, I remember."

"You're on Page Six. Not literally but figuratively."

I tilt my head to the ceiling and let out a heavy sigh. "Your point, Eva?"

"If everyone's going to assume you had sex with Carter anyway, why not actually have sex with Carter? That way, you get something out of this, too."

Her mind works in depraved ways. It really does. But she's planted the thought in my brain, and it's growing like a weed. I shake my head as if to clear it. I must remain strong. I must. "Having sex with Carter would not help the situation."

She shrugs. "Fine. But I'm putting a Google Alert on him anyway. Just in case."

"I worry about you."

She sticks her tongue out at me. "I worry about me, too. *And* I worry about my best friend."

I drop the clothes on my chair and pull her up from the bed for a hug. *She* has my back. Always.

With her mouth at my ear, she says, "Can you at least tell me this: If you were to use an emoji to represent his penis, would you use a banana or an eggplant?"

I push her off me and roll my eyes. "Eggplant."

She hoots. "*Get it*, woman."

I pick up one of my tank tops and toss it at her. "*Get out*, woman."

Her eyes are teary with laughter as she leaves. "I'm going, but report back later. Can't wait to hear about Nate losing his shit."

I'd happily wait decades for that.

IT COMES AS no surprise to me that a reporter is waiting for me when I arrive at Hard Core. She appears young, and she's chewing on her lip as she scribbles furiously in a reporter's notebook. She just might have more butterflies in her belly than I do. Still, she has a job to do, so I steel myself for the barrage of questions that are sure to follow her friendly greeting.

"Tori Alvarez, I'm Maisie Hunt from *Philly Water Cooler*. Could I have two minutes of your time?"

Hunt's approach differs from the rapid-fire questions I'd anticipated. I'm inclined to listen to her, if only to prepare myself for any future harassment.

Mouthing hello to the front desk clerk, I hand him my ID and tighten my hold on my gym bag before I face Ms. Hunt. "Sure, I'll give you two minutes."

Her eyes startle. "Great, great. Well, uh, I just wanted to ask if it's true that you're dating Carter Stone."

I motion for her to follow me to a spot away from the desk. "I'm not dating Carter Stone. I'm his personal trainer."

"Um, okay. But *Celebrity Watch Online* is reporting otherwise."

"That may be, but *Celebrity Watch Online* doesn't have the facts. Plus, Ms. Hunt, the picture doesn't show Carter kissing my forehead. He was wiping my tears, about something unrelated to him. Something you would have known had you contacted me before republishing unoriginal gossip. That was sloppy journalism. There's no story, and your job is not to make one up."

She fidgets with the pad in her hands. "I'll correct that."

"Please do. Anything else?"

"No...um...nothing else," she stutters.

"Have a great day, Ms. Hunt."

"You, too," she says, a dazed expression on her face before she spins and walks away.

I have no control over what she writes, but maybe she'll be more thoughtful about her reporting in the future. Now to deal with Ben and Nate.

I take back my card and shove it into my bag's side pocket. I don't attack the stairs as I typically do, mostly because I'm dreading the conversation I'm about to have. With my gut churning, I enter the office, where Ben and Nate are huddled together. They straighten when I collapse into my seat.

"Everything okay?" Ben asks.

I blow out a long, ragged breath. "A reporter intercepted me on the way into the gym to ask about my relationship with Carter Stone, but otherwise I'm doing splendidly."

Nate and Ben both lift their brows and glance at each other.

"I detect sarcasm, Ben. Is that what you're picking up?"

Ben nods. "Yes, it has a certain *je ne sais quoi* to it. Inappropriate sarcasm under the circumstances, maybe?"

Chin in one hand, Nate purses his lips and nods. "Yes, that seems right."

Why are they joking around? I thought they'd be pissed. Now my knee won't stop bouncing. I adopt an authoritative tone. "You asked me to come in, and I'm here. Before you berate me for making poor choices, I'd just like to point out that he is *not* kissing me in the photograph, and I went to Aruba after the Mason debacle, *not* with Carter."

"Tori—"

"Also, we're not dating. This is mostly fabricated by the gossip peddlers."

Nate raises a brow again. "Mostly?"

I should just shut up, shouldn't it?

Ben peers at me and drums his fingers on the table.

"What?" I ask him in a strangled voice.

As usual, Ben and Nate lob digs at me as though they're playing volleyball with them.

"We knew you'd be upset about all this," Ben says.

"Feeling guilty," Nate adds.

"Thinking you betrayed us."

"Ashamed."

"Oh, the shame."

Ben slices a hand across his neck, signaling to Nate that the comedy set is complete. "We're not going to pretend we think what you did here was appropriate—"

"But we're *not* dating—"

Ben raises a hand to stop me from defending myself. "Tori, give me a chance. Look, we don't need to know anything as long as you tell us whatever is happening involves two consenting adults. If that's the case, then this discussion is over."

I stare at Nate. In the past, he's argued that the gym should adopt a formal policy about relationships between clients and trainers. "You're on board with this?"

Nate clears his throat. "Yeah, I'm on board."

"That's surprising," I say.

"The longer I'm in this business, the more I realize nothing's black-and-white. Sometimes we can't help who we fall in love with."

If I had any gauze handy, I'd spin around and wrap myself in it like a dummy. I can't believe I'm having this conversation. It's mortifying. And I need to end it, so I tell them what they want to hear, which also happens to be the truth. "Whatever it is, it's between two consenting adults."

To sum up, celebrity gossip sites are reporting that Carter and I are dating, I've had to field questions from a reporter about my love life, and I've just had the most uncomfortable conversation in the history of conversations—with my bosses. Eva's right. Not exactly in the way she put it. But maybe since my all-or-nothing approach to dealing with Carter hasn't worked in my favor, I could try to bend a little and get something out of this, too.

So far, the media coverage suggests only a passing interest in our relationship status. We don't have to announce to the world that we're dating. We could just enjoy each other here in Philly in private, for as long as we choose. Take it slowly. Avoid the cameras in the meantime. Reassess as the need arises. Right now, I simply need to be with him.

I hope he's ready.

Carter Stone, I'm coming for you.

Chapter Twenty-Four

Carter

I'M HOLDING MY phone away from my ear as Julian barks at me.

"Are you listening to me, Carter?"

My publicist, Dana, gave Julian an earful when she heard about the Tori story, so now he's passing on the love to me.

"I'm listening, Julian. This was taken out of context. There was nothing to tell Dana. There's no relationship to acknowledge. Not yet at least. It'll blow over on its own."

Julian grumbles on the other end. "She didn't know what to say, Carter. That's all. Usually you give her a heads-up about these things. Just keep us in the loop, okay?

"Sure, I get it."

"And refresh my memory, is this the woman you planned to apologize to?"

"Yeah, she's the one."

He lets out a harsh laugh. "You and I have different definitions of *closure*."

I ignore his observation. "Let's not pretend I can ever control what the press decides to report."

I also can't control how Tori reacts to being the subject of press attention. But I need to make sure she's okay. Which I'll do as soon as Julian is finished berating me.

He sighs. "Fine. Is there anything you need to give me a heads-up about?"

"Nope."

"Good. Now, in other, better-guarded news, you have a date for your read-through with Gwen Styles."

"When?"

"Next Tuesday or Thursday. You get to choose."

"But they said I'd have six weeks."

"Well, now you have four."

Shit. More games from Samantha Bell. She probably never intended to give me six weeks. Just trying to throw me off my game. I would have preferred more time. But as is the case with most aspects of this business, I don't decide the when, I only control whether I show up on time. "I'll be there, of course."

"I've already asked Jewel to make your travel arrangements. Just let her know which date."

"Thanks, J."

"You got it, man. I'll check in next week."

I end the call and pace the length of the living room. Tori and I are due to meet again this evening, but I'm not even sure she'll want to.

I send her a quick text.

Me: **You okay?**

A minute later, my phone buzzes.

Tori: **I'm fine.**
Me: **We should talk. Can I see you?**

She doesn't answer immediately. I tap my phone on my thigh as I wait.

Tori: **Sure. When?**
Me   **Now? I'll come to you.**
Tori: **No, I'll come to you. I need fresh air. Address?**
Me: **230 W. Rittenhouse Square. I'll tell the doorman to send you up.**
Tori: **Okay. Also, fancy.**

Her side note gives me hope that she hasn't written me off.

My stomach gurgles. I haven't eaten in three hours, a passage of time that's been unheard of the last three weeks. I'll scarf something down while I wait for her to arrive. Which is good. I need to focus on something.

Otherwise, I'll tie myself in knots trying to predict how she'll react to my decision.

Twenty minutes later, my intercom buzzes. I hit the push-to-talk button. "Yeah, Bill?"

"Ms. Alvarez is on her way up, sir."

"Thanks."

I straighten the pillows on the couch and set a few stray glasses in the sink. I scan the room, picturing it from Tori's perspective. It's nothing like my condo in West Hollywood. Most of the furniture in here looks like it belongs in my parents' house. But from the bedroom I can see Rittenhouse Park, and the massive stone half wall separating the bed from the rest of the bedroom is a nice touch.

I sprint to the door when the bell rings. Fuck pretending to be unaffected by this woman. She's occupied my thoughts since the day I met her. To pretend otherwise would be a waste of time. I swing the door open. "Hi."

With her head bowed, she lifts her hand in a weak wave. "Hey."

I want to lift her chin and kiss her worries away, but her demeanor tells me she won't appreciate a show of affection. *Go slow, Carter. She's probably wrecked by the gossip.* "Come on in."

She inches across the threshold and tightens her hold on her purse. She's wearing a peach T-shirt dress and navy-blue Chuck Taylors. She points to my bare feet. "Should I take off my sneaks?"

"Only if you want to."

She scans the living area. "Then I'll keep them on."

I stand behind the kitchen counter as she takes a seat at one end of the sofa.

"Want something to drink?" I ask.

"No, thanks."

I grab a bottled water from the fridge and join her. After taking a quick swig, I set it down on the coffee table and place my elbows on my knees, making a steeple of my fingers. "I'm sorry about the press coverage. I did a piss-poor job of protecting you from their attention, didn't I?"

"You sure did."

I snap my head up at that.

She floors me with a quirk of her lips, and the tightness in my chest loosens.

"Welcome to my life," I say.

Her gaze on me softens. "A small price to pay to do something you love, I'm sure. But I didn't choose this. In fact, if given a choice I'd never have to deal with this again."

I have so many questions about her reluctance for media coverage, but my brain snags on the consequences to her job. "Your bosses. Have you talked to them?"

"Yes, they were good about it, but it was a painful conversation." She wedges her hands between her thighs. "Essentially, they told me they didn't need to know what was going on between me and you if I could assure them we were proceeding as consenting adults."

"What did you tell them?" I ask in a low voice.

She leans forward and stares at the floor. "I assured them we were two consenting adults. And I came here intending to do something about it." Sighing, she lowers her chin to her chest. "But we shouldn't. It's inappropriate."

"Is it?"

She raises her head, her mouth open. "*Yes*, it is."

"Because you're my trainer?"

She rolls her eyes. "No, because I'm your urologist, Carter. Jesus, what am I missing here? Of course because I'm your trainer."

"I think you're using that as an excuse."

"I'm not," she says weakly.

She is. Dammit, I *know* she is. And in a minute, she's going to know it, too. "What if I told you my audition's been bumped up a couple of weeks, so I'm happy to consider your work with me done. What would you say then?"

Her eyes widen, and she gulps.

Yeah, that's what I thought. *Gotcha, Tori.*

Chapter Twenty-Five

Tori

WE WON'T BE working together anymore? Shit. What do I say now? "Is that true?" is all I manage to say in response.

"It is. Julian called me about the change less than an hour ago. So as much as I'd love to keep working with you"—he stands and lifts his T-shirt to show me his flat abs—"this is as good as it gets."

Oh, it's good all right. Like lick-the-contours-and-suck-on-his-skin good. Still. "I'll work with you until your audition. Another few days can make a world of difference."

"I can continue to work out on my own in that time." He waggles his eyebrows. "And keep those few days open for more interesting activities."

I huff at him. "Carter, this isn't funny and doesn't solve anything."

His eyebrows shoot up. "Yes, it solves everything. You claim a relationship with a client is inappropriate."

I cross my arms in front of my chest. *"It is."*

He tilts his head and regards me with a suggestive grin. "So now I don't have to be your client." He pretends to dust off his hands. "Done. Problem solved. And before you get upset about it, consider this. I've accomplished what I set out to do within the time frame I've been given. Ending our business relationship now only means we can enjoy each other the way we both want to. Do with me what you will. You have my permission. This should be good news…unless being my trainer never was the reason you didn't want to be with me."

Balling my hands into fists, I jump up from the sofa and push him out of my way. "This conversation is ridiculous."

"I'll tell you what's ridiculous," he says behind me.

Whirling around to face him, I am momentarily stunned by the view that greets me. His inky-black hair is in disarray, a victim of his fingers. The effect is so compelling I want to be their accomplice. With his hands jammed into the pockets of the jeans that hang loosely from his trim hips, he tries to exude an easy confidence, but his ice-blue eyes are trained on my face with an intensity that matches the tension in the room.

"I know you want me as much as I want you," he continues. "But you refuse to take the leap."

I throw up my hands. "Yes, I refuse to take the leap, because I don't know what *this* is. Where should I jump exactly? And how high? Are we jumping into bed, or into something else? You're an *actor*, Carter. You live in California. And you have a life that's incompatible with mine."

He tilts his head, and his tight expression relaxes. "You're scared."

Well, duh. "Hell, yes, I'm scared."

"Would it help if I told you I'm scared, too?"

My mouth hangs open. "You are?"

He nods and removes his hands from his pockets. "For as long as I can remember, acting has been my life. It's consumed my time, my attention. It's made me who I am. Other than my family and Julian, I don't open myself to anyone. I'm scared because how I feel about acting pales in comparison to how I feel about you."

I can't control the gasp that escapes my mouth. "Carter," is all I say.

"I'm not going to pretend it'll be easy. Hell, I don't even know the questions, let alone the answers. But we can figure it out together." He steps closer. "I'm not playing games, Tori, and in my mind, this isn't temporary. If you want me, you have me."

If I take this step with Carter, I'm opening myself up to so much more than even I can imagine. But God, I want to. I'd like to tell him that his feelings are reciprocated, but the words never come. They're lodged in my throat, refusing to leave the comfort of being inside me. I do know how to show him my affection, however, so I lunge at him and cover his mouth with mine.

Yes, I know. Very subtle.

Carter chuckles against my lips and deepens the kiss.

After I've sufficiently reacquainted myself with his mouth, I draw back. "I took a leap, because I want to be with you, too."

He cups my cheek and ghosts his thumb across my bottom lip, after which he straightens and rubs his hands together. "So what would you like to do next? Watch a movie? I could throw some popcorn in the microwave."

The change in his demeanor causes me to blink furiously. "What?"

"We should take this slow, right? Get comfortable with the idea of being together, huh?"

He flashes me a smile.

I shake my head in response. "Cute."

He walks backward, removing his T-shirt and tossing it at my feet. "Or I could give you a tour of my bedroom."

I scan him from the top of his silky hair to the toes that peek out from the hem of his jeans. This is going to be *so* good. Screw my bones, I can feel it in my lady bits. So I follow him like a panting puppy begging for a treat. Yes, yes. Kibbles and dicks! Kibbles and dicks! And because I'm an excellent facilitator, I raise the hem of my dress and pull it off, my gaze never leaving his.

Carter stumbles. "You can't take off your clothes without warning me. It's dangerous."

"I'll bear that in mind for the future," I say with a wink.

Before we cross his bedroom's threshold, he stops me with a raised hand. "Hang on. I need a minute to soak this in. You in a bra, panties, and Chuck Taylors. Fuck me, that's hot."

"I'm even hotter with absolutely nothing on."

He drags me inside and palms my ass to draw me to him. His chin makes a new home in the crook of my neck, while my hands make quick work of the top button and zipper of his jeans. Out of the corner of my eye, I note there's a view. I won't be paying attention to it anytime soon, though. Instead, I delve inside his pants, my hand seeking his erection, and he hisses when I cup him.

"Tori, I want to do this right," he whispers against my ear.

"I don't want this to be right, Carter. I want it to be all kinds of wrong. Show me what you've been holding back this whole time."

Swallowing hard, he leans back. His chest is heaving, and goodness, his pupils are dilated to three times their normal size. Not even the adrenaline generated by our training sessions brought Carter to this state.

He circles me and presses a kiss at the nape of my neck. I shiver at the brief contact, wanting much more. His fingers are hot against my skin when he unsnaps my bra. With the lacy material discarded at my feet, he reaches around and cups my breasts, alternating between massaging them and tweaking my nipples. As he caresses me, he grinds his sex against my backside, and there's no mistaking his thickness.

Content to temporarily play his trusty assistant, I toe off my sneakers and reach for the side strings of my bikini underwear.

Carter swats my hands away and growls against my ear. "Leave that to me."

The front of his body is flush with the back of mine. In that position, he walks me to the wall and slides my hands up and over my head. I register the rustling behind me and gasp when his lips meet the small of my back. Then his hands glide over my ass before he tugs my panties down my legs. I step out of them, and Carter places his hands on my waist, spinning me to face him. I look down, and my heart races. He's on his knees at my feet and licking his lips in anticipation.

He taps my thigh. "Put your leg over my shoulder."

Oh. My. God. He expects me to stand against the wall? I will crumple into an embarrassing heap at his feet. He swipes a finger against me, groaning as he tests my wetness. My knees buckle. "Yes, Carter, yes. Please put your mouth on me."

His fingers massage my folds, and then his tongue flicks against my clit.

I shift against his mouth, chasing his tongue, needing more, but he doesn't suck on me the way I want him to, and I bang my hand against the wall because I'm going to die if he doesn't give me what I need.

"Is this what you want?" he asks before he lays his tongue flat against me and slides up to my nub.

Pleasure courses through me like a never-ending circuit of sexual energy, and I don't ever want it to stop. "Yes, yes, fuck, Carter, yes, more."

He pulls back and places a finger against my clit, teasing it. "There it is. So fucking pretty, Tori. I've been dreaming about having this in my mouth." He licks his lips. "Soon you'll be all over my face."

Oh God. My clit pulses with each flick of his finger, and my stomach tightens in response to the onslaught. "Please, Carter," I say in a pained voice.

"I've got you, baby," he says.

And then he draws my clit into his mouth, sucking it softly and then more aggressively, until my legs shake from the pressure of holding myself up while he ravishes me. But it's not enough. Somehow, he senses I need more, and he slides two fingers in and out of me while he laps at me with long, strong strokes.

I don't recognize my voice or the sounds coming out of my mouth. Some of the words are intelligible, but mostly I'm moaning, and wailing, and hissing. And it feels so good I want to shout.

"Carter, I…I need to ride you. Right now."

He looks up at me, the hunger in his gaze pinning me to the spot. "Baby, you can have anything you want."

I'm not hiding from this anymore: This is happening.

Chapter Twenty-Six

Carter

As TORI RIDES me, her eyes closed, her breasts bouncing in tempo with her gyrating hips, the surrealism of the moment overtakes me. My brain processes the tingling in my cock just fine. But the fact that Tori is the woman inducing that tingle is hard to grasp.

Tori is riding me. I repeat. Tori is riding me.

And what a magnificent sight she is. Her long curly hair brushes against the tops of her tits, and her brown skin glistens, damp from her efforts. Her lips are wet, slick from the constant press of her tongue against them. Each time she raises her body, the strain in her facial features disappears, only to return when she bears down on me.

Again and again.

Over and over.

So fucking perfect.

I'd like to do more than groan and grunt. I'd like to tell her that there's no need to break me, that repeatedly bringing me to the brink constitutes a special brand of torture I'd be happy to repay, but the part of my brain that regulates my ability to form coherent sentences has shut down.

I need to regain control of the situation, although somewhere in the recesses of my mind I question whether that's even possible. I squeeze her waist, urging her to ride me faster. Harder. She opens her eyes, widening them to baby-doll proportions. "Oh God...yes...Carter...yes, that's it...I..."

When she leans over and presses her lips to mine, I breathe in the scent of vanilla that kisses her skin.

Nuzzling her neck, I whisper, "Hang on. Let's switch places."

She raises her torso, an unfocused gaze contributing to the sexy image that imbeds itself in my brain for safe-keeping. "What's wrong?"

"Nothing's wrong. You wanted me to show you how much I've been holding back, and to do that I need to fuck you hard."

Her eyes blaze with desire, and she shifts, stretching out her legs so we can roll over and swap positions. Sweat drips from my face as I lift her legs into the air and place them on my shoulders. Her legs are smooth to the touch, distracting me from my mission. I can't resist leaning in and pressing my mouth against her inner thigh, stretching her body to accommodate my weight. The result is that she's open to me, and I drive into her like a man possessed. And I am. Possessed by her.

I have enough sense to choke out, "Is this too much?"

She shakes her head from side to side. "No, no. Keep going."

My arms burn from the effort of holding myself upright, but I can't stop. I won't stop. I'm close, and she is, too, our bodies vibrating against each other. Her cries of encouragement grow louder with each thrust, and I watch her dazed expression for signs that she's approaching the summit. But then she reaches up and caresses my face, her soft hands slowing the moment, taking ownership of its significance. "I can't believe this is us," she whispers.

My body tenses in response to her words, and I fall fast. Hard. Long. I freeze as the orgasm crests and washes over me, a riot of sensation that hits my body like an earthquake, my dick at its epicenter. A heap of a man reduced to nothing by the force of his orgasm. But she isn't there with me. And although my arms begin to protest, I push through the discomfort, grinding into her, until her cries mingle with my heavy breathing. A few seconds more and she practically sings her release, her back arching in abandon as she tightens around me.

Fuck. That was good. Like mind-bendingly good. Like I-want-to-do-this-with-her-every-day good. Only her. She's wrecked me for anyone else, and I'm not worried about that fact at all.

Minutes later, we lie across each other in silence, a tangle of body parts amid the rumpled sheets. Raising my head to gauge her mood, I kiss her shoulder and wait.

She turns to me and gives me a lazy smile. "I'm going to need that popcorn now."

Hollywood Observer

9:00 a.m. PDT 6/4/2017 by Lisa Gibson
Los Angeles, California

Early Review Special

Hard Times suffers from a case of trying too hard, and not even its all-star lineup could save it. The latest casualty among major studio (melo)dramas masquerading as indies, the movie chronicles a week in the lives of a married couple whose previously successful daughter (Emily Garamond) succumbs to heroin addiction. Maggie Boyd is convincing as a mother undone by the rapid deterioration of her previously perfect life, while Dennis Satch struggles to connect with the broader themes of the story or his role as a father wracked by guilt for pushing his daughter beyond her limits. Unfortunately, the film manages to come across as a long public service announcement with stereo surround sound and haunting (read: dark) cinematography. Newcomer to film Carter Stone, who plays the daughter's drug-addicted classmate, wows the audience with his emaciated physique and deathly pallor, but his performance is otherwise uninspiring and emotionless. My advice? Don't quit your day job, Carter. Oh, wait...

WE SAY: You shouldn't leave the house for this one. Catch it on Netflix on a rainy day instead.

Chapter Twenty-Seven

Carter

MY CELL PINGS with the ringtone I've downloaded and assigned exclusively to Julian: the opening bars of the *Mission Impossible* theme song. He hates it, which is why I love it.

I reach over, grab the phone, and lean my back against the headboard. Beside me, Tori shifts, her arms winding their way around my waist. I use my free hand to brush back a few strands of her hair so I can fully see her sleeping face.

"What's up, Julian?"

"Just wanted to let you know that *Hollywood Observer* published an early review of *Hard Times*."

"No shit?"

"It's not good, Carter."

My heart pounds, and my stomach clenches. "They trashed my performance?"

"They trashed the entire movie, but yes, you're a part of the trashing."

Fuck. Hearing about a bad review hurts just as much as reading one. "Do I want to read it?"

Julian sighs into the phone. "Is not reading it even a realistic option for you?"

"No, you're right. Let me take it all in, and then we'll talk, okay?"

"Sure."

Before I can disconnect the call, Julian stops me. "Carter," he says with hesitation in his voice.

"Yeah?"

"I'm sorry about this, man. But remember, it's a single review, and another critic will love it."

It's then that I remember this can't be easy on him, either. His reputation suffers when his clients bomb. "Thanks, J. And I'm sorry about this, too."

He chuckles. "We'll be fine, Carter. I'm not worried. And don't beat yourself up about this. It's a hiccup in the scheme of things."

"Yeah. Later."

After ending the call, I disentangle myself from Tori, who turns on her side with one eye open and asks if everything's okay. "Yeah," I tell her. "Go back to sleep. I just have to check something."

She grumbles an unintelligible response and closes her eyes.

I slip on a pair of jeans and walk barefoot to the living room. A simple search produces the review in question.

Uninspiring. Emotionless. Don't quit your day job. Holy shit, the reviewer didn't hold back. At all.

I jump at the sound of Tori padding down the hall.

She approaches the living room, her steps tentative. One of her cheeks is lined with my comforter's pattern. She's wearing my white T-shirt, which ends just below the tops of her thighs, and she's holding her own phone in her hand. Tori's the bright spot in my dreadful morning.

"Hey, what's going on?" she asks as she leans against the archway.

After dropping my phone on the couch, I stride across the room and pull her toward me. "It's nothing." I nuzzle her neck, but not long enough for my liking.

She pulls away and peers at me. "Carter, what happened?"

I take a long breath. "*Hollywood Observer* published an early review for *Hard Times*. Apparently, the movie and my performance did not impress the critic."

"Oh, shit. Sorry. Is a review in *Hollywood Observer* a big deal?"

I nod. "It's the equivalent of a book review in the *New York Times*."

She winces. "Didn't you just finish filming the movie like six weeks ago? How is it finished already?"

"The production was largely complete months ago. The only scenes left to edit were the ones after my weight loss."

She nods and reaches for my hand. "Can I read the review?"

"Why?"

Her fingers intertwine with mine, and she squeezes. "It's hard to console you when I don't know the nature of the critique."

I pull up the article on my iPhone and hand it to her. "I'll warn you now. It's painful."

She drops on the couch, sets her own phone down, and pats the sofa cushion. "Come." I'm too jumpy to sit, so I motion for her to start. It's fucking annoying that this is how we're spending our morning-after.

As she reads, I watch her face for signs of her reaction. The entire time, she alternates between furrowing her brows and pursing her lips, and when she's done, her mouth drops open. "Wow. She's a snide one. Ever get one like this before?"

"No. And I'm not used to being raked over the coals in the press like this. Have I been embarrassed at an audition? Passed over for a part? Received faint praise? Sure, plenty of times. But this is different. This is a professional review that's nasty as hell, and hundreds of thousands of people will see it."

"I'm sorry, Carter. I don't know what to say. But it comes with the job, right?"

"Yeah. It does. But this one hurts more than any criticism directed at me in the past. *Hard Times* was an opportunity to demonstrate my range, to show that I'm capable of playing more than the handsome-neighbor love interest. I failed."

She snaps her brows together. "It's an *opinion*, Carter. *One* person's *opinion*, which by definition, means it's subjective."

I scrub a hand down my face and grasp onto the back of my neck. She's right. But what if there are others? What if this is one of many bad reviews to come? "You're not telling me anything I don't know, but my head doesn't know how to put this in its proper perspective."

"Okay, let's say this review isn't a one-off. Suppose several reviewers trash the film. You're not going to stop acting, are you? Of course not. Besides, every actor's entitled to a *Gigli*."

I shake my head at her, still distracted by the zingers in the review. "A what?"

"Oh, c'mon, Carter. A *Gigli*. Ben Affleck? Jennifer Lopez? Almost universally regarded as one of the worst films of the modern age."

Understanding dawns then. She makes a good point. "Well, it's technically not true that *Gigli* was a one-off. Affleck also starred in *Jersey Girl* and *Daredevil*."

She rolls her eyes and shakes her head. "My *point* is that not every film is going to be a critical success, and even great actors get caught in the crossfire. Judi Dench in *The Chronicles of Riddick*. What the hell was she doing in a movie with Vin Diesel? Jon Voight in *Anaconda*."

My mind whirs. "Matt Damon in *The Brothers Grimm*."

She stares at me with a blank look on her face. "Never saw that one. Straight to DVD?"

"I think so." I pace the room, snapping my fingers. "Bradley Cooper in that movie where he's an author—"

"*The Words*," she calls out, smiling.

"Denzel Washington—"

She raises a hand to stop me and pulls me down next to her. "He's off-limits. My mother would have my head if I talked badly about him."

She swivels to the side and wedges one of her legs in the space between my back and the sofa cushion. I turn and fall back against her so that we're lying together, her hands sifting through my hair. This woman gets me in a way I never expected. If I were upset and had to flash a smile for the cameras, she'd know it wasn't genuine. I've never put on a façade with her, even when she didn't know I was Carter Stone. With her, I embrace my realness, whether good, bad, or embarrassing. Maybe it's because she wants me for me, not for what I can give her.

I tilt my head up. "Thanks for listening."

"I want to be there for you, Carter. That's what...girlfriends do, right?"

Her voice halts midsentence, telling me this isn't a casual observation. No, this is big for her. I reach behind me and caress her neck. She leans into my touch and runs a finger from my navel to my chest.

Her phone buzzes on the table, and she shifts our positions to grab it. After a few swipes and a bit of typing, she says, "Eva. Wanted to make sure I'm okay."

"Did you tell her that I rocked your world last night?"

Her body shakes with laughter. "No, I told her I rocked yours."

She continues to read her phone, and then she gasps.

I sit up. "What is it?"

She shakes her head, and I glance at her screen. She's reading an email, and her lips curve into a slow smile, calming my rapidly beating heart. "It's nothing. We can talk about it later."

I sit up. "Tori, it's something. I can tell by the look on your face. Don't hold back on my account."

She chews her bottom lip as she studies me. "It's from an investor group I contacted a while ago. At first, they told me they weren't taking applications. Now they're saying one of their deals fell through, and they'd like to know if I'm interested in submitting a proposal. Look."

I read the email as she bounces next to me. "Dreams Inferred LLC. Cool name."

She grabs my forearms. "Do you know what this means? I might be able to get backing for my own studio."

I drop the phone onto the couch and pull her into my arms. "That's fantastic news, Tori."

She scratches her bottom lip as she stares into space. "But they're only giving me a week to submit, and they'd like to schedule the pitch meeting soon after that. That's not a lot of time."

"I have no doubt you'll get it done with time to spare."

The tension in her face eases. "Thanks."

She stands, and I rise, too. She moves into my arms as though it's the most natural response to being this close to each other. "I have to get to the gym." Then she sighs.

Uh-oh. "What?" I ask.

"Your training. You can't slack off completely. How about I give you some ideas for a more intense home training program…until you return to California?"

"That would be great. I'll purchase a set of weights and have them delivered here. Julian and I usually work out together. I'll hook up with him when I get back."

She drops her gaze to the floor. "When will that be?"

"Two weeks or so. I have to return to LA to do the table read for *Man on Third*."

She lifts her head and gives me a quizzical expression. "What's a table read?"

"It's when the cast sits around a conference table and reads the script aloud. We do it before the filming of the current season. I was supposed to do it sooner, but I asked for more time so I could work on getting a part in *Swan Song*. I'd love to take you on set. You could see what it's like. Hang out with me at my place, maybe?"

I don't tell her that I'm hoping she'll love that. Best-case scenario: She doesn't find the attention too much to handle.

She widens her eyes and gives me a hesitant smile. The look on her face guts me. Julian's right. I'm whipped.

"I'd like that," she says. But then she frowns. "But I'll probably be meeting with the investment group that week."

"Right. Another time, then."

"For sure," she says.

I don't want to press—but then again, I do. "When?"

She tilts her head to the side. "When what?"

"When would be a good time for you to visit me?"

She sighs. "I'm not sure, Carter. This meeting with the investment group is all I can focus on right now. Let's revisit when I know more, okay?"

"Sure, I understand," I tell her.

And for the first time, I really do understand. She'll never be thrilled about dating an actor, so an opportunity to come to LA and go on set isn't going to entice her. This isn't just about me and what I want. This is also about Tori and what she *doesn't* want.

I remind myself to keep Ashley's advice in mind: *Baby steps, Carter. Baby steps.*

Chapter Twenty-Eight

Tori

ASKING SOMEONE FOR *money sucks.*

I'm suffering through the application process for my funding request while Carter studies the script for *Swan Song*. He's relocated the small desk that once resided in his bedroom to the living room. That's because we learned that having the desk near the bed undermined my ability to get any work done.

I'm hunched over the keyboard, and I have the strangest urge to yank my hair out. "Grrr."

"What's wrong?" Carter asks from his spot on the couch.

He's barefoot and bare-chested, and an even bigger distraction than having the desk in the bedroom.

"These questions are frustrating," I say over my shoulder. "Example. Question Four: 'Tell us how you're uniquely situated to develop the market or service that is the subject of your proposal.' Can I just say I'm a personal trainer and leave it at that?"

Carter chuckles. "If you'd like a rejection, sure."

I drop my head onto the keyboard. Within seconds, Carter's behind me, massaging my neck and shoulders and generally making me feel like putty.

"I hate this. I have a hard time selling myself."

He kisses my neck. "Luckily for you, I'm the master of self-promotion. It's time to pad your resume."

I twist my body and look up at him. "I will not."

He rolls his eyes. "I'm not saying you should lie. Just take the facts and elevate them."

"You sound like a judge on *Top Chef.* Should I deconstruct my resume, too?"

He licks the side of my face and puckers his lips. "You've committed the ultimate sin. You're too salty."

I try to playfully swat him away, but he dodges my hands and rubs my shoulders instead.

"What do you have to offer that no one else does?" he asks.

I turn as I rise, slip my fingers in the loops of his jeans, and pull him toward me. "Okay, how's this? I'm the girl-friend of one of the hottest actors in television today, and I'm responsible for his smoking-hot physique. That should qualify me on the spot."

He narrows his eyes before he turns away. "That's definitely not what I had in mind."

He's poised to put distance between us, but I grab his arm and spin him around. Standing on my toes, I pull his chin down and force him to make eye contact with me. "Carter, I was kidding. I'd never try to trade on my relationship with you."

He throws his head back and draws in a long breath. "I know, I know. Sorry." He straightens and envelops me in a tight hug. As his lips float across my forehead, he murmurs, "Bear with me, okay? I'm trying not to say or do stupid shit, but I'm not one hundred percent there yet. I blame it on *Swan Song*."

It's not *Swan Song*. He knows it. I know it. But I'll let him use this excuse. Just this once. Because I really don't want to fight with him about something that has no basis in fact. "Are you nervous about the audition?"

"Technically it's not an audition. I'm reading with the actress who's already attached to the film, so it's a chemistry read."

I wrap my arms around his neck and try to look stern. "I don't want you to have chemistry with anyone else."

"But if Gwen Styles and I don't have chemistry, I don't get the part."

I give him a fake pout. "Well, when you put it like that, I suppose it's all right."

He inches backward. "Hey, would you read with me?"

Shaking my head, I laugh at the notion. "Me? Act? That would be painful for you."

"No, no," he says. "Just read. It'll help me with my prompts."

"Oh…um…okay."

Carter flies across the room and grabs a stack of paper. "I just got the entire script a few days ago. We'll have to sit together since I don't have a copy."

He flops onto the couch and motions for me to join him. We sit side by side, the pages of the script in front of us on the coffee table.

He gives me a quick summary of the film. Oh my heart, it's sad. The scene he wants to rehearse depicts the moment his character realizes he's been deceived by the woman he's fallen in love with while participating in a pen-pal program.

"Ignore the stage direction and prompts," he says. "Just read Pam's lines. That's Gwen Styles's part."

I nod. "Got it."

PAM

Say something. Tell me what you're thinking.

I read this line with about as much emotion as an inanimate object. But Carter, apparently assuming the role of Alex, regards me with a dispassionate expression, and I'll admit to being unnerved by his transformation.

ALEX

I don't know what to say. I don't know who you are. I don't know what's real. You've fucked with me and my life for eighteen months. What kind of person does that?

PAM

I never intended to deceive you.
But the more we communicated, the
more I realized you needed an
escape. I wanted to be your escape.

ALEX

By pretending to be someone else?
By making me fall in love with a
person who doesn't exist?

PAM

(eyes brimming with tears)
I never meant for it to go this
far. I'm ashamed, and sorry, and
so upset with myself.

ALEX

(grabs her by the arms)
Did you laugh with your friends?
Did you tell them how you convinced a stupid soldier boy that
you were a young widow trying to
get her life back together?

PAM

I *am* a widow. I *am* trying to get
my life back together. But I'm not
young. That's the only difference.

                    ALEX
              (he pushes her away)
That's not the only difference, and
you know it. You manufactured your
life, made me think you'd lost your
military husband a year ago. You're
sick, and you might not survive
this. You're a wretched person, and
you're nothing like the woman I
fell in love with. And I hate you
for making me think she existed.

The anger in Carter's expression disappears, and he
smiles. "We can end here."

Holy shit, he's good. I'm stunned into silence. For a
minute there, he'd convinced me that *I* was a wretched
person who'd done a terrible thing.

"Say something," he says softly.

He chews on his bottom lip as he waits for me to
respond. This beautiful man is anxious about my reaction, and I just want to kiss away his fears.

I swallow and clear my throat. "I'm no expert, but I
think you're made for this part. Carter, you're talented."

He releases a long breath. "Thank you."

"Also, this film sounds depressing as shit."

After barking out a laugh, he pulls me into an embrace
and gives me a sweet kiss.

When we separate, I tip him over onto the sofa cushion and straddle him. "Are there any sex scenes in the
movie?"

"No. Just a few kisses."

"That's disappointing. I was going to offer to rehearse those with you."

He grabs a fistful of my hair and pulls me down so that our faces are centimeters apart. "Let's practice anyway."

My world shrinks to the ten square feet around us. "Yes, let's."

I nip his lip and slide my hand down his stomach. When I find his erection, I rub it through the fabric of his jeans, my gaze never leaving his.

His mouth falls open, and he flicks out his tongue. "Yeah, Tori. That feels good."

The sound of his arousal makes my clit pulse, and I can feel myself getting wet.

Overwhelmed by my need for him, I bury my face in his neck and whisper against his ear. "Please tell me you have a condom in your back pocket."

He growls his response. "Fuck, yes, I do."

"Then let's practice a quickie."

After that, everything happens in double time. He unbuttons his jeans and pulls down his zipper. Ready for the handoff, I tug off his jeans and briefs as he lifts his ass from the couch.

I reach into his back pocket for the condom before tossing his pants behind me. I want him inside me so badly that I fumble with the wrapper. We kiss and nuzzle each other, our breathing harsh and ragged, and then I place my hand around his rigid cock and pump him a as he strains against me.

"Yeah, Tori, I'm beyond ready," he grits out.

Together we place the condom on his erection, and then he pulls down the spaghetti straps of my dress and lifts the skirt to my waist.

"Please, baby," he whispers. "Fuck me now."

With one hand on his slick chest, I push my panties to the side, center myself, and bear down as I tighten around him. It's so fucking snug I gasp.

"Tori, Tori, Tori," he chants.

Then the sound of Carter ripping apart my lace panties fills the room. It makes me desperate to know he's desperate, and I fall over, pressing my breasts against his chest and capturing his mouth with mine.

He palms my ass, squeezing it every time I reach the base of his dick. My hair is everywhere, and several strands are plastered against his shoulders. We rock against each other, until I sit up, my mind intent on riding him until we both come. But Carter's got other ideas. He readjusts our bodies, lowering himself on the couch lengthwise and taking me with him. Then he bends his knees and surges into me, so quickly and forcefully that I scramble to gain purchase and finally settle on hanging on to his waist. I'm a rag doll in his hands, the muscles of his arms flexing in response to the demands he's putting on them.

"Tighten around me, baby," he says in a voice so low and rough I don't recognize it.

The friction devastates me, reaching a point where the pleasure momentarily stuns me, and all I can do is hold on to him. "Yes, yes, Carter. Oh God, yes."

"I'm going to come, Tori," he says. "Are you close?"

"Not yet," I say in a strained voice.

One of his hands trails up my back and snakes around my shoulder. "Milk my cock, Tori. That's it." And then he alternates between caressing and tweaking my nipples.

I'm so fucking close I want to cry. It's going to slam into me any minute now, but being on the brink is taking its toll on my body. I'm so tense my back and thighs ache. "Carter," I cry. I'm begging for release.

Sensing my need, Carter slips his hands between my legs and rubs my clit. Once. Twice. Oh yes. And then I detonate, the pleasure emanating from my core and fanning outward to the very tips of my toes and fingers.

And Carter's with me, seized by his own orgasm. "Yes, Tori. Yes. Fuck. Yes."

Afterward, we're breathless, spent, an utter hot mess. And I'm deliriously happy because that was incredible. He pulls me down and hugs me tightly, his warm breath tickling my ear.

"Carter," I say in a serious tone.

He pulls back slightly and regards me with adoring eyes. "What, baby?"

"Don't let anyone ever tell you that you don't have range."

His eyes crinkle at the corners, and he caresses my back. "I won't, Tori. I won't." After we cuddle for a few minutes, he pulls my torn panties from between the cushions and winces. "My body can't handle sex on this couch. I need more room."

"We have a big bed twenty feet away."

ACTING ON IMPULSE 301

"I have an even bigger bed at my place in California. Can't wait to get you in it."

Yes, I suppose I can't avoid LA forever. But just a little longer would be nice.

After several seconds of silence, he sits up, dislodging me in the process. "You don't want to go." Without giving me time to respond, he jumps up, grabs his jeans, and yanks them on.

I slip my arms through the straps of my dress. "I didn't say anything."

He narrows his eyes at me. "Exactly. And you stiffened in my arms. What am I supposed to think?"

"That I'm hesitant to deal with being in the public eye?"

"Or you never intended for us to be serious so you're biding your time until I return to California."

He's so wrong I could scream. Essentially, we've been dealing with being in the public eye since the Twitter fiasco. LA, though, is…just more. Of everything. And I'm trying to shore up my emotional reserves to face it, but I'm just not ready yet. I rise from the couch and pull the skirt of my dress down. "I was overwhelmed when it was one or two reporters in Philly. I can't imagine what it would be like in LA. All those people wanting to take your picture, shouting at you, prying into your life. Just give me time, okay?"

He gives me a smile, but it doesn't reach his eyes. "Take all the time you need."

But now I feel like I'm running out of it.

Chapter Twenty-Nine

Carter

"Carter, we have great chemistry."

Gwen Styles and I are sitting at a table in the tree-lined courtyard of New York's iconic Tavern on the Green. Classical music plays from speakers camouflaged as rocks and nestled in the shrubbery framing the space. She's wearing the biggest sunglasses I've ever seen, and the server just delivered Styles's second Tom Collins.

While she sipped the first TC, she asked me enough questions to ghostwrite my autobiography. A thin sheen of sweat covers my arms. I'm not nervous. It's just hot as Hades.

The read went well per Styles, which is good news because ten minutes into it, I realized her opinion trumped virtually all others in the room. The director, John Paulson, consulted her on everything, much to Samantha Bell's annoyance.

Styles is an attractive woman with a regal bearing. The fluidity of her movements makes it easy to imagine that she was a professionally trained dancer in a former life. She also has a sharp tongue. When we arrived at the restaurant, she looked around and said, "Fucking great. It's a tourist trap now."

I wait for her to say more.

"Do you have a girlfriend, Carter?"

I nod. "I do."

"Is she an actor, too?"

"No," I say, picturing Tori's terror-stricken face when I asked her to read with me. "She's actually averse to all things Hollywood."

"Here's my advice. If you find someone who doesn't care about the lights or the cameras, a person who'd rather sit with you on the couch than walk the red carpet, you should grab onto her and never let go."

"Do you have someone like that in your life?" I ask.

"Yes," she answers with a smile. "But it took me a long time to find them."

I don't disagree with her theory entirely, but Tori should be willing to bend, too. I'm a young male actor whose livelihood depends on being in the public eye. My perceived popularity fuels my actual popularity. If Tori wants to be with me, she can't ignore that reality. "I'm trying to make it work, believe me."

Fifteen minutes into the lunch, she passes me the bread basket, takes a long sip of her drink, and gets to what must be the true point of this meeting. "I've dealt with enough dirtbags in my life, so I refuse to spend the next three months with a jerk. You seem like a good guy, but there's just one thing that concerns me."

My stomach plummets. "What's that?"

"I know Simon Cage. He doesn't have great things to say about you. He seems to question your abilities."

I choke down on all the negative information I could share about my former agent. Hearing that he's still trashing my name, I regret that I didn't go after Simon legally. In my mind, it was easier to let our business relationship end quietly. I reasoned that bringing a lawsuit against him would make industry types skittish to work with me. He misused his position and stole from me, yet I'm the one still experiencing the repercussions of that failed relationship. "If I may be frank?"

Styles tips her head forward. "Please."

"Simon Cage is a snake who took advantage of me. Even if I'm as bad as Simon claims, why would he share such negative information about a former client? I'll tell you why. He's deflecting."

The easiest way to shut up Simon forever is to get this part. If I land the lead role in *Swan Song* and deliver a kick-ass performance, Simon's criticisms won't carry much weight, and I'll have proved him wrong in the process.

"We all have a Simon Cage in our lives, Carter. It's an unfortunate but inevitable fact of every actor's life. Some of us are unlucky enough to have several."

"Do you?"

"A few. I've been doing this a long time. I've met so many people on my journey, and here's what I realize: This business makes users out of people who never even set out to harm us. It's hard to resist latching on to someone else's success when the opportunity arises."

That's Simon in a nutshell. And now that I think about it, the shit-for-brains doctor in Philly went there, too. I don't think he set out to sell photos of me, but when he realized there was something to be gained, he jumped at the chance to make money at my expense. And I'm sure it'll happen again. Maybe not tomorrow or the next day, but someday.

"So how do you protect yourself against the users?" I ask Styles.

"I'm very selective when it comes to choosing the people I let into my life."

So am I. Usually. Tori's my exception.

I welcomed her into my life with relative ease, never questioning her motives. And there was no reason to, given how she initially resisted being with me. But if Tori were presented with an opportunity to trade on our relationship, would she?

Now that I've thought about it, I'm finding it difficult to think of anything else. Because if Tori betrayed me in that way, I'm not sure I'd recover. *Trust her, Carter. She hasn't given you any reason not to. Besides, what other option do you have?*

I'm AT THE airport when Julian calls me.

"Good news," he says without preamble. "The word is, you're still in the running. It's down to three: you, Andy Winn, and Drew Cherry."

My meeting with Styles messed with my confidence, so I'm relieved to hear I remain a contender. "Any other intel?"

"Just that the director, Paulson, is nervous about the reviews for *Hard Times*. Wants to be sure you're still a hot commodity. So I called him and told him about your upcoming appearance on *The Actor's Couch*, and he seemed mollified by that. My advice? Don't hide in your condo. Get out there and be seen. Spend time with your Hollywood counterparts. Banks, Conner, Madlin. Conner's celebrating the opening of his new restaurant and club this Thursday. Dana says she can get you on the guest list."

Ace Conner is an ass, and we don't move in the same circles, but his star is on the rise, so it's not a terrible idea. "Tell Dana to get me that invite. I'll be there."

"Will do. And congrats on making it to the final three."

"Thanks, J."

I make a quick call to Jewel and explain the change in my itinerary. Within minutes, she's got me on the next flight to LA.

I'm not due to board for another hour, so I call Tori. No matter how frustrated I am by our situation, I know she cares, and that knowledge sits in my pocket as a constant reminder that she's worth waiting for.

She picks up after three rings. "Hey. How did it go?"

I hear weights clanking in the background. "It went well. Julian says it's now down to three actors for the lead, and I'm one of them."

"Carter, that's great," she says. "I'm so happy for you, and I'm not at all surprised."

There's a genuineness about her response that soothes my soul. I'm not ashamed to say I want her with me all the time. "Thanks, baby." I hesitate to bring it up, but she needs to know I'll be leaving from New York. "I have to head back to California for a bit. A week probably. I'm just going to leave from here."

"I'll miss you," she says in an uneven voice.

"Listen, there's a thing this Thursday. An event I need to go to. Part of the song and dance to make myself appealing to the *Swan Song* producers. Any chance you'd like to join me?"

The silence lasts several seconds. "Carter, I can't. My pitch to the investors is scheduled for Friday morning. I need to prepare, and I don't think there's any way I'd be able to get back to Philly in time."

"Yeah, no. I get it. Just thought I'd ask. So I'll check in with you when I get home, okay?"

"Okay. Have a safe flight…and enjoy your…thing."

"Thanks."

Patience, Carter. This pitch is important to her. It could open so many doors.

Gwen Styles's observation pops into my brain: "This business makes users out of people who never even set out to harm us."

And no matter how hard I try to, I can't force the thought out of my head.

Chapter Thirty

Tori

I'M NERVOUS ABOUT this pitch.

Friday morning, I quickly shower and get dressed, practicing parts of it as I go. When I arrive at the Center City high-rise where Dreams Inferred LLC occupies an entire floor, I've recited the key points more than twenty times.

I check in with the receptionist, and a short while later, my only contact so far, Gary Evans, greets me with a firm handshake.

"It's a pleasure to meet you, Ms. Alvarez," he says as we walk down a narrow hall whose walls are decorated with photographs of iconic people and places related to Philadelphia. *City Hall. Benjamin Franklin. The Liberty Bell. Rocky Balboa with his fists in the air at the top of the steps of the art museum.*

Mr. Evans opens the door to a room and ushers me in. He then motions for me to sit across from him at the conference room table. I place my purse in the chair beside me and settle my hands over the manila folder protecting the pages of my pitch.

"Ms. Alvarez, my partners and I have reviewed your package, and we're impressed. The concept behind your fitness plan is simple and accessible. Many Americans don't have access to a gym, and another subset of your target population travels extensively. The concept of using only your body to attain fitness isn't new, but no one's presented it in this way as far as we know, and we're impressed with your research on differently abled individuals."

Wait. Why is he pitching my program for me? I drop my hands to my lap. Let the hand-wringing begin.

"We have a few concerns with the proposed program, however."

Ah. The good ole compliment sandwich. I should have known a *but* was coming. "I'm happy to address them if I can."

He straightens in his chair, adopting an authoritative stance. "First, we don't see much scaling potential. Your proposal only mentioned two locations in Philadelphia. If the program succeeds, what opportunities do you see for additional revenue? What are the synergies?"

I open my folder, pull out the relevant pages of my proposal, and hand him a summary page. He retrieves a pair of reading glasses from his suit pocket and puts them on. "Go on, Ms. Alvarez."

"As you'll see, I envision You Are What You Move as a fitness movement of sorts," I continue. "It's taking the simple idea that physical activity using your own body as resistance can be more effective than expensive gym memberships or personal exercise equipment."

His eyes flash with a hint of annoyance. "Right. The concept isn't the problem. Talk to me about execution."

"Okay, I'd like to build an online community that will also be an attractive demographic for advertisers. Although gyms and exercise retailers aren't targets, other manufacturers would jump at the chance to reach this community. Think exercise apparel, including You Are What You Move apparel, exercise mats, water bottles, and so on. Also, the program relies on my personal training experience and education. Other personal trainers could design programs for clients based on the concept. Groups of differently abled people working out together in the outdoors, for example. No exercise studio needed."

"So one could become a certified trainer?"

"Yes, like Zumba."

"Then you'll need a catchier name."

I don't want to smile at that, but I do anyway. "I'm sure I could come up with something better."

Mr. Evans nods. "I think we'd like to see that fleshed out a bit more."

"Sure. I can revise the proposal to include data on this aspect of the program. What are your other concerns?"

Mr. Evan leans forward and considers what he's about to say.

Just spit it out. *Please.*

"As you said, the program relies on your education and experience as a personal trainer. But you don't have extensive business experience. You've managed a gym for three years, but you're not bringing any ownership experience to the table."

My hands are sweating now. "I do have a minor in business administration."

"That's education, not experience. We're interested in how you'll run this company. What support you'll have. We're angel investors, Ms. Alvarez, and although we're not investing our life savings, that doesn't mean we're not looking for the typical indicia of a good risk."

"I intend to use some of the money from your investment to hire a business consultant who'll assist me with starting the company."

Mr. Evans doesn't respond to this. Instead, he rolls his chair back and rises. "And finally, how do you intend to draw people to your doors? Showing a physically fit personal trainer demonstrate exercises using her own body weight isn't as effective as using the real people who've used the program. You need testimonials. Before-and-after pictures. People need visuals. They want to be convinced that achieving their goals is possible."

He's pacing, and my stomach's churning. I'm losing him. Where the hell's the compliment in this sandwich? So far, it's been bad, bad, and more bad. I could solicit people to sign up for a beta program. But I need to keep the investors' interest in the meantime.

He pulls out his chair and takes a seat. "Ms. Alvarez," he says as he straightens his cuffs. "I think my partners and I would be willing to overlook certain risks associated with investing in your program if you had a secret weapon."

I stare at him with what I'm sure is a blank look, because I have no idea where he's going with this.

"Suppose you were able to secure a celebrity endorsement, for example. That might be of particular interest to us." He pulls his phone out of his pocket, swipes left, and glances at the screen. "Do you know anyone you could convince to vouch for the program?"

His question hits me upside the head like a sledgehammer. It all makes sense now. I'm here because of my relationship with Carter, not my proposal. Dreams Inferred LLC didn't have an "unexpected opening" in its potential portfolio of investments. No, the investors somehow learned of my connection to Carter and suddenly "rediscovered" their interest in my venture.

But even if I were willing to trade on my relationship with Carter—and I'm not, of course—the truth is that he wouldn't be able to vouch for the program. His training and my proposed program are two different animals.

"Mr. Evans—"

"Call me Gary."

"Gary, although the idea of securing a celebrity endorsement is a good one, Carter Stone isn't a viable option. He hasn't followed the program, and in fact someone like Stone actually wouldn't be on brand. We're trying to reach John Q. Public here."

"You could always put him through the program or fudge the details to make it appear as if he completed it.

The key point is that you've worked with him. It's a golden opportunity for you, isn't it? Given his recent weight loss, if he transforms his physique, he'll be the 'it' guy in Hollywood, at least when it comes to hot bodies."

Did he just use the term *hot bodies*? I think I just threw up a little in my mouth.

This must be what Carter experiences on an almost daily basis: people wanting a piece of him, people assuming they're *entitled* to a piece of him. I'm angry on his behalf. But Carter accepts it and presses on, because he loves acting, and he's willing to take the bad with the good. And I'm sure for him, the good outweighs the bad.

Oh.

Oh, damn.

It pains me to be this dense.

If I really want to be with Carter, shouldn't I, too, be willing to take the bad with the good? And doesn't the good, in fact, outweigh the bad?

Yes, and yes.

And if I had to choose between dealing with the intrusion upon my life that follows from being with Carter or not being with Carter at all, which choice would I make? The answer is a no-brainer.

So what the hell am I doing here?

"Mr. Evans, am I right in assuming the group isn't interested in my proposal unless I can secure an endorsement from someone like Carter Stone?"

Mr. Evans blanches, but he recovers within seconds and gives me a curt nod. "You're correct, Ms. Alvarez."

I stand and offer him my hand, which he takes reluctantly.

"Then I think we're done," I say in a clear and steady voice. "Thank you for your time."

Keep it moving, Tori. This is a minor setback. I'll find another way to open the studio.

For now, though, I'm going to visit my man.

AFTER A FORTY-MINUTE taxi ride, I arrive in Carter's West Hollywood neighborhood. The driver takes a wrong turn onto a dead-end street and swings around until he finds Carter's home, which is situated on a surprisingly quiet cul-de-sac. The exterior is midcentury modern, its first level a wall of white with a gray front door. Windows span the second level, suggesting that the house has a spectacular view. The landscaping is minimal, but I spy two palm trees flanking the end of the cobblestoned walkway, and their presence makes me smile.

The driver whistles. "Who lives there? Someone famous?"

"Not sure. I'm just a dog walker."

A dog walker who flies from out of town and brings a suitcase with her? Ugh, Tori, your subterfuge skills are weak.

I ring the doorbell, and the sound of padded feet tells me this trip wasn't futile. After adjusting the straps of my oversized purse, I lick my lips and smile.

The woman who opens the door scans me from head to toe and returns her gaze to the carry-on at my side. She's young and pretty, with dark brown hair and golden-brown eyes, and she's not unlike the women I've seen on Carter's arms in gossip magazines. I don't know what to think. But I don't jump to conclusions. Yet.

She places her hands in the air in surrender and grins. "I'm his sister, I swear. And you must be Tori-not-short-for-Victoria."

I like her immediately. "You're Ashley?"

She nods and swings the door open. "The one and only. I'm crashing. You planning the same?"

"Yeah," I say, pointing to my travel gear. "A weekend visit...but I guess I should have cleared this with him first."

"I wouldn't worry about it. If anything, he'll kick me out. Come on in. It's so great to meet you." Ashley picks up the newspaper outside the door before she closes it, and then I follow her past the foyer into the living area.

"Great to meet you, too." I pull my luggage up one step, walk through the short foyer, and scan the living area. "Wow, this is gorgeous."

It's a study in light and space with floor-to-ceiling windows, vaulted ceilings, and hardwood floors. And sculptures. Lots and lots of sculptures. Which is the only clue I need to confidently conclude an interior decorator furnished Carter's place.

I glimpse Ashley's bare feet and toe off my sandals before I go any farther into the room.

"Yeah, the views are amazing," she says. "Do you want a tour? I'm not sure when Carter will be back."

"That would be great. Could I, uh...use the restroom first?"

Her eyes widen. "Yes, I'm so sorry. You must be exhausted. The powder room's down this hall to the left. Would you like something to drink?"

"Water would be great."

I drop my purse on a kitchen stool and walk down the hall.

I'm not sure why one would need a double vanity in the powder room, but I'm not complaining. I trail a finger against the marble counter, admiring the intricate tile backsplash surrounding the massive mirror. It's the kind of mirror that reveals every imperfection, and I stick my tongue out at myself because I will not let this soul sucker kill my joy.

When I return to the living area, Ashley hands me a glass of water.

"Would you like me to get him back here somehow?" she says with mischief in her eyes.

I swallow and shake my head. "No, no. I don't want him to change his plans for me. If it's okay, I'll just hang out here until he gets back."

"Sure. Let's get you that tour, then."

We both freeze, however, when the lock on the front door clicks and Carter walks in. He has his phone to his ear, and his mouth is set in a scowl. The moment he sees me, he smiles and his eyes brighten. How I wish we were alone so I could have my way with him.

He ends the call and places his phone on the kitchen counter. "I thought you weren't able to come this weekend."

"I left as soon as I could. It didn't feel right to be away from you."

He lowers his eyelids to half-mast. "I'm glad you're here." His voice deepens a notch. "*Really* glad."

Oh. Whatever he's communicating, I'm here for it. Because I'm certain it involves a bed and a mind-numbing orgasm—maybe even two or three. "I'm glad I'm here, too."

Ashley waves her hands between us like an NFL referee. "Oh my God, you two. I'm right here. Get. A. Room."

Carter and I laugh.

"Sorry, Ashley," I say. "We're in the easily-carried-away stage."

"Don't worry about it. It's just…he's my older brother." She covers her eyes. "I can't look." She scurries away. Seconds later, a door clicks shut.

"Come here, you," he says as he tugs me close. I fall into his arms easily and snuggle against his chest. I breathe him in, his familiar scent clean and crisp, like a towel that's been air-dried near the beach. I place my hands at his waist and drag my hands over him, my fingers traveling over the dips and swells of his powerful back. Someone's been keeping up with his exercise plan.

He threads his hand under my hair, drawing my head back, and plants an openmouthed kiss on my neck. With his mouth still pressed against my skin, he bends and lifts me by my ass so that I have no choice but to wrap my legs around his waist. Okay, I have a choice, but I choose to do this. In truth, I want to climb him and rub myself against every inch of his body until we're fused together for the next hour.

"Oh shit, you guys. Wait until I leave at least."

I scramble off Carter, and we spring apart like two teenagers caught necking in the back of a car. Ashley gathers items in the living area, avoiding eye contact with us as she does. She slings her purse over her shoulder. "I'm out. Julian took pity on me and is letting me crash there. Says he won't be home anyway."

Carter swipes his hand down his face. "Ashley, you don't have to go."

Even I can tell it's a lackluster protest. The man does this for a living. What happened to his acting skills?

She raises her brows. "I assure you, I do. And don't worry about me. I have the rental." To Carter, she says, "I'll check in with you before I leave." Then she waves at us from the door. "Have fun, kids."

The front door closes, and Carter again lifts me off the ground. "I missed you."

I thread my hands around his neck and hang on for the ride down a long hall to his bedroom. "I missed you, too."

"I have an idea," he says in between kisses to my neck and jaw.

"Tell me," I say as I squirm against him.

"Let's stay in bed for the rest of the weekend."

"You have the best ideas. A think tank would be lucky to have you."

He smiles against my neck, and then he deposits me in the center of his bed. I'm in an unfamiliar place, so I survey the room, just to get my bearings. It's dominated by windows, and his furnishings are sparse. The most significant décor is the sunlight filtering through what I'm sure are ridiculously expensive blinds.

Carter toes off his shoes and unsnaps his jeans. My gaze darts to the sliver of skin above his boxer briefs before it returns to his face. Next, he dispenses with his royal blue T-shirt, pulling it overhead so that I get a first-row seat at an entertaining display of flexing muscles. I want to clap my hands and cheer, because it deserves a standing ovation and an encore. But Carter wants me to play a part in the show, too.

With his unbuttoned jeans still hanging from his hips, he pulls me to the edge of the bed. My feet hit the cold marble floor, and I spread my legs. He drops into the space I've created for him.

"Sit up," he instructs.

Oh, this is different. I was usually the one telling him what to do in the gym. I like being on the receiving end of his bossiness here. He pulls up my top and lifts it over my head, but he doesn't remove it completely, which binds my arms. With a single finger, he pushes me back down and massages my breasts until they pop out of the cups of my bra. "There they are," he says with a smile. He traces my nipples with his index fingers, drawing circles around them, and then he pulls them gently, lengthening them. "So swollen," he whispers.

I rock my hips in response to Carter's ministrations, and my movements draw his gaze to the junction of my thighs. "Let's get these pants off you. I want to see your bare pussy."

With a whimper that shall never be acknowledged again, I raise my hips off the bed. He unzips my pants and tugs them down my body, throwing them behind him and returning to rid me of my panties next. But he doesn't pull them all the way down my legs. Instead he pulls them off my mound and ass and leaves them around my thighs. Then he bends over and breathes me in. "You smell like you want me to fuck you so badly."

I quiver in anticipation, already picturing his cock filling me to the hilt. In the meantime, he's left me a mess: shirt secured around my arms; bra cups resting below my breasts; and panties binding my legs. I want to touch him, but my shirt is constricting me, which is just what he wants. It leaves me vulnerable to his desires, and I like that, too. My position should make me feel helpless, but not for a second do I worry that Carter will take advantage of me. This is just as much for my pleasure as it is his, and the continuous roll of my hips, along with my soft moans, tells him he's succeeding.

"Carter, please," I beg him.

He stands and steps back, admiring his handiwork. "Look at you," he says. "I'm honored."

"And I'm horny," I say after taking a harsh breath.

He unzips his jeans slowly, revealing a hint of pubic hair and the underside of his rigid dick. "Do you want me to take it out?"

"Yes, that's how this usually works."

He curls his hand and then slides it up and down his cock. "I don't think you're ready."

I can't do anything but shift my ass and hips and squeeze my core. The pressure is deliciously frustrating. But I need more. So I lick my lips. "Carter?"

"Yes?"

"I'm warm, wet, and tight, and I'd love you to fuck me into next week."

"I don't think I can trust your assessment of the situation. I should confirm it with my own hands."

He gets on the bed this time and pulls me to my knees. "Let's see, now," he says as he slips a single digit inside. "Oh, that's warm. Very warm. I think we can get you wetter, though."

I collapse against him and cry out. "Yes, please. Do whatever you want."

Carter kisses me and draws my bottom lip into his mouth. "Do you need a second finger?"

"Oh God, yes. Please."

He adds a second finger, and my gut clenches from the dual tension of being pleasured and having limited mobility.

"I can't quite determine how tight you are. Two fingers aren't a reliable guide. How about four? Can you take four?"

"I'll take whatever you give me, damn you."

He fills me with four fingers and twists them. "Oh shit, you *are* tight, Tori."

My wetness coats his fingers as he slips them in and out of me. He groans against my ear, apparently appreciative of the slick heat between my legs. It's not enough, though. My body tightens from the pressure of being on the brink of orgasm, and I desperately need relief. With his fingers inside me, I raise one leg and press my foot onto the bed. That tweak in our positions allows me to ride his fingers as though they're his cock. I use his hand to feed my need to be filled—and his mouth drops open as he stares at the place where my pussy and his fingers meet.

I kiss his chest, obscuring his view. But I don't care, because we need to move this along. "Do you feel that all over your fingers? That could be me pulsing around your cock."

"Fuck," he cries. "I surrender."

He squeezes his eyes closed, groans, and pulls out his dick, fisting it tightly. For a minute, he appears disoriented, and then I realize he's searching for something. He shucks his jeans, crosses the room, and flips open a black case filled with condoms.

"If you release me from all this, I'll put it on for you."

"Nope. You stay right there. You're a devious orgasm extractor, and I have to last."

I snicker at his earnestness as he makes quick work of putting on protection.

Once sheathed, he climbs on top of the bed and releases me from my constraints, tossing my shirt, bra, and panties on his side table.

"Turn around. Ass in the air."

I do so without delay, using my elbows to support my upper body. Carter rubs his cock over my pussy and pushes inside. There's a second of discomfort as I adjust to his size, and then he grinds into me slowly.

"You okay?" he asks.

"Yes, Carter, yes. Don't be sweet. Just fuck me hard. *Please.*"

He caresses my shoulders and gathers my hair in his hands, and then he tugs on my curls as he folds his body over mine. He pulls out, leaving only the broad head of his cock inside, and then he pounds into me, his breath hot and ragged against my ear. "Still okay?"

"Unless I say otherwise, you can assume I'm okay."

My advice pushes him to action. He rises off my back, digs his fingers into my waist, and strokes me wildly. And oh, I don't know what I love more: Carter's groans and moans, or the way he's filling me.

Over and over he sinks into me, his cock creating the friction that makes me teeter on a deliciously precarious edge. I'm *almost there*, and the push and pull between us, the tingling that fuses my nerve endings into a continuum of pleasure, is as satisfying as the climax we're trying to reach.

He releases my waist and massages my back as he pumps. "That's it, Tori. Tighten around me. Let me feel you."

"Like that?"

His answering groan shoots to my achy clit. "Yes. Fuck, yes. Touch yourself, baby. I'm going to come."

I slide my arm under me and rub two fingers against the nub. Round and round in circles I go until my arm shakes from the pressure of it. Carter spreads my ass, achieving a deeper penetration I didn't think was possible, and plunges into me with abandon.

My mouth hangs open as he works me from behind, and it's so intense that I can't do anything but drop my hands to the bed, grasp the sheets, and rock my hips back to meet his thrusts. His hands knead my shoulders, and then he guides my torso lower so that my face and breasts are pressed against the mattress. Holy shit, this position tilts my pelvis just so, and each successive thrust brings me one step closer to a body-numbing orgasm.

When I reach my peak, it crashes into me without warning, and my entire body trembles in response to the waves of pleasure spreading through it. And then a deep groan rumbles from Carter's chest, joining my high-pitched cries, followed by a stream of *fuck*, *shit*, and *that's so good*.

We are loud. And I love it so much.

Carter collapses against me, and we drop to the bed in an inelegant heap.

Still on my stomach, I swallow several times. My throat is parched, and my lips are chapped, but I don't care because that orgasm wrecked me in the best way.

Carter pulls out of me slowly, rolls off the bed, and tosses the condom in the trash. He slides back into the bed and pulls the covers over us, turning me to face him. "It's been a long time since I've seen this pretty face." He takes a section of my hair and twirls it around his fingers.

I nuzzle his neck. "You were focused on my ass."

He pushes me away, and I pull back.

"You're ticklish," I observe, my mouth agape.

He plants a soft kiss on my parted lips. "Am not."

As I contemplate how to uncover the truth, he pins my arms behind my back. "Okay," he says. "I'm ticklish. Please don't use it against me."

I drop my head to his chest. "Never."

He takes a deep breath, his face surrounded by a cloud of my curls. "Hey, Tori."

"Yeah?"

"I'm so glad you're here."

I lift my head and stare into his eyes. There is *nowhere* I'd rather be. "I'm so glad I'm here, too."

THE NEXT MORNING, I wake and discover that I'm alone in Carter's so-big-it-must-be-custom-size bed. Now that I'm not being stroked to oblivion, I can appreciate the view of the Hollywood Hills that spans the entire length of the room. What a stunning view to wake up to.

He's rustling about in the other room, if the banging of pots and pans is any indication. I reach over to check the time on my phone just as it buzzes.

> **Eva:** I just heard. So sorry, sweetie. Did he have an explanation?

I have no idea what she's talking about, but I suppose "he" is Carter since she knew I was traveling to California to visit him this weekend.

I could pretend all is well, but Eva's my best friend, and I want to know what's going on.

Me: I haven't heard anything. What
explanation?

A minute later, my phone buzzes again. Eva has sent another text, this one including a link to a website. I pull up the page and scroll through until I see a picture of Carter with his crotch against a woman's ass in a tightly packed room. His hands are in the air, suggesting that they're dancing, and his head is thrown back, but not far enough that you miss the big ol' smile on his handsome face.

Maybe I'm naïve to think this, but I don't believe Carter did anything other than dance with that woman. In a suggestive way, sure, but I'm not lying here thinking she was in his bed last night. In any case, Carter knows as well as I do that in Hollywood reality is valuable only if it's interesting or scandalous, and if reality is boring, innuendo takes its place.

Still, the caption accompanying the photograph hurts. It reads: "Has Carter Stone found a new love interest? Hmm. This photo suggests the answer is *hell yes*."

Lovely.

Welcome to life with Carter. If we're going to have any chance of a future together, I'll have to deal with situations like this one. And if Carter values his balls, he better give me a good explanation for that photo.

I quickly type a response to Eva.

Me: Thanks for this. It's fine.

Eva: Fine? Not fine. I'll cut his ass too. Just
say the word.

Me: I'm going to give him a chance to explain. Check in with you later.

Carter returns to the bedroom holding a tray of eggs, pastries, and juice. He's also grinning from ear to ear, but as soon as his gaze lands on my face, he sets the tray down on his nightstand.

I prop myself up with a pillow and toss my phone on the mattress, the screen still showing the photograph of Thursday's festivities. "I'm having a hard time looking at that."

His face crumples. The change in him is so swift and complete it's as though I'm watching a sunny day unexpectedly turn into a stormy one.

"It's a photo of a single moment," he says. "That was a sneak attack on my crotch, I swear. I told you about the event, remember? The point of going was to show that I'm not drowning in the sea of bad reviews for *Hard Times*. I *knew* there would be paparazzi there. We were *just* dancing, and yeah, she got a little frisky with it."

I trust him, and I don't think he's deceiving me now. More than that, he's right that I knew about the event. In fact, if it weren't for my meeting with the investors, that might have been my ass on his crotch in the photo. "I believe you."

The tension around his eyes fades, and he dons a hesitant smile. "Thank you."

"Eva's going to kick your ass, though."

"Shit. I'm sorry about this. All of it." He points to my phone. "You'll explain this to her?"

"Yeah. I'll get you off the hook."

"And maybe next time, you'll be the woman in the photo?"

Great minds. "Yeah, I'm ready to try."

He blows out a breath, and his answering smile lights me up inside.

I pat the bed. "Now come here and feed your woman."

He sets the breakfast tray on the bed and sits next to me, his back pressed against the headboard. After planting kisses on my cheek and forehead, he nibbles on my neck, and I use my chin to shoo him away. Then he pulls the tray closer to us, so we can both enjoy the food.

"You made this?" I ask him.

"Don't be too impressed. The pastries are from a bakery a mile away, and the eggs are probably runny."

"I'll stick with the muffin, then, thanks."

"Ingrate," he teases.

"I'm grateful. Just protective of my digestive health."

"Tell me about the meeting with the investors," Carter asks between chews of his whole-grain bagel. "Was it really a dumpster fire?"

I snort when I remember the text I sent Carter after I'd walked out.

Tori: Meeting over. Total dumpster fire. Guy was a *pendejo*. Will explain later.

I take a sip of my orange juice before answering. "It *was*. We were never going to be a match, and although I'm bummed that I lost a prospect, I'd rather find the right partner than get stuck with the wrong one. The guy didn't understand key aspects of my proposal and said some crappy stuff about my lack of experience." Laughing off Evans's rudeness, I mimic his gruff tone. "Ms. Alvarez, you have three years of management experience but you know *nada* about running your own studio."

Carter chuckles, his eyes gleaming with mischief. "Yeah, I could tell immediately Evans was an ass."

I rush to pick up a slice of apple, but then my hand hovers over the plate, my laughter petering out like a stalled engine as Carter's comment sinks into my psyche.

I could tell immediately Evans was an ass.

A ton of bricks lands on my chest, making it difficult to breath. I've never mentioned Evans by name, so how does Carter know he's an ass? "You could?" I say in a strangled voice. Somehow, I manage not to wince at the sound of it, the evidence of my own gullibility in high-definition audio. "How the hell is that possible, Carter?"

His grin collapses, and his face turns ashen. "I talked to him…but I can explain."

Why would Carter meddle in my affairs? It makes no sense. "What possible reason could you have had to speak with him?"

He jumps up from the bed and runs a hand through his hair, but he's not meeting my gaze. Instead, he paces the room and stares at the walls as though the answers to his troubles can be found in them.

Screw this. I jump up from the bed and wrap the sheet around me.

"Tori, don't," he says. "Give me a minute."

Ignoring him, I scramble around the room picking up my discarded clothes. I can't find my damn jeans. Turning away from him, I hastily throw on my top and underwear, my heart racing as though the finish line is outside my chest. No more than five feet separate us, but we're miles apart in understanding each other. I stand there, pantsless, and put my hands on my hips. "Your minute is up."

Chapter Thirty-One

Carter

I CAN'T GIVE her an excuse because I don't have one.

Earlier, when I walked into my house and saw Tori in my living room, I felt like I'd climbed a mountain and reached the summit. She was here. She'd come on her own. She was willing to try to make our relationship work. I'd planned to take her for a ride up Mulholland Drive, where we'd eventually head to my secret spot near the overlook and I'd tell her I love her.

My own stupidity pushed me off the mountain, and now I'm free-falling. All I can do now is tell her the truth. "I contacted Evans yesterday."

"Why?" she says. "Were you trying to influence my pitch?"

The confusion in her voice guts me. I shake my head, realizing only at this moment how she could have made that assumption. "No, just the opposite. I called him *after* I got your text. I knew it hadn't gone well, so I didn't think I'd be influencing it in any way."

She shakes her head as she speaks. "But just because *I* thought it was a crappy interview doesn't mean they thought it was, too. You hadn't even talked to me. So you *could* have influenced the outcome."

Fuck. She's right. This is a mess. "Yeah. I'm not trying to excuse what I did."

She throws up her hands. "What *did* you do, Carter?"

"I asked him if you'd mentioned me. If you'd used my name to promote your pitch. I just…I needed to know."

Now that I've said that out loud, the idiocy of my thought process mocks the fuck out of me. I know in my heart that Tori wouldn't have betrayed me like that, but I let my own insecurities guide my actions. I convinced myself a quick call would confirm that my trust in Tori was well placed. That a person in my position couldn't be too careful and there'd be no harm. I was wrong.

She stares at me, unblinking, her lips parted in an O. Then she drops her chin and studies the floor. She's disappointed in me, and that's the worst part. "You were checking to see if I was using you."

She's not asking. She's telling.

"Yes. It was a stupid thing to do. In here"—I pound on my chest—"I know you'd never do that, but I let my head get in the way. I'm sorry. I'm so fucking sorry."

She straightens and looks around the room. Then she drops on her hands and knees and drags her white jeans from under my bed. "I don't understand any of this," she says as she struggles into her pants. "Did Evans tell you I nearly bitch-slapped him for trying to get to you through me?"

"He didn't describe it that way, but yes, that was the impression he gave me. I—"

She lets out a heavy sigh. "You asked me to trust you, and I did. I even held it together when I saw the photo of you with that woman. Because you'd earned my trust. Now I realize I haven't even earned yours."

I stride to her and place my hands on her shoulders. "You have my trust, Tori. It was a momentary lapse. Please forgive me."

Her eyes are cold, and her mouth is pressed into a thin line. She shakes my arms off her. "You had one pass, remember? I have none left to give you."

She's shutting down on me, trying to put me in her past. "I know what you're doing, Tori. You're pulling away. What's your go-to phrase again?"

She tilts her chin up and looks at me defiantly. "*Siempre pa'lante, nunca pa'tras*. It's fitting for this situation."

"I'm not a *situation*, Tori. I'm your boyfriend, and I want to be with you, and I want to make this right. Tell me how to do that."

She says nothing for what seems like an eternity. When she finally speaks, her voice is calm, eerily so. "This was always going to be a bit of a gamble, you know. My fear of being in the public eye guaranteed that. And I thought I could meet you halfway, at least try to work through this because I thought you were worth it. But if we don't have trust, Carter, none of this works."

"We *do* have trust, Tori. Please don't take this instance of stupidity and make it the poster child for our relationship. It's not."

"Carter, you're not getting it. For weeks, I've been operating as if I'm the reason our relationship can't move forward, but I'm not the only one who needs to work through some issues. I know people have used you before, but I don't think you even realize how much it's affected you. You don't believe in yourself, in your own abilities, in the qualities that make you special. You're on this quest to be taken seriously as an actor because you don't think you're enough. You assume everyone's out to take advantage of you because you can't possibly imagine that people could want you for anything other than your fame. I didn't fall in love with Carter Stone. I fell in love with Carter Williamson. But as long as Stone is running the show, you're bound to make choices I can't live with."

She's so right I don't know what to say. Too many people have fucked with my head—Simon Cage, ex-girlfriends, the paparazzi, the freaking doctor—and I've been on the lookout for the next person who's going to hurt me. But I want to work through this. *With her. For her. For us, dammit.* "Help me make the right choices, Tori."

"These aren't my choices to make," she chokes out. "I've done *nothing* to warrant your distrust, yet here we are."

"So what? You just move on?"

"I don't know. I need time."

She means time apart. But I know this is just a stopgap measure for her. She'll run back to Philadelphia and stuff me in the closet of boyfriends past. She honestly believes that's the right way to go, just as much as I honestly believe it's not. "Fine. But while you're figuring things out, think about this. That phrase you love so much is bullshit."

She narrows her eyes and flares her nostrils.

Yeah, get mad, Tori. If it takes getting her angry, then so be it. I pace the room as I speak, unable to remain still as I fight for us. "Listen, part of moving forward is embracing your past, not ignoring it. Part of life is working through your problems, not searching for a problem-free existence. Think about you and your family. You can't talk to them about your fears, and it's killing you. You think you've moved on from that? You haven't. The whole You Are What You Move concept is practically an homage to your father."

She's been following me with a wary gaze. Now her eyes widen and her breath hitches.

Because she knows I'm right. Hell, *I* know I'm right regardless of what she thinks. "You can't help him, so you're helping others like him," I continue. "But you're never going to be truly happy unless you work through that issue with your family."

She folds her arms over her chest. "You're right. Which means we both have issues to get through. We should take the time to do that."

Fuck. In her head, she's already gone, and I can't do this alone. My chest deflates, and I sigh heavily. Then I scoop up my T-shirt off the floor and slip it on. "I'm going to head out and give you space. Let me know if you need a ride somewhere."

As I'm walking out the door, she whispers, "I'll be fine."

Great. That makes one of us.

Chapter Thirty-Two

Tori

AFTER THE FRONT door slams shut, I flop onto the bed and groan. Somehow, I pull myself out of the dark abyss and gather my toiletries.

Minutes later, the doorbell rings, and I freeze. I'm not even sure I should answer it, but whoever is out there is resting a finger on the doorbell and isn't going away.

I stomp to the door and peek through the side window. An impeccably dressed black man with the longest eyelashes I've ever seen is standing outside. Now he's resting his hands in the pockets of his pants, his expression pinched and impatient.

I crack open the door. "Yes?"

He smiles, and his dimples appear to say hello as well. "You must be Tori."

"Are you Julian?"

"I am. Is Carter here?"

"He's not, and I don't know when he'll be back." I open the door wider. "Would you like to come in?"

The corner of his mouth quirks up. "Sure. But I do have a key."

My face warms. Of course he does.

Julian enters Carter's home like he's been here a million times before. I laugh to myself, because he probably has. He drops an envelope on the sofa table and sits in one of the accent chairs across from the couch.

I stand by the sofa table, unsure what to do. "We had a fight," I blurt out.

Julian's eyes widen, and then he grimaces. "If Carter were any other client, I'd pretend I didn't hear that and point out the great weather we're having. But he's my best friend, too, so I'm here to listen if you think that would be helpful."

I take a seat across from him. "He doesn't trust me."

He nods. "There are very few people who fall into that camp for Carter."

"Yes, I can see why. But I thought I was among them. In that camp. And then he did something that revealed I wasn't. I'm not sure I can get past it."

Julian fiddles with his tie. "Guys like Carter are naturally magnetic. He's a nice guy who does stupid shit sometimes."

"You sound like him."

"I prefer to think he sounds like me."

My mouth twitches. "Fair enough."

Julian studies the view from the living room window. "I'm not sure it's my place, but I'll give you my advice anyway. It's easy to get drawn into Carter's circle. But after a while your life might revolve around him, and that's not healthy. He's a bit of a lost soul himself, so it's not wise to lose yourself in him. He won't grow if you don't challenge him."

"Sounds like you're speaking from experience."

Julian turns his head, and his eyes bore into mine. "I am. And I'll be the first to admit I don't always get my own advice right."

"How long have you known him?"

"Since we were kids. We've been best friends for over fifteen years."

"How'd you end up being his agent?"

He shakes his head. "You ask a lot of questions."

I shrug. "I'm an inquisitive person."

Julian returns his gaze to the scene outside. "My parents were entrepreneurs, so I grew up in a household that valued business acumen. An MBA seemed to make sense. When I graduated, I thought I'd head to New York for a few years, work for a consulting firm or something, and then join my father's company when I was ready. Around that time, Carter found out his then agent was skimming him, taking more than the customary commission and underreporting the pay he was getting for jobs. He asked me to look at his books, his contracts, everything. It snowballed from there. Before I knew it, I was interning at a talent agency in California."

Julian's professional and authoritative, "together" in a way that inspires confidence. Carter's lucky to have him in his corner. But as Julian alluded to moments ago, there's an undercurrent of discontent between them that worries me. Julian's life revolves around Carter—and I suspect he's not happy about it.

"What happened to his former agent?"

Julian grinds his jaw before answering. "Simon Cage is a sleazy piece of work, and I wish Carter would let me do something about him. When Carter accused him of stealing, he ripped Carter a new one, told him he was and always would be a B actor and he didn't need this shit from him. Started badmouthing Carter with casting directors. It's the reason Carter's been more successful in television, it's a different community."

He leans forward and glances at his phone. "He's not responding to my texts. I'm going to let him be. Work beckons."

"On a Saturday?"

"Every day is a workday." Julian rises, and we walk together to the door. "It's great to meet you, Tori. I hope we'll see each other again."

I can tell from his tone it's as much a question as it is a statement. "Maybe."

Before he opens the door, he turns back to me. "Don't misunderstand anything I've said. I owe Carter a lot. If it weren't for him, I'd still be a junior agent somewhere, fetching coffee and copying contracts. But you've got to carve out your own space, otherwise you'll get sucked into his world and have no space of your own."

There's no concern there. I'm not getting sucked into Carter's world. I'm returning to mine.

RETURNING TO MY world isn't easy. Even less so now that Carter's not around. I'd planned to bring him to my father's birthday party this week, but instead I'll be going alone.

The party is no small deal. Each year, my mother closes Mi Casita during a weekday on or close to my father's birthday—Saturdays are moneymakers and can't be spared. She throws a serious bash with a live band whose members are my father's good friends.

My job is to bring alcohol. In my family, a standard liquor order consists of lots of rum and two cases of Budweiser. If you've been tasked with supplying drinks and forget either of those items, you might as well turn around and not show up.

Because I refuse to lug a case of beer when I'm wearing a dress, I bring the alcohol to the restaurant Wednesday morning, figuring I'll return to the apartment after work and change before the party starts. Holding a case of beer against my stomach, I kick the door to get someone's attention.

I peer inside and see my mother and sister at a table, a mountain of green plantains resting between them.

Bianca rises, unlocks the door, and holds it open for me. "Just one case?"

"No, just two hands. The other case is in the trunk." I give her a saccharine-sweet smile. "Good morning, Bianca."

"Good morning, Tori," she says in a singsong voice that sounds remarkably like "Fuck you, Tori."

Surprise, surprise.

I set the case on the counter. *"Hola, Mami."*

She smiles and continues to score the green plantain in her hand. *"Hola, mijita."*

After bringing in the remaining liquor, I rinse my hands in the sink behind the counter. "What are you making? *Mofongo?*"

My mother glances at me. "Your father's favorite."

It's my favorite, too. What's not to love about fried green plantains mashed with garlic and pork cracklings? "Can I help?"

As usual, Bianca rejects my offer. "It's okay, we've got a good system going."

Translation: *We don't need or want your assistance.*

I'd usually throw up my hands and leave, but I can practically feel Carter pushing me in their direction. I purse my lips and blow out my breath softly. "Actually, I don't have anything else to do this morning, so I'll peel."

Bianca purses her lips but doesn't object. I suspect that if my mother weren't here, though, she'd kick me out the door.

I settle into my seat and grab a plantain and a knife. Just as Abuela taught me, I score the plantain along the seams, making sure not to cut too deep, and then I cut off the heads and tails before carefully peeling back the skin.

My mother and sister stop what they're doing and watch my handiwork, perplexed expressions on both of their faces.

I scan the table behind them, which is filled with ingredients for various dishes. "Where's the salt water?"

Bianca rises. "It's in the back. I'll get it."

"*¿Quién te enseñó cómo hacerlo?*" my mother asks.

"Abuela Clara taught me how."

When I was a teenager, Abuela moved from the house she'd once shared with my grandfather in Carolina, Puerto Rico, to a small bedroom in my parents' home above Mi Casita. The transition did not go well. She missed her backyard, where she'd raised chickens and tended to a small garden. She resented not having her own kitchen in which to cook her meals and stuck her tongue out behind my mother's back when Mami tried to clean up after her the few times Abuela cooked in her presence. Most of all, she hated the noise, whether it was an ambulance siren or the steady thumping of a bass beat from a car driving past our building.

But for the few years she stayed with us before she died, Abuela and I spent many afternoons together while my mother and Bianca worked in the restaurant. This was when she'd sneak in our kitchen and cook, and I'd help, cutting vegetables, sifting and rinsing rice, and peeling potatoes.

If Abuela were alive, I'd be in the kitchen with her today, pounding out my frustrations on whatever root vegetable she needed for the dish she was making. I'd tell her about Carter and the mess we've made of our relationship. I'd tell her that I have no idea how to turn my dreams for my career into a reality and that I'm nervous about my future.

"Is that what you two were always doing up there?" my mother asks.

I smile and nod. "Yes. And watching *Wheel of Fortune*. I was responsible for returning the kitchen to its original state."

"I thought so. You were always so heavy-handed with the air freshener."

Bianca returns with a pot of salt water.

After slicing the plantain in one-inch pieces, I use my knife to slide the chunks from the cutting board to the pot, and then I pick up another plantain, ready to score and peel. Holding my knife in midair, I take a deep breath before I speak. "We should do this more often."

"We didn't think you'd want to be bothered," Bianca says. "You're never around anymore. And then you drop by and expect us to be thankful for your presence. What's it like having a life outside this restaurant? I'd love to know, Tori. What's it like to go to college? Please, educate me."

My mother grasps Bianca's forearm. "*Mija*, you don't want to work at the restaurant?"

Oh, wow. She's the self-professed princess of Mi Casita. I never imagined she resented that position.

Bianca bows her head and slumps her shoulders. "I do. It's just…No one ever asked me what I wanted. The responsibility just fell to me. And then I kick my ass working here, and my little sister comes back from college with her fancy fitness degree and criticizes our food. This is our *culture*, Tori. I'm sorry if you think it's incompatible with your"—she makes air quotes—"healthy lifestyle."

"I'm not criticizing our culture. I love this food as much as you do. I just want us to be able to talk about Papi's health without everyone shutting down or thinking that I'm looking down on them. Can we all agree that Papi shouldn't be having fried foods all the time?"

"*Sí,*" my mother says. "Of course."

"Yes," Bianca says in a low voice.

"Abuela talked about our food all the time. Even little things, like how she used to share her best mangoes with the family next door. How to pick the perfect one. There are so many wonderful ingredients we can use. I just think maybe we could expand the menu, so Papi can enjoy more of the foods he loves. Abuela had so many recipes she passed on to us. *Pescado y chayote.*"

"*Asopao* as the main meal," Bianca adds.

"I know them all," my mother says as she stares wistfully at the bowl of plantains in front of her.

I reach over and link my pinky finger with hers, a move that's a throwback to my youth. "Maybe I could help you write them down—for me and Bianca. Maybe share them online?"

"Oh, I don't know about that, *mija,*" my mother says. "Those are our family recipes."

"Yes," my sister says. "But I suppose there's nothing wrong with sharing them with others."

"And we could also be creative ourselves," I add. "I think it would be fun to come up with new ways to prepare dishes. Experiment more with boiling *yuca* or baking *empanadillas*, you know? Give Papi a few different options."

"I never imagined you'd want to do any of this," my mother says. "But I'm very glad you do."

Bianca nods.

"This is important to you and to our family." I gesture around us. "I want to be a part of this. And if I question something about the food, please know I'm doing it because I care, not because I want to criticize. Okay?"

They both nod at me, and the cloud that usually hovers above me when I visit Mi Casita breaks. "Next, I'll work on getting Papi to take my class."

Bianca shakes her head. "You're asking for a miracle there. Good luck with that."

My father walks in at that exact moment, and we all laugh hysterically at the table.

"What?" my father says. "Have you been talking about me behind my back again?"

We exchange knowing looks, and then my mother rises from her chair and pulls my father toward the kitchen. *"Vamos a comer frutas,"* she says to my father.

"Fruit?" he asks. Then he turns back to me with a smile. "This is your fault, isn't it?"

Bianca and I laugh together at the table. Then we each return to scoring plantains, until she clears her throat.

After blowing out a long breath, she says, "I know I haven't always been the easiest sister to have, and I can't promise we'll ever be the best of friends, but I'd like to try to get us back on good terms. Okay?"

"It goes both ways, you know. And I'd like to try, too."

We give each other tentative smiles. Then she tips her head to the side and studies me.

"What?" I ask.

"Um, I saw the picture of you and Carter Stone in that online magazine, the photo that was taken right outside."

My gaze darts to the ceiling and back, and then I set down my knife. "Yeah, I saw it, too. The paparazzo didn't even throw us a bone and include Mi Casita's signage."

Bianca rolls her eyes. "I don't care about that, and I know you don't care about that, either. But I saw something that I thought was interesting."

"What?"

"Did Abuela ever tell you her theory about how to tell if someone cares about you?"

I place my hand on my chest and nod. "Yes, yes. You'll always know if someone cares, because you'll see it in their eyes, right?"

"Right," Bianca says. "I couldn't see perfectly, because it wasn't a great angle, but I'm pretty sure the way Carter was looking at you in that photo comes close to what Abuela was talking about."

The man has my sister on his side. That's...scary. But I must admit she's right. Even when he doubted me, he cared. Nothing he did undermines my belief in that fundamental truth. Carter's not perfect, and neither am I. But we care for each other—deeply. Now I just need to figure out how to make my way back to him.

Chapter Thirty-Three

Carter

JULIAN ARRANGED FOR my appearance on *The Actor's Couch* after I'd landed the role in *Hard Times*. He leveraged the film credit to convince the show's producers that I was on the brink of hitting A-lister status. It's been a few days since Tori left LA, and I've heard nothing from her in that time. I'm not in the right headspace to field questions about my personal life, but withdrawing now would be unprofessional, and I don't need any additional hits to my reputation. My one consolation: The show isn't filmed before a live audience.

As I walk onto the set, the poor reviews for the film hover over me like a rain cloud. The producers of *Swan Song* will see this interview. If there's any possibility they'd still cast me as the lead, this is my shot to show them I'm still the budding heartthrob they think

I am. I'll have to project confidence in my work and assure anyone who's watching that *Hard Times* was an anomaly.

The set literally consists of a couch for the guest and a club chair for the host. It's a comfortable couch, at least.

The host, Elaine Daubert, and I exchange pleasantries, and then she gives me a brief rundown of what to expect during the interview. "Our most popular interviews are ones in which the actor looks relaxed. If it's scripted, the audience will pick up on it, even if your acting skills are extraordinary."

She's probably given this speech countless times and knows it by rote. "Sure, sure." I settle into the couch as a sign of my good intentions. "I'll do my best."

The cameras roll, and Elaine introduces me to the TV audience. "Our featured actor on the couch this evening is Carter Stone, a man who's made many ladies swoon with his roles on two popular sitcoms, *My Life in Shambles* and *Man on Third*."

As expected, Elaine asks me about my roles in those shows and tries to share a few spoilers about the upcoming seasons. Here is where I generally thrive.

Seven minutes or so in, Elaine shifts her body a few inches away from me. The move is so subtle the audience probably won't notice it. "So, Carter, let's talk about your first foray into film."

Ah, so that's what that shift was about. She's going to broach a topic she knows I'll be unhappy about. It's not a surprise. After all, this wouldn't be entertaining without some conflict.

"*Hard Times* is different from anything you've ever done before. What was it like working with Hollywood legends Maggie Boyd and Dennis Satch?"

"I was in awe of them. Intimidated, too. I mean, these are the folks you aspire to be as an actor. Counterparts of Nicholson, Streep, and so on. And they were so gracious, sharing their expertise. There's a scene in the movie when Dennis Satch's character grabs my character, Chris, by his collar and is screaming in his face. And to be honest, at that moment, I was thinking, *How is this my life?*"

Elaine laughs, but then her face turns sober. "The early reviews are in…"

I nod. "They are."

"They're calling it 'bad.'"

I pound my fist against my chest as though I'm being stabbed in the heart. "It hurts," I say with a laugh.

"Why not take the skill set you've mastered and start with a romantic comedy? Wouldn't that have been a wise career move?"

The wise career move would be to say that my acting skills aren't limited to romantic comedies and move on to the next topic. But I'm tired of pretending, tired of making decisions to shield myself from criticism. Tired of being ruled by what others think of me. Sometimes the best approach is to speak from the heart and see where it takes you.

"I suppose starting with a romantic comedy would have been a sound career move, but my decision to take on *Hard Times* was about more than getting a film deal. Look, I've been in this business a long time. I grew into a man on-screen. I don't know who I am without acting. And for me that was always okay, because I loved what I was doing. But after years of playing the same kind of character, I need more. I need to stretch myself. Being the cute guy or the funny guy just isn't enough."

"And *Hard Times* is the kind of role you were looking for," she offers.

"Exactly. I'll be honest, I'm worried as hell. I'm worried that the career I've given my life to isn't enough to sustain me, and even worse, I'm worried that I'm not good enough to stretch myself in the way that will make me happy. If it turns out I'm not suited to dramas, I'll do something else. But I think it's too early to make any big decisions. One movie will not make or break my career."

"You're entitled to a flop, is what you're saying."

Tori's reaction when I told her about the early reviews of *Hard Times* comes to mind. "Yeah, I'm entitled to one *Gigli*."

Elaine blinks before she breaks out into a smile. "Well, you've just guaranteed you won't be starring in any films with Ben Affleck."

I return her smile. "Probably. But I'm more concerned about closing off any possibility of dating Jennifer Lopez."

Elaine throws her body forward as she cackles. When she recovers, she wiggles her ass into her seat as if to say, *Now comes the juicy part.* "Speaking of dating, is there someone special in your life?"

If self-preservation is the goal, my answer would be simple. I'd make some quip about not having time or say something charming or self-deprecating to deflect attention from the answer I don't want to give. But I just told Elaine about my fears as an actor, and I never would have risked being vulnerable that way if Tori hadn't called me out on my insecurities.

"The truth is, I'm not a great boyfriend. I have a hard time letting people in my life. I'm always wondering about their motives, questioning why they're befriending me. That has everything to do with my own issues about my self-worth. A friend once told me my need for validation leads me to make bad choices."

Elaine's eyebrows disappear under her bangs. "A friend, you say?"

"Yes, a friend, and looking back on some of the things I've done, I can't disagree. I'm not perfect, far from it. Hollywood can convince you otherwise, but we're all struggling with something." I look directly at the camera. "Read my lips, fans. I. Am. Not. A. Catch."

Wide-eyed, Elaine leans back against the couch. "You're blowing me away here."

I chuckle. "I don't mean to. Believe me, I don't think this is going to up my likeability factor at all."

In fact, I need to climb out of this train wreck and talk to Julian. He'll help me figure out how to fix this.

But Elaine's not done with me. "Have you ever been in love? And before you answer, remember that your response might crush a sizeable part of the female population."

Yeah. If Tori were sitting on the couch with me, she'd gag at that one. God, I miss her so much. "I've been a serial dater for most of my adult life, so until six weeks ago, the answer would have been an emphatic no. But

ACTING ON IMPULSE 353

now I can say yes, I've been in love. Still am in love. But I don't deserve her. If I did, she'd be the special person in my life. So. Yeah."

I glance at a glossy-eyed Elaine, whose face is tilted to the side. *Awkward* doesn't even begin to describe how I feel. It's time to wrap this up. "I've said too much."

Elaine squeezes her eyes shut and reopens them. "Not at all. This has been eye-opening. Care to tell us the name of the person who captured your heart?"

"Definitely not."

"And I'd be remiss if I didn't ask you about your weight loss for *Hard Times*. What was that like?"

"Brutal. And it's not something I'd wish on anyone. I consulted a physician to ensure I had enough essential nutrition to avoid a total collapse, and I ran the equivalent of a half marathon every day. I don't ever want to run again."

"You do what you need to do for your craft, right?"

She has no idea how shitty that question makes me feel. Essentially, that's been Tori's point all along—and not in a good way.

"I did what I thought I had to do at the time, but going forward I'm going to be more selective about the things I do for my craft. Acting doesn't define me."

"Are you looking forward to the premiere next week?"

Not really. Not without Tori by my side. "It's my first in a movie I'm in. Should be interesting."

Elaine directs her gaze to the camera. "Well, there you have it, folks. Up close and personal with Carter Stone." She glances at me and stretches her hand out. "It's been a pleasure, Carter."

I shake her hand. "Thanks for having me."

She again turns to the camera to sign off. "Tune in next week for a dose of double trouble. We'll have the husband-and-wife acting and directing team *everyone* in Hollywood would love to work with, Jim and Cassandra Lang. Have a great evening."

A voice from the control room directs the camera crew. "Standby, Camera One, closing wide shot in thirty seconds."

Since I know I'm still on camera, I paste on a carefree smile, though my chest feels like it's going to fold into itself. What the hell did I just say? I can't remember, but I doubt it paints me as the carefree, easy-to-work-with actor whose star is on the rise.

Julian's going to kill me, but for the first time in a long time, I simply don't care.

Hollywood E-Gossip

Casting Round-up
By Lisa Maxen
Posted 9:02 a.m. PT

A Win for Winn

Sources tell us Andy Winn has been cast in the lead role opposite Gwen Styles in *Swan Song*, the film adaptation of the best-selling novel of the same name. Winn, who's best known for his breakout performance in *The City's Stories*, will play a soldier stationed in Iraq who befriends and falls in love with his pen pal (Styles). Other actors considered for the part include Drew Cherry and Carter Stone. "The film's producers were confident Winn had the chops to play the challenging role," an anonymous source close to the casting process confided, whereas Cherry and Stone were deemed better suited for romantic comedies and action films.

Chapter Thirty-Four

Tori

AFTER MY FATHER'S party, I return to the apartment and tiptoe inside. Eva wasn't feeling well when I left and passed on joining me.

I leave my shoes by the door and head straight to the bathroom, where I run into a body that's not my roommate's.

"Nate! What the hell?"

My boss is in my apartment.

Wait. What? Why?

The door to Eva's bedroom flies open. She's wearing a black nightie. "Oh, fuck," she says when she spots us in the hall. "You're supposed to be at your dad's party."

"You're supposed to not be"—I point at Nate—"with him."

Nate rubs his bald head. "I'm just going to get the rest of my stuff and head out." He ambles into Eva's room, and she looks at me wide-eyed before she closes the door, leaving me alone in the dark hall wondering how Mr. Stickler for Personnel Issues ended up in my best friend's—*and his employee's*—bed.

I'm still cackling when Nate emerges from Eva's bedroom. She's nowhere to be seen. *You can't run or hide, hussy.*

Nate stops in front of me. "This is awkward."

"That it is," I say.

"I should explain—"

"No, you shouldn't. She's my best friend. I talk to her first. Always."

He puts up his hands. "Okay, okay. Have you heard from Ben?"

"Ben? No, why?"

"Carter contacted us yesterday."

The contents of my stomach are in danger of being ejected. "About what?"

"He thanked us for making you available to him for training. And he passed along a video snippet of your class, the one you teach at the community center. Said he thought we should reconsider our objections to the class. The guy's obviously smitten."

What video? I had no idea Carter had taken any video. And he gave it to them? Oh, my heart. "He did?"

"Yeah. Ben and I were impressed with it."

"So you're ready to let me teach the class?"

Nate leans against the wall. "No. It's still not on brand."

"Yeah," I say, trying not to let my disappointment show. "I can see your point."

"But we'd like to talk to you about investing in your studio."

It's hard to take in any air. "What? Are you serious?"

"*We're* serious. You're talented, and we think you're on to something."

"Wow. I'm floored. And I'm definitely interested in talking." After I've digested this new information, I add, "Um, sometime down the road, I might want a studio out in California." I can't believe that came out of my mouth, but yeah, if I want to be with Carter, that's likely where I'm headed. Or am I being too presumptuous? "Nothing's definite," I clarify. "Just a thought. Would that...be a deal breaker?"

Nate's chin rises slowly, and he grins at me. "Well, all right. And no, that's not a deal breaker. We're investing in you, not a location."

I glance at Eva's closed bedroom door. "You should know, though. This isn't going to color how I feel about you and Eva. I'll take my cues from her."

Nate pushes himself off the wall and salutes me. "I wouldn't expect anything less of you, Tori. Good night."

"Yeah. Good night, Nate."

After using the bathroom, I get undressed and tumble into bed.

And, of course, I think about Carter until I fall asleep.

THE NEXT MORNING, I wake to discover Eva threading her fingers through my curls. I push up on my elbows and shake my head. "Goodness, woman, you're a creeper. Did you snip a lock of my hair while I was sleeping?"

She shoves my shoulder. "I was admiring how your face looks when you're not stressed out by life."

I pull the sheet over my mouth to cover my morning breath. "That's a thing? Not being stressed out by life?"

"A rare phenomenon that happens every seventy-five years or so, like the appearance of Halley's Comet, or in your case, when you sleep."

"I love that this stuff tumbles out of your mouth at six o'clock in the morning."

She smiles. "Well, you're going to love something else about me because I made you breakfast."

"What's the occasion?"

"Breakup therapy."

"That's a thing, too?"

She nods. "Absolutely."

"What did you make? A smoothie?" I ask hopefully.

"Nope. Eggs, bacon, and toast. And coffee. So much coffee."

I'd usually pass on the bacon, but doing this for us makes her happy. "I want *all* of it."

We decimate the breakfast at the small table in the eat-in kitchen, and as we sip coffee, she leans over and places a hand over mine. "I have another surprise for you."

"Stop being weird, Eva. I'm not even sure it's fair to call this a breakup, but even if it is, I'm not going to shatter into a thousand pieces."

"I'd never think that of you, *mama*, and my surprise proves it." She stands and motions for me to follow. "It's in my bedroom."

"Is it...Nate?"

Then I laugh so loudly I'll probably wake our neighbors.

She huffs. "We're not talking about that now. Not yet."

"Whenever you're ready," I singsong behind her.

At the threshold, she places her hand on the doorknob and turns to me. "Now cover your eyes."

"Oh, for heaven's sake, Eva."

"Just do it."

I slap my hand over my eyes and wait. Eva grabs my other hand and pulls me through the door.

"Okay, open them," she says.

When I do, I jolt, because there's a freestanding punching bag in the middle of her room—and it has a photo of Carter's face taped to it. "What am I supposed to do with this?"

"Punch it, pinch it, kick it, whatever you need to do."

"I don't want to punch Carter in the face, not even in jest."

Eva tilts her head to the side and regards me with a quizzical expression. "So why aren't you in California?"

I groan and bend over so my face is completely hidden by my hair. "I don't know. I'm the worst. My brain's one big stew of second-guessing my decision to see him again."

"So take your frustrations out on the bag."

It's not a bad idea. Maybe it'll help me to sort out what to do next. I rip off the photo Eva taped to the bag, crumple it into a ball, and toss it in the trash can. "Give me the gloves."

Eva cheers and hands them to me. After I throw them on, she checks the laces like she's a boxing coach and a championship match is set to begin after the bell rings.

"You hate that your relationship with Carter played out in the press," she prompts.

Hitting the bag hard, I yell, "Yes."

"You hate that he was photographed with another woman even though you know he has no interest in her."

I punch the bag again. "Yes." I'm feeling better already.

"You miss his eggplant-emoji-sized dick."

I can't help snorting. Dammit, that warrants two jabs and an uppercut. "Yes, yes, yes." I resume my fighting stance.

"And you're annoyed that Carter has his own hang-ups just like anyone else and that you have to work through them with him."

I drop my arms. "No, no, that's not true."

"And your relationship with Carter is doomed because despite how you obviously feel about each other, you refuse to live the kind of public life that comes with dating a Hollywood actor."

Leave it to Eva to pull my head out of my butt. I love the man. And even though he hasn't said the words, I know he loves me, too. I'm wasting time being apart from him. So what if our life won't be easy? He's right. I shouldn't chase after a trouble-free existence, not when the alternative is an imperfect but full life with the man I adore.

I give Eva a weak smile, pull off the gloves, and drop them on her bed. "Thanks for the entertainment. I've got to get ready for work."

"I'm sensing a lot of tension," she calls after me. "The punching bag will be here whenever you need it."

"It worked, Eva," I say over my shoulder. "You gave me the final kick I needed. I'm going to book a flight after I shower."

Behind me, I hear her shout *"Yes!"*

Back in my bedroom, I pull out my phone and look up Maisie Hunt from *Philly Water Cooler*. The way I see it, she owes me for misprinting information about Carter and me. Let's see if she agrees. Hopefully, she has a friend in California who can get me what I need.

Chapter Thirty-Five

Carter

THE BLACK SEDAN that will take me to the Westwood Village Theatre for the *Hard Times* premiere arrives promptly at six in the evening.

"Good evening, Mr. Stone. I'm Elijah. Will you be traveling alone?"

I shake Elijah's hand. "Yes."

I'm ignoring Julian's advice and attending on my own, for one reason only: Tori.

The possibility that we won't be together devastates me. Even the news that I didn't get the part in *Swan Song* didn't affect me as much as Tori's absence from my life.

I don't care about projecting confidence in the face of the brutal reviews *Hard Times* continues to receive. I couldn't care less about speculation concerning my relationship status. And I don't give a rat's ass about what people might be whispering behind my back.

I just want Tori to know that she's irreplaceable, that if she were willing, she is the only person I'd want by my side. Does attending a premiere without a date communicate all that? Probably not. But in the end, I don't want to go with anyone else anyway, so I'm sticking with this plan.

As I climb into the car, my cell phone rings. Jewel's name and image appear on the screen. "What's up?"

"Hey, Carter," she says in a hushed voice. "Glad I caught you. Julian just called and asked me to tell you that Dana's approved a red-carpet interview with *Hollywood Insider Live*, so don't be antisocial, and answer the reporter's questions, all right?"

Huh. That's bizarre. Dana hates live interviews because they're unpredictable. And I don't want to talk to reporters, period." I sigh into the phone. "Jewel, are you sure Dana cleared it?"

"What, Carter?" Jewel shouts. "I can't hear you. There's something—"

Our call is disconnected. Great. Now I'll have to suffer through a live interview that might end in disaster depending on the correspondent's questions.

When the sedan pulls up to the Westwood Village Theatre, a few of the film's stars are being interviewed on the red carpet, and several others stand in front of the media wall while photographers behind the velvet ropes take their photos. A small crowd assembles near the media wall, but otherwise it's a low-key event.

The display includes an oversized official movie poster, and I get a small thrill seeing my name on the sign. Elijah opens the passenger door, and I exit the vehicle. A few bright pops of light cause me to dip my head as I wave.

The small crowd applauds my arrival, but I suspect some of them are tourists who stumbled by the premiere and have no idea who I am.

A woman in a sleek black dress and flats calls me by name and ushers me along the red carpet. I don't have a starring role in the film, so there's no need to coordinate my appearance with other actors in the film. I stop at the media wall for a few photographs and then look around for the correspondent from *Hollywood Insider Live*.

Failing to see anyone interested in what I have to say, I fuss with my cuffs and then wave at the crowd. Impatient to get inside, I scan the area in front of the photo backdrop. My heart explodes like confetti in my chest when I see her.

Tori's here.

She's wearing a stunning gold-and-white gown that emphasizes her athletic figure. Her hair is swept up in an elegant hairstyle with a single sparkly hair clip at her right temple. And she's holding a microphone.

I swallow several times before I find my voice. "What's going on?"

She winks at me and gives me a saucy smile, but the microphone in her hand is shaking. "Go big or go home, right?"

She doesn't wait for my response, which is a good thing, because I have none. Instead, she points at the cameraperson behind her. "Ready?"

He nods and counts down with his fingers. "Three… two…one."

She takes a deep breath and blows it out before she begins. "This is Tori Alvarez filling in for Laura Beck for a super special edition of *Hollywood Insider Live*. I'm here with Carter Stone, who we all know and love from *Man on Third* and *My Life in Shambles*. Carter appears in a supporting actor role in *Hard Times*. It's, um, great to have you with us, Carter."

"Uh, thanks…thanks for having me."

"So is this your first premiere?"

"It's my first premiere for a movie I'm in, yes."

"Awesome. Congrats on the accomplishment. Can you tell us what audiences can expect from your performance in this film?"

"It's gritty, I think. I'm stripped bare, figuratively and literally. And I think audiences will be surprised by the rawness of the film as a whole."

"Well, I, for one, cannot wait to see it. Now, Mr. Stone, your appearance on *The Actor's Couch* was inspired, but I'd like to dig deeper on some of the issues you touched on. Would that be okay?"

"Sure."

"Before we go any further, I just wanted to point out that you look fantastic in that tuxedo, which probably can be attributed to the amazing physique underneath those clothes, am I right?"

Tori nudges me with her shoulder and waggles her eyebrows. Who is this woman? This is Tori 2.0, and I'm having a hard time processing that she's doing this in front of a camera.

"Mr. Stone?" she prompts.

"Oh, my physique—yes, I'd say that's right."

"And did you work with a trainer?"

"I did. Her name's Tori Alvarez."

"Was she effective?"

I give her "the eyes," and then I say, "Very."

The cameraperson chuckles. "I have no idea what's going on."

Tori widens her eyes and mouths "be quiet" to the cameraman.

Turning to me, she asks, "Are you still working with Ms. Alvarez?"

"No."

"Why not?"

"I let her go."

Tori clutches her necklace. "Goodness. Why'd you do that?"

"She'd completed the task I hired her for. It opened us up to new opportunities."

"Ah," she says, giving me a knowing smile. "And is there anyone special in your life now?"

"I want there to be, but it's really up to her."

"You didn't share this person's name on *The Actor's Couch*, but would you be willing to share her name now?"

"Absolutely."

Her hands tremble as she holds the microphone in front of my mouth. "Go ahead, Mr. Stone."

I position my body flush against hers and cup the nape of her neck. "It's you, Tori. It's always been you."

Her breath hitches and her lips part, and since I'm an opportunist, I sweep in for a tender kiss. She wraps her arms around my neck, and the kiss intensifies within seconds. Cameras flash, and the crowd cheers.

Drawing back, I catalog her appearance—the flushed cheeks, the sparkling eyes, the incredible dress—because I want to remember every second of this moment. "I love you. I want to be the person you wake up with, the person who holds your hand when you need it, the person who kisses you sweetly, the person who makes love to you, the person who listens to your dreams, the person who laughs with you. The person you yell at on the rare occasion when I do something to make you mad. I want all of it."

"I love you, too," she says.

I narrow my eyes. "And?"

She purses her lips and shrugs as if the declaration's no big deal "That about covers it." Her intense gaze tells a different story, though. Staring into her eyes, I have no doubt she wants everything that I want.

I pull her close and kiss her forehead. "You're right. Our love is all that matters. But what just happened?"

"I figured if we put it all out there, anything else would be boring, and they'd leave us alone."

"It could backfire."

"I don't care," she says as she rests her head in the crook of my neck. "Whatever happens, we'll work through it, okay?"

I squeeze her hand. "One thing we won't have to work through is my trust. I won't doubt you ever again. We're in this together."

And I'm so sure of that fact that all the other issues fade away.

Someday Tori will be my wife, and God willing, the mother of my children. And it all started with a flight to Aruba. I smile at the memory of that little girl wailing at my terrible impression of a bear.

Okay, so maybe I will tell our kids the *real* story of how I met their mother. After all, it's a good one.

Hollywood Observer

9:00 a.m. PDT 2/13/2018 by Observer Staff
Los Angeles, California

A Surprise Audition

Carter Stone is on fire lately. The Hollywood A-lister is promoting his first starring role in a feature film, *The Mash Up*, which has been showered with rave reviews, including ours <u>here</u>. We're betting Stone's hilarious performance gets him a few Best Supporting Actor nods this year. The movie's directors, Jim and Cassandra Lang, say Stone was a dream to work with and they're lucky to have nabbed him when they did, because now he's on every director's must-have list. They also revealed that they'd settled on Stone as part of their dream cast after watching his interview on *The Actor's Couch* in preparation for their own appearance on the show a week later. How's that for an undercover audition? Although Stone is enjoying his critical success, his time and attention appear to be focused on his girlfriend, Tori Alvarez. Just last week, Carter and Tori were reportedly spotted at a jewelry store—in the engagement and wedding rings section. Tori, meanwhile, has a lot on her plate, too. This fall, she'll be celebrating the opening of her West Hollywood fitness studio, Every Body, and in her "spare time" (our quotes, not hers), she'll be working with her mother and sister to develop recipes for their upcoming cookbook, which will feature traditional Puerto Rican recipes and their lighter-fare counterparts. We're licking our lips just thinking about it!

THE END

Acknowledgments

MY HUSBAND DOES ALL THE THINGS and gives me ALL THE FEELS. I can't thank him enough for being my partner in every sense of the word. Love you like crazy, sweetie.

Now to my girls. Being your mother is one of my most important obligations in life and the source of my greatest joy. Just so you know, I'll cuddle you even when you're in your thirties, which is when you should be reading this.

Mãe, eu te amo. It always comes back to you.

My critique partner, Olivia Dade, means the world to me. Your support, guidance, and friendship have been invaluable to me, Olivia, and I can't imagine traveling on this writing journey with anyone else. Love you, lady.

My agent, Sarah Younger, continues to champion and guide me. I wouldn't want to run this marathon without you cheering me on.

My editor, Nicole Fischer, is a rock star at what she does. Somehow, she read my manuscript and knew exactly what needed to be done to whip it into shape. I'm thrilled to be working with you, Nicole, and I'm looking forward to growing as an author with you in my corner.

Which leads me to my shout-out to the rest of the Avon Impulse family: Thank you for welcoming me into the fold and for everything you've done on my behalf. Also, that cover. Goodness, you nailed it.

To my beta readers, Soni Wolf, Ana Coqui, and Susan Scott Shelley: Thank you for your kind and wise words. Your insights helped me write a better book.

Finally, to you, dear reader: Thank you for embracing my words. I hope you enjoyed reading this story as much as I enjoyed writing it.

Read on for a sneak peek at the next book in Mia Sosa's
Love on Cue series...

PRETENDING HE'S MINE

Coming February 2018!

Chapter One

Julian

THERE'S A WOMAN experiencing a toe-curling orgasm in my condo. And to my knowledge, this is the first time I'm in no way responsible for it.

Because this dumpster fire needs more tinder, the person bringing herself pleasure within the confines of my not-so-humble abode is my best friend's little sister.

The best friend who's also my most high-profile client.

The best friend who would pin my balls to the textured wall framing my fireplace if I had anything to do with his little sister's orgasms.

I'd prefer to sustain a thousand paper cuts than listen to her moans, the catch of her breath, the rustling of the sheets around her body. But she's crashing at my place, and she's left the door of the guest bedroom open. Just a crack. The sliver of soft light coming from the adjoining bathroom beckons like a portal to another world. *Come*, the voice of James Earl Jones says. *The embodiment of your hidden and fucked-up fantasies lies in this realm.*

Is she naked, or has she tugged her pajama bottoms to her ankles? Is she using one finger or more? Is she a multitasker who massages her breasts, too? My erection wants answers to these pressing questions.

I squeeze my eyes shut. Dammit. This isn't right. It's a private moment, and I'm a lecherous asshole. Summoning what's left of the self-control that's served me well for more than a decade, I turn away from the light and slink down the short hall to my kitchen. There, I refit my wireless headphones and find a tall glass for the water that brought me out of my room.

I'd resigned myself to remaining as far away from Ashley as possible while she stayed the night, but I didn't expect an innocent trip to the fridge to leave me thirsty for something else altogether. I'm not even sure why I took off my headphones as I passed her room. But I did. And now I know what she sounds like when she comes.

I didn't cross the line; I hurdled over it.

It began more than a year ago, when Carter asked me to check in with his little sister, who'd been in town during a layover in her flight schedule. She was mopey because she'd just broken up with her boyfriend. While consoling her, my arms circled her waist, and she rested her head on my shoulders. It's a foggy memory, but I recall pressing my lips against her forehead, a friendly show of affection that came as naturally to me as breathing, and then she raised her lips to mine, suggesting she wouldn't object to more.

With regret but a clear sense of purpose, I shut it down. Which is what I need to do now. Now that the portal is open, though, I want to step through and explore this other world. Until that day, I'd never imagined acting on my attraction to Ashley. She's supposed to be the little sister I always wished to have. Since then, however, I can't think of anything else.

Picture her in pigtails and remember what it was like to help her stand after an epic fall on the bike she'd just learned to ride.

Forget that she's now a sexy adult woman with a maddening power to pierce your prickly exterior and make you laugh.

Banish any inappropriate thoughts about her to a parallel universe that will never intersect with this one.

Although temporary, the solution is simple. Fifty push-ups will round out my workout and help settle my libido. With my get-over-my-lust-for-Ashley plan in place, I set the glass in the sink and cut the light switch. I spin around, and a warm body skids into me, a soft mouth connecting with my bare chest.

She yelps. "Julian? Please tell me it's you."

The tremor in her voice pulls me out of my stupor, and I take in an unsteady breath as I step back. "It's me, Ashley."

Fuck the fifty push-ups. I'm going to need a hundred.

Ashley

THIS WAS A test.

In the event of an actual sexual emergency, I would be climbing Julian's body like a cat in heat. Julian dislikes cats, however, and he dislikes women who invade his personal space even more. Still, *this woman* needs to know if her lifelong crush has feelings for her.

Hence, Operation Fake Orgasm.

Moments ago, I sat on the bed in Julian's guest bedroom and flipped through the copy of *Sports Illustrated* I'd picked up from the magazine rack.

I moaned. I groaned. I smacked my lips. I think there were a few *yeses* in there, too. Then a high-pitched cry. To heighten the atmospherics, I also rustled the sheets.

Meg Ryan would have been proud.

Did I do all this knowing the door to the bedroom was open? Affirmative. Will the ruse reveal whether Julian's attracted to me? Hang on. I'll let you know in a minute.

He flips the light switch. Julian's dark gaze settles on his hand, which is gripping the counter's edge.

"Sorry, Julian. I didn't realize you were out here. I just wanted to grab a glass of water."

He raises his head, and his gaze finally lands on me. In a matter of seconds, he regards me with interest, his dark brown eyes cataloging my face and body, and then he shuts down his perusal with a shake of his head. It's willpower at work, and the fact that he needs it is promising.

Before I can revel in that knowledge, he taps his ears and pulls out his headphones. "Hey. I've been in my own world here."

My eyes blink repeatedly, so much so that the kitchen appears to be bathed in strobe lights. "You've been listening to music?"

Julian smiles, and his dimples say hello. "Yeah, I've been working out, and I didn't want to disturb you."

Drat. My fake orgasm was a waste of my time. But that's neither here nor there when I consider that Julian's bare chest is in my field of vision. I haven't seen it since my last year of high school—and Julian's last year of college. There have been significant developments in the interim.

His smooth brown skin still makes me yearn to touch it. But maturity—and probably the effects of a heck of a lot of exercise—has etched itself into the dips and planes of his torso, broadening the span of his waist and hardening his abdomen. How would the landscape change if he contracted his muscles in response to my touch? God, I'd love to know.

"So what's next for you?" he asks.

His voice, a smooth baritone that slides over me like silk, adds to his appeal. Even in college, Julian spoke like a man well beyond his years, but now that he's older, his voice complements his persona, serving as the right accessory for any outfit or occasion.

As he awaits my answer, he lifts his body and settles on the kitchen counter, his small and large muscles contracting like well-oiled gears. Needing something to do with my twitchy hands, I search for a glass.

"Upper cabinet above the sink," he says.

I round the counter and open the cabinet door. "I'm working mostly in Dallas and Philadelphia next week." I turn halfway, giving him my profile. "Why the sudden interest in my work schedule?"

Julian presses his lips together and stares at me. "That's not what I meant."

I face forward, my hand behind me as I fill the glass with water from the fridge dispenser. "What *did* you mean?"

He throws his head back. "When will you be done with this stint as a flight attendant? It's been about a year now."

The "stint" reference causes me to straighten and square my shoulders. After taking a sip of water, I say, "I'll be done with it when I'm ready. For now, it's giving me the means to travel and experience new places." I meet his stare. "And people."

His nostrils flare. "I'm sure."

Except for his annoying tendency to judge my choices, Julian would be close to perfect. "Anyway, to answer your thinly veiled question about my purpose in life, I'm thinking I might try my hand at real estate."

Julian groans. "Right. Because the housing market is booming, and there's a shortage of qualified real estate professionals in..." He squishes his eyebrows together. "Where are you living now, anyway?"

It's a simple question—with a complicated answer.

Last week, I would have said Hoboken, New Jersey. But that was before my roommate's seedy boyfriend, Paul, cornered me in my kitchen and squeezed my ass as

I rinsed out my favorite coffee mug. That was also before I slammed said mug against the side of his face. Elisa screeched at me when she saw the blood smeared against his cheek. The cut was superficial, but her response to what had prompted me to cause it hurt much more. In the end, she blamed Paul's wandering hands on the tightness of my pajama bottoms.

Needless to say, as long as either Elisa or Paul occupies the apartment, I won't be returning.

Which means I'm homeless. But Julian doesn't need to know all of this. For his own good. Because if he knew what had happened, he would head to Jersey for an unfriendly visit with Paul. And trouble would surely follow. So I tell him the truth, the *partial* truth, and nothing but the *essential* truth. "My living arrangements are in flux right now. I'm working on finding a place to stay."

"What's wrong with Carter's place while you"—he makes air quotes—"figure things out?"

I chuckle. "He *literally* has his hands full with his girlfriend. New love, it's a bit much, you know?"

Julian dons his trademark half smile—the one I pretend he reserves just for me—and adds a wink for good measure. "Is that what had you running to my place tonight?"

"Exactly. They appear to be spreading their DNA over every surface of his condo. I'm worried one morning I'll find a pubic hair in my cereal."

Julian shudders and pretends to wretch. "Stop, please."

Satisfied I've made my point, I nod and purse my lips in displeasure. "Now you know how I feel."

"I'm sure your parents would welcome you with open arms."

I inwardly cringe at the thought of returning to my parents' house. "I think you meant they'd welcome me into their smothering arms. No thanks."

He tilts his head as if to downplay my objection. "Would going home be such a bad thing?"

Um. Yes. It would be a terrible thing.

My hometown Harmon, with a population under three thousand and two different bakeries within a block of each other, often makes the list of quaint and idyllic towns in Connecticut. But its demographics leave much to be desired: 90 percent of its residents are assholes, while the other 10 percent are members of my family, students attending the boarding school down the road from our family's home, or owners and employees of those lovely bakeries. I'd rather describe my sexual history in graphic detail to my parents than return there for more than a two-day visit during the holidays.

Julian knows I hate Harmon and all the bad memories I left there, which is why I simply stare at him in response to his ridiculous question.

He drops his head, his fisted hands lightly pounding his thighs, but he says nothing.

I hate silence. Without sound, which I prefer at high decibels, my thoughts often threaten to consume me. Julian enjoys silence, however. A room with no music or chatter is his happy place. His comfort in the absence of noise is one of the reasons I'm drawn to him; it looks and feels like confidence, something I either lack or have in abundance depending on the people around me. When I'm on my way to Harmon, my confidence drops me off at the airport and waves at me as it heads to a sunny destination in another country.

After a half minute in which I struggle for something to say, Julian lifts his head. A sense of foreboding blankets the room, and I wince at the pained expression on his face.

"If you need a place to stay while you sort out your living arrangements, you can stay here. In one of the guest bedrooms."

His voice is even and emotionless. Goodness. Does he abhor the idea of having me here *that* much?

I thought...I don't know what I thought. Maybe Julian's dating someone and he doesn't want me to interfere with his lifestyle. Maybe to him I'm still his best friend's annoying sister, and he suggested I stay here only to keep his best friend and client happy. Or maybe, just maybe, he suspects being in close quarters with me would test his resolve to keep our relationship platonic. Although his reasoning is unclear, his lack of enthusiasm about the idea is not.

And that's why I'll accept his offer. Because I need to know once and for all whether Julian's attracted to me.

If he isn't, I'll move on.

If he is, I'll climb his body like a scratching post. And finally take him off my to-do list.

Julian stares at me, his mouth slightly open as he waits to see if I'll accept his offer.

"I won't stay long, I promise." I give him a reassuring smile. "And I'll be traveling a lot, so you won't even know I'm here."

"I doubt that," he says under his breath.

Ha. Given what I have in mind, I doubt that, too.

About the Author

MIA SOSA is an award-winning contemporary romance writer and 2015 Romance Writers of America Golden Heart® Finalist. Her books have received praise and recognition from *Library Journal*, *The Washington Post*, Book Riot, Bustle, The Book List Reader, and more.

A former First Amendment and media lawyer, Mia practiced for more than a decade before trading her suits for loungewear (okay, okay, they're sweatpants). Now she strives to write fun and flirty stories about imperfect characters finding their perfect match.

Mia lives in Maryland with her husband, their two daughters, and an adorable puppy that finally sleeps through the night. For more information about Mia and her books, visit www.miasosa.com.

A Letter from the Editor

Dear Reader,

I hope you liked the latest romance from Avon Impulse! If you're looking for another steamy, fun, emotional read, be sure to check out some of our upcoming titles. We have something for everyone next month!

If you're a fan of bad boys, you'll definitely want to grab a copy of BAD FOR HER by Christi Barth! This is the first in a hilarious, sexy new series about three brothers in witness protection who are forced to start over in a tiny Oregon town. With a fake identity and too many secrets, ex-mobster Rafe Maguire can't get serious with the gorgeous local doctor…but trying to be good doesn't mean he can't be a little bad.

We also have a fun new sports romance from Julie Brannagh! The latest installment in her Love and Football series, NECESSARY ROUGHNESS is a fun, steamy story of a gruff, grumpy football star with an injury that's put him out of commission and his sexy, spunky physical therapist who is almost too tempting to resist.

And finally, for a quick, sexy, suspenseful read, you'll want to one-click the new novella from HelenKay Dimon! THE NEGOTIATOR is about a woman who discovers her supposedly long-dead husband's body on her kitchen floor and must team up with sexy, savvy Garrett McGrath to uncover the truth before she's accused of murder!

You can purchase any of these titles by clicking the links above or by visiting our website, www.Avon Romance.com. Thank you for loving romance as much as we do…enjoy!

Sincerely,

Nicole Fischer
Editorial Director
Avon Impulse